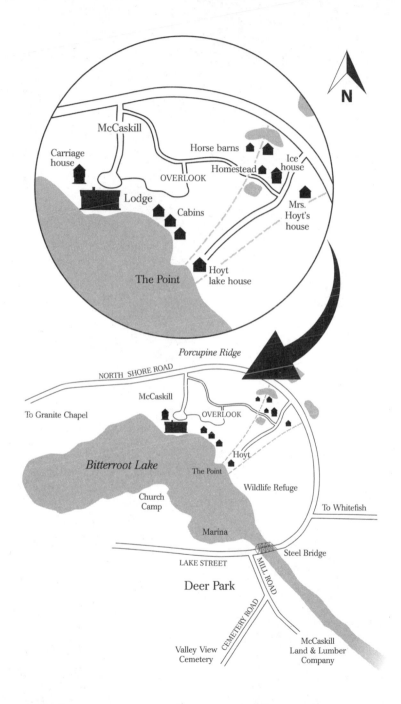

BITTERROOT LAKE

BITTERROOT LAKE

A NOVEL

Alicia Beckman

CROOKED
LANE

NEW YORK

Copyright © 2021 by Leslie Ann Budewitz

Published in the United States by Crooked Lane Books, an imprint of The Quick Brown Fox & Company LLC.

Crooked Lane Books and its logo are trademarks of The Quick Brown Fox & Company LLC.

Library of Congress Catalog-in-Publication data available upon request.

ISBN (hardcover): 978-1-64385-580-6
ISBN (ebook): 978-1-64385-581-3

Cover design by Nicole Lecht

Map by Francesca Droll/Abacus Graphics, LLC

Printed in the United States.

www.crookedlanebooks.com

Crooked Lane Books
34 West 27th St., 10th Floor
New York, NY 10001

First Edition: April 2021

10 9 8 7 6 5 4 3 2 1

For Ramona DeFelice Long
in friendship and gratitude

It was already late
enough, and a wild night,
and the road full of fallen
branches and stones.
                    —Mary Oliver, "The Journey"

What Sarah remembered most about that day twenty-five years ago were the sounds.

The words that twisted Lucas's full lips, that ripped away all the innocence of the weekend, that scraped her to the bone even still.

Janine sobbing, rasping for breath.

Lucas revving the engine of the little red sports car, grinding the gears as he pulled away from the lodge. Michael and Jeremy yelling, then jumping in as they tried to keep him from certain disaster.

The tires squealing on the highway. Metal crumpling. An animal bellowing.

And all of it echoing off the rocks and water and mountains, drowning out the birdsong and the chirping squirrels and the laughter of people at play on the lake. Winding through the spruce and pine and piercing her in the gut.

The siren. Jeremy moaning, strapped to the gurney, its wheels snapping as the EMTs loaded him into the ambulance.

The doors slamming shut. The ambulance screeching back toward town.

Did they cry, the girls left to watch and wait? Scream, shout? They must have. She didn't remember.

Fear and terror, and grievous loss, erase every other sense, wiping the memory blank, leaving time as clean and empty as her grandmother's ironstone dishes. As she had too recently been reminded.

MONDAY

Seventeen Days

1

A light glowed in the window of the far cabin, the cabin closest to the lake.

Sarah McCaskill Carter squinted and tightened her lips. She was seeing things again. She'd thought that once she came home to Montana, to Whitetail Lodge, the apparitions, the ghosts, the specters—whatever they were—would go away. That she would be herself once again. Although the therapist in Seattle had told her it might take months, or longer, to feel she was back on solid ground. Everyone responds to grief differently, the woman had said, in their own way, on their own time.

The light was gone. Sarah blew out a breath and took her foot off the brake, aiming the rented SUV down the last stretch of the winding lane that led to the lodge. She touched the gas and focused on the road. Deer, even elk and the occasional moose, were known to jump out of the shadows that filled these woods, especially when twilight was fading. She knew what damage they could cause, to a car and to a life.

She glanced back at the cabin. The light was on.

"Get a grip, girl," she said out loud. "Or your next trip will be to the funny farm."

Moments later, her headlights hit the double doors of the carriage house. Even in the fading light, the roof appeared to be sagging and the siding dull, in need of oil. Less schlepping if she parked in front of the lodge. But high winds and evening rainstorms were common in the mountains, and it was better to be safe and sore than sorry.

Wait. Was one door ajar?

"Don't get spooked," she told herself. "It's just loose. There's no one here." When her mother asked her help getting the lake place ready for the summer and making a plan for the future, she'd warned her that the lodge needed serious cleaning. Sarah could deal with that. She'd dealt with worse than a little dirt.

Even so, her mother would have expected her to stop by the house in town first.

Not yet. Sarah could not stomach the thought of staying in Seattle one more minute, but she wasn't ready to be smothered by mother love.

Tomorrow. She'd call her mother tomorrow and let her know she was here.

The words "better safe . . ." echoed in her brain. It had been seventeen days since her husband's death, and she had not felt safe for one minute.

Nothing in reach might double as a weapon. She stepped out of the car, leaving the engine running. Opened the rear door and dug in her suitcase for her heavy black flashlight, its heft a comfort.

The ten-foot-high garage door groaned at her touch, then slid open with a squeal. Her headlights picked out a white van, mud-splashed, Missoula County plates reading CKLDY.

She caught her breath. It had to be—it couldn't be anyone else.

But why was the woman here?

"Janine?" Sarah called into the darkness. No answer. She tried the driver's door. Locked. Circled the van, straining to see in each window. Empty, as far as she could tell. Touched a muddy tire. Fresh. Laid a palm on the hood—not hot, not cold.

What was going on? She slid open the other door, then pulled her SUV inside. She'd come back for her bags later.

The lodge loomed, tall and dark, casting deep shadows over the circular drive. She strode past the stone steps of the front porch, aiming for the forest path that led to the three log cabins. The evening clouds had begun to part, but there was no moon, leaving only the last hint of twilight to guide her.

It was enough. Her feet knew the way, and she didn't want to telegraph her presence with a stray flashlight beam. Because who knew why her old friend was here, or if she was alone? With all the time and distance between them, Sarah could not count on being welcomed, even though this property belonged to her family.

Between the first two cabins, she paused to gaze out at Bitterroot Lake, listening to the waves lapping on the shore. Its waters ran deep, frigid even in summer. Now, not quite mid-May, the lake could be deadly.

Her steps slowed. She paused and took a deep breath, intent on the last cabin. The curtains had been pulled tight, but a soft glow leaked out, and she could see a battery-powered lantern on the window sill. Whitetail Lodge and its grounds had been a haven and retreat since early in the twentieth century, when a railroad tycoon built the lodge as a summer home. Her family had acquired the property—several hundred acres and a long stretch of lakeshore—in 1922. Her mother would have told her if any cabins were occupied.

No, this visitor had come here on the sly. Sarah did not begrudge the refuge or the intrusion. But she deserved to know the reason.

She strode to the weathered pine door. One foot on the path, the other on the stone step, she raised her hand and knocked. Heard the silence within. Knocked a second time.

"Janine? It's Sarah Carter. Sarah McCaskill Carter."

Silence, then footsteps, followed by a soft sound—a meow?

The door opened a few inches, a narrow swath of light playing on the worn wood floor. Janine Chapman peered around the edge of the door, gripping it with both hands. Her dark eyes were huge and red-rimmed, her olive skin tear-splotched. Was that blood on her white T-shirt?

"Lucas Erickson is dead," she said. "And they're going to think I did it."

And with those words, all the ghosts in Sarah Carter's past came back to life.

2

Half an hour later, Sarah clutched a mug of hot tea and
stared across the kitchen table. Her mother may have
started cleaning the lodge—a bucket and sponge had
been left in the deep white farmhouse sink—but she hadn't gotten very far. Sarah had wiped down the chrome-trimmed Formica table and chrome chairs, their red vinyl seats showing
wear at the corners, while the kettle heated. The tea was old,
Twinings in bags, the sugar clumped with damp. She'd picked
up a few things in a market not far from the train station, but
tea and sugar weren't among them—she'd make a full grocery
run in a day or two, if she decided to stay.

But tea wasn't the point.

"Tell me again," Sarah told the woman she'd known since
the seventh grade but hadn't seen in years. "Start from the
beginning."

Janine spread her hands across the wrinkled letter that lay
between them, smoothing the white paper. Capable hands, the
fingers strong and supple. No rings, not worth the trouble of
scrubbing them clean of flour and sugar, let alone keeping a

shine. Despite their strength, the baker's hands could not iron out the angry marks she'd made when she'd crumpled up the page and thrown it at the unseen, anonymous writer.

But the folds and furrows in the paper did not obscure the words, typed in a standard font, undated, unsigned.

"Only you know the truth of what happened twenty-five years ago," the letter read. "Only you can decide what to do."

"Did you bring the envelope?" Sarah asked. The cat—compact, its fur dark chocolate, coffee-tinged at the ears and paws—finished its circuit of the room and jumped into her lap. Her hands instinctively steadied the creature, and she added cat food to her unwritten shopping list.

Janine's dark, wiry curls swung back and forth. "No return address." Sarah had lent her a clean shirt, Janine's bloodied T-shirt now draped over the back of a chair.

"The postmark?"

"Missoula."

Montana's second-largest city, home to the University of Montana. One hundred and fifty miles south. A long drive, simply to confront a man.

Nothing simple about it.

"But he lives here, in Deer Park. Why would you think he sent it?"

"Post office closed the sorting facility years ago. All the mail in western Montana goes through Missoula now. Unless it's local, from one Deer Park address to another. And he might have gone down there, for court or legal business." Janine drew her tea closer. "But it has to have come from him, doesn't it? No one else . . ."

Her voice trailed off, not saying what didn't need to be said. Twenty-five years ago this month, Sarah had graduated from the university, along with their friend Nicole. The new grads and Sarah's sister Holly, a year younger, had come to the lodge to celebrate, Janine in tow. For a week, the four friends and roommates had been the only ones here—swimming, hiking, laughing, drinking too much wine, and falling asleep in the sun. Enjoying their last carefree days before time and plans separated them.

Then Lucas and his buddies showed up. And everything changed.

"Oh, God, Sally, it was awful. It was hideous. I wanted to throw up." Janine bent over, clutching her elbows. Then she stood and began to pace between the ancient white enamel range and the equally ancient refrigerator.

No one had called Sarah "Sally" in decades, except occasionally when someone in the family slipped. Or a friend from way back.

"He wanted to make sure I kept my mouth shut. Rumor is he intends"—Janine paused—"*intended* to run for office."

"Political office?" As if there were another kind. But *Lucas*?

"Congress, I heard. He might have lacked political experience, but he never lacked confidence."

Why not Lucas? He'd been smart and ambitious. Lawyers often leaned toward politics. And officially, he had no criminal record.

"Lucas?" she repeated, this time out loud. The cat shifted in her lap.

"I thought—I thought—" Janine stopped, then grabbed her chair and rocked it backward. "He always blamed me for the wreck. Because I said no, because I wouldn't sleep with him—"

"He attacked you. He all but raped you." Sarah didn't bother stemming her anger as the memory spilled out of her. "I saw you, we all saw you, racing out of the cabin, your shirt ripped,

your shorts half off. Running barefoot down the gravel driveway to get away from him."

"Instead, he jumped in Jeremy's car and tried to leave."

"I remember," Sarah said, her voice breaking. She would
never forget. Jeremy had left the keys in it. He and Michael ran
after Lucas. Somehow, both young men—boys, really, barely
older than her son was now—had ended up in the car, too. Trying to get Lucas to stop, to figure out what had happened, to
keep him from careening up the road and down the winding,
two-lane North Shore Road in a blind, foolish rage. Holly had
jumped in their father's old Jeep and raced after them. She'd
seen Lucas picking up speed on the blacktop, weaving across
the center line and back again. Seen Jeremy trying to wrench
control of the car. Seen the moose amble up out of the borrow
pit and straight into their path.

Sarah could see it all as if she'd been there. She could hear
the squeal of rubber, the rip of metal on asphalt, the wild bellowing. The terrible sounds had rolled down the slope to where
the other three had stood, clinging to each other, in front of the
lodge. Nic—Nicole, always the sensible one—had run inside to
call for help while Sarah and Janine rushed up the hill, terrified
of what they would find but too terrified to stay put.

"Lucas may have blamed you," she said quietly, "but Jeremy
never did. He knew what Lucas had done. Even though you'd
told him no over and over, all weekend, Lucas boasted that he
could get you into bed, one way or another. Michael and Jeremy told him to shut up, to let it go. He always knew it wasn't
your fault."

Janine collapsed onto the chair and buried her face in her
hands. Careful of the cat in her lap and the years between her
and her friend, Sarah touched Janine's arm, then scooted closer
and slid her hand onto her old friend's back.

Jeremy had been raced to the hospital in Whitefish, then flown to the trauma center in Seattle. He'd been in one hospital or another for the better part of the summer. And when Sarah had gone to visit him, they'd begun building a serious relationship. His parents hadn't welcomed her, not at first. Not until they saw that their only son was determined to keep her close.

And no one ever said that Jeremy Carter lacked determination.

Lucas's injuries had been minor. So minor that people assumed he was drunk, the way it often seemed to happen— the passengers or the innocent occupants of the other vehicle bore the worst of the trauma while the drunk driver walked away with barely a scratch.

But he hadn't been drunk, except maybe on anger and pride, and there had been no other vehicle. Just Jeremy's little red sports car, a graduation gift from his parents, flipped on its top, Jeremy seriously injured and Michael Brown, sweet, playful Michael Brown, thrown across the highway and killed.

And the big cow moose dead, her calf standing beside her, bawling. A neighbor, George Hoyt, had taken charge of the calf until state wildlife officers could come for it.

Janine straightened, letting Sarah's hand fall away, and sniffed back her tears. "What are we going to do?"

"We're going to call the sheriff," Sarah replied. "Like you should have. I still don't get why you didn't."

Janine turned to face her, her words urgent. "Lucas was dead, and I didn't see the gun. I was covered in blood, and I was not going to be the next person shot." Her shoulders slumped. "Besides, the cops don't believe women like me."

Her simple statement was a gut punch. An echo of the past.

Maybe Montana hadn't changed so much after all.

"The sheriff is my cousin, Leo," Sarah said. "I'll make him believe you."

Janine lifted her chin a few degrees, then nodded. She'd moved to Deer Park in seventh grade with her mother, a waitress at the Blue Spruce. Town was small enough that rumors flew, and the kids all heard their parents talk about Sue Nielsen and her errant ways. Sarah and Holly had thrown a Halloween party at the house in town that year and Peggy McCaskill suggested Sarah invite Janine, saying "that girl needs a friend." Becca Smalley and her beady-eyed buddies said if Janine came, they would stay home. "Too bad, so sad," Sarah replied—they'd miss out on the fortune teller, the games, and her mother's popcorn balls. After that, she and Janine had become fast friends. Janine had stayed in Deer Park for a few months after high school, then moved to Missoula herself, picking up restaurant work. The next year, they got an apartment together. Leo had been a couple of years ahead, but Sarah bet he'd remember Janine, too striking not to notice.

She pulled out her phone. "Cross your fingers for reception."

"Mine's dead," Janine said, laying her phone on the table, the screen shattered. "It cracked when I dropped it, when I thought . . ."

"Thought what?"

"When I thought the killer saw me. I ran for the door, I tripped, it went flying. I grabbed it and got out of there, fast as I could."

"Did they see you?"

"I don't know. I think so. I don't know."

Sarah pushed a few buttons, but nothing happened. Her mother had said the landline was shut off, but hadn't mentioned trouble with cell reception. Of course, her mother regularly ignored her cell phone, often for days. Sarah eased the cat onto the floor and stood. "Why don't you hunt up some quilts or blankets while I try outside? It's clear enough, I might get a signal without having to drive up to the highway. We'll sleep on the couches tonight."

"Sarah," Janine said. "About Jeremy. I'm so sorry. I meant to call, or write, but . . ."

Sarah swallowed, her eyes stinging. When would her eyes stop stinging?

"He didn't deserve to die so young," Janine continued.

"No one does," Sarah snapped. "Cancer doesn't care how old you are or what you deserve."

Two minutes later, she stood outside, her twill jacket with the belt and too many pockets zipped tight. She'd spoken too harshly, she knew. Part of the fallout of losing your husband at forty-seven. The therapist had said she might feel anger at the wrong things, say something she hadn't intended to say. Might yearn for alone time, though she'd always welcomed company.

That's why she was here. Where the unexpected presence of an old friend in need had changed her plans yet again.

"Focus," she muttered, staring at her phone. Leo and his wife had come to Seattle for Jeremy's funeral—the McCaskill clan had outnumbered the Carters—and he'd enveloped her in a hug meant to say that everything would be just fine. Even though she knew nothing would ever be fine. Leo had always been that way.

She trusted him. But that didn't mean Janine would.

Two bars. She scrolled through her contacts, then punched CALL. "Go through, go through." The body must have been found by now, by a secretary or partner. By a client, coming for an appointment. Or his wife, wondering where he was and why he didn't answer his phone. Did Lucas Erickson have a wife?

If anyone else had been in the building, anyone besides the killer, he or she would have called it in. If he, or she, had seen Janine, there would be a lookout for her—what did they call it? All-points bulletin—APB? BOLO—be on the alert? Despite her cousin's job, all she knew about law enforcement came from TV or the paper.

The line rang on the other end. "Pick up, pick up." Maybe Leo was still at the scene, his personal cell on mute. Should she call 911? But this wasn't an emergency, was it? Surely the body had been found.

A voice began speaking. "Leo, it's Sarah," she managed before realizing she'd gotten voice mail. She started over, more slowly. "Leo, it's Sarah. I'm at the lodge. Call me when you get this. It's urgent. I'm okay, I'm not in trouble, I'm not in danger, but—call me."

The stars shone down on her. The scent of the woods enveloped her. She gripped her phone tightly and wrapped her arms around herself.

Only a few weeks ago, she and Jeremy had talked about the crash. He'd been growing weaker and they'd had to admit it was time for hospice. Hospice was for the elderly, she'd always assumed—decades away, until it wasn't. He'd still been coherent, his usual calm self—she was the angry one—replaying his life. They talked about Michael Brown, imagining his future had he lived. Michael's quirky smile was easy to recall, the dimples in his dark brown cheeks. Tall, six-six or seven. Not good enough for the major college teams in Southern California, his home, but plenty good for UM.

And they'd talked about Lucas. She'd heard he'd taken up the life of a small-town lawyer, but when Jeremy had told her Lucas lived in Deer Park, she'd been sure he was confused. Mixing up the present and the past. But he'd been insistent, and he'd been right.

Had it been prescience, that the subject had come up? They say the dying are in touch with the other world, the world where unseen connections become visible, and Jeremy had at times seemed to be slipping beyond her grasp. But then he would return to her, giving her that smile that always made her tingle, even when she knew the end was near.

Until that Saturday night seventeen days ago. Both kids had flown home for a visit. He'd told them all he loved them, they were the light of his life, and closed his eyes one last time.

"Oh, Jeremy," she said out loud, her voice cracking and squeaking, her hand flying to her mouth. "What am I going to do without you?"

But there was no answer. She glanced at the phone. No answer there, either. No call, no message, no signal.

She was on her own. She and Janine and the cat. So much for her plan to sit on the deck with a glass of wine and watch the stars blink twice—once in the sky and again reflected in the dark, glassy lake.

This day wasn't turning out at all like she'd expected. Her life wasn't turning out like she expected.

"Deal with it, Sarah," she muttered, then slipped the phone into her pocket and went inside.

TUESDAY

Eighteen Days

3

here was she?

Sarah opened her eyes to light streaming in through the windows. The dirty windows, her first clue that she wasn't in the house in Seattle. Besides, the sun was streaming in the wrong way, the windows facing south.

And this was definitely not her bed, the cat curled up on her feet.

The cat. She hadn't had a cat in years.

It came back to her then, how she'd reached the lodge last night and found Janine, and the cat. Janine's gruesome discovery, her attempt to call her cousin the sheriff. The cups of stale tea they sipped as they tried to piece it all together.

And a night wrapped in a musty wool blanket on the bumpy old leather couch. No wonder her dreams had been unsettled, vague images slipping away with the morning light.

She slid one foot up, then wriggled the other free, not wanting to disturb the cat. Too late. It turned its head and gave her the stink eye.

"Figures." She sat up, pulling the small, warm body closer. "You a he or a she?"

"It's a she," Janine said as she approached, two heavy white mugs in hand. "I checked."

"Oh, coffee. Bless you." Sarah pushed the blanket aside with one hand, put her feet on the floor, and set the cat next to her. As if unsure how to respond to the indignity of forced relocation, the cat stood, circled, and settled back down, tucking her tail beneath her.

"My grandmother's ironstone, what she always called her railroad dishes." She took the mug Janine held out, its shape familiar and comforting, and let the first sip linger in her mouth. Hot, bitter, perfect. "You know, I don't think anyone's made me coffee, at home, since Jeremy got sick. He'd start the pot before he went out on his run and it would always be a toss-up whether he'd get back before I got up."

"Bakers and runners," Janine said. She still wore Sarah's T-shirt and black leggings, both long on her. "We get up early and spend the best part of the day on our feet."

The world beyond the windows shimmered despite the grime. Bitterroot Lake was shaped like an uneven piece of elbow macaroni, the lodge at the outer edge of the bend, town to the southeast, hidden by the curve.

What time was it? Sarah had no idea. Where had she left her phone? Odds were the signal wasn't coming through anyway, not in the daytime, despite the clear skies, making the phone a pricey clock. If she stayed more than a few days, they might need to reconnect the landline.

If. The controlling word in her world right now.

She took another sip of the Italian roast she'd brought with her from Seattle. Even a thirty-year-old Mr. Coffee knew what to do with good beans.

But coming back to Montana hadn't changed the key fact. Each day brought so many questions. Why, just as they were getting used to being empty nesters, getting to know each other again as people, not just parents, had the cancer come back and killed him? Quickly, too—less than six months from that first sharp pain in his low back to the end. To the ashes she'd brought with her. She and the kids had spread a handful on Lake Washington, not far from their house in Seattle, but she'd saved some for Bitterroot Lake, where it had all truly begun.

Now Lucas Erickson was dead, too. Had the three young men been cursed? Michael and Lucas had been roommates in the dorm, Jeremy a friend, jumping at the chance to visit the girls at an old lodge on a mountain lake. What young men wouldn't have?

Something soft swished against her bare arm. The cat. "You hungry? Me, too."

She took another sip and glanced at Janine, sitting on the other couch staring at a phone, her striped Pendleton blanket neatly folded. The letter lay open on the coffee table. "I thought your phone broke."

"I borrowed yours while you were asleep. Walked up toward the highway until I got a signal." She set the phone next to the letter. "Still no reception down here."

"Did you call Leo?"

"I called Nic."

Nicole. "Why? What can she do from four hundred miles away? Oh. You think—"

The sound of a car outside interrupted her and she stood. Strode to the nearest window and pushed the lace curtain aside.

"Better wash another cup," she said. "We're going to need it."

*　*　*

"I have to confess," Sheriff Leo McCaskill said after Janine had told her story, "I don't get why you didn't call us. Smart to leave the building—the killer could have been hiding anywhere. But you should have called us the moment you got to safety. Or driven over, if you were too scared to stay, or your phone wasn't working. The courthouse is only two blocks away."

"Leo," Sarah said, resting a hand on the kitchen table and leaning toward her cousin. "You have to understand. There's history here."

"So you say. But without a report . . ." Though Leo had the McCaskill height, he didn't have the classic Irish coloring of Sarah and her siblings. His nearly black hair was shot with gray and his eyes were the same dark brown as his uniform shirt and the matching stripe on the outer seam of his tan pants. "Look, it's not that I don't believe you about the assault—what, twenty-five years ago? But history is no defense to failure to report a crime. That's a crime itself, you know."

At least he hadn't said history was no defense to murder. Fingers crossed that meant he didn't consider Janine a suspect.

"I didn't know that," Janine said. "And Sarah did try. How did you know we were out here?"

"You, I had no idea. When I got Sarah's message, I tried to reply, but no luck. So I called your mother," he said to his cousin. "She knew you were coming home, but not when. And hearing you'd already arrived from me did not make her happy. You have to call her."

"I have to call her," Sarah repeated, staring into her empty coffee mug. "How did you find Lucas? Did you find the gun?"

"His secretary, Renee Harper, found him when she came back from the post office. She swears he was alone when she left, and that she was gone no more than half an hour." He swallowed the last of his coffee and set the mug on the table. "And no, no weapon. Just the body and the blood."

He'd already taken Janine's T-shirt into evidence, tucking it into a paper bag he'd sealed and initialed. He'd taken the letter, too.

"A lot of blood," Janine said, her voice thick with the memory.

"And you don't own a gun?" he asked, though he'd asked once before. The answer was the same—a shake of the head.

"Was Lucas popular?" Sarah asked, thinking of that possible run for office. "Well liked?"

"Well known," Leo replied, his careful choice of words saying plenty. "Soon as you two are cleaned up and dressed, come into my office and give official statements. We'll need both your fingerprints."

"Mine, too?" Sarah asked. "Why?"

"You touched the letter, right? Getting prints off paper isn't easy, so there's no guarantee we'll get a match. But at least we can eliminate yours." He rubbed the cat's head one more time. "And pick up some cat food."

*   *   *

Thank goodness she'd remembered to switch on the water heater last night. The hot shower had felt so good.

There might come a day when Sarah McCaskill Carter would walk down the streets of her hometown wearing second-day clothes and second-day hair, but this was not that day.

She took pity and set the last of her yogurt on the floor for the cat, who polished the bowl clean before sitting on her haunches and asking for more. "Don't get used to it. People food isn't good for you and I have no patience for picky eaters."

The cat did not reply.

Sarah found a tunic for Janine to wear over the borrowed leggings, then pulled on slim-cut black pants, a white silk T-shirt, and a bright blue blazer with a notched collar and rolled-up sleeves. Black flats. She'd only brought one bag, a woven straw tote with a leather strap. Finger-combed her light brown hair, the red flecks catching the light. It would do.

They drove the ten miles to Deer Park in the rented SUV, Janine's face ashen, hands clutching her elbows. Sarah kept her eyes on the road, barely seeing the land she'd once known as well as her own face.

On the courthouse steps, Janine paused.

"The last time I was here, I was twenty-two, claiming what my mother left behind."

Sarah grabbed Janine's shoulder and looked her square in the eyes. "You. Are not. Your mother."

Inside the office, the sharp smell of cleaning spray mingled with the scent of daffodils from a bouquet on the counter. The fortyish woman on duty said Sheriff McCaskill wanted to see Sarah first, and a young officer who introduced himself as Deputy Pritchard escorted her to the interview room. The fluorescent lights buzzed slightly and gave his pale skin a bluish tinge, though the table and chairs were not as old and scarred as she'd expected. Then Leo entered.

It didn't take long to repeat her story for the digital recorder that lay on the table between her and the two men. No, she replied to Leo's final question, she had nothing more to add.

"If you're sure—" Leo said. She was sure.

Back in the lobby, he beckoned to Janine. "No reason to wait," he told Sarah. "We could be a while."

She turned to her friend. "Text me when—" But Janine had no phone.

"I'll ping you when she's free," Leo said. A good sign, right? He didn't plan on clamping on the handcuffs and tossing Janine into the jail. Which surely did not smell of spring flowers.

Outside on the sidewalk, Sarah checked her phone. Replied *Gorgeous day in Montana—love you!* to a text from her daughter, no doubt sent while scurrying between classes. She'd texted both kids from the train station in Whitefish yesterday, letting them know she'd arrived safely. Her son might not reply for a day or two. They had their own lives now, which was the point of raising kids, right? But though she'd been happy to see them choose their dream schools and move halfway across the country while their father was alive and well, now she wanted to drag them home and never let them out of her sight.

Which was exactly what she couldn't do.

She dropped the phone into her bag. The courthouse anchored Main Street—literally; it stood in a circle at the south end of downtown, a few blocks from the lake. Despite the sunshine, the air held a slight chill. Mountain air. Fresh, and yet, filmy. Like a thin curtain had fallen between her and the rest of the world when Jeremy died.

This is your hometown. There is nothing to be afraid of.

She took a deep breath. One step, then another, and another.

At half past ten, Main Street was open for business. Flower baskets hung from hooks on some of the wrought-iron lampposts, while others sported nylon flags with bright images of birds and butterflies. "OPEN" signs glowed in the windows of the copy shop and the liquor store, and petunias and verbena spilled from window boxes outside the florist's shop. Her grandmother had had a standing order for a fresh bouquet every week, and Sarah had loved going in with her to pick them up, even when the owner was away and they had to deal with the prickly woman who worked there. As a little girl, she'd wondered why someone who worked with pretty things always seemed to be in a bad mood, but her grandmother had said the woman had a hard life.

"Good morning," an older man called as he came out of Deer Park Hardware and crossed the sidewalk. She returned the greeting, though she didn't know him. This was how she remembered town. Not like Seattle, where default mode was to pretend you didn't see the woman who pushed her grocery cart between you and the shelf you were scanning for the right kind of mustard or the man next to you studying his phone while you waited for your latte at Starbucks.

And yet, though it all looked so familiar, so friendly, it felt so different from when she'd last visited, a year ago.

No. It was she who was different.

And she whose tummy growled. The few bites of yogurt she'd eaten before giving the bowl to the cat had worn off.

But when she glanced down a side street, a sharp tang swelled in the back of her throat. Between the quilt shop and the locksmith, across from the school playfields, stood a single-story sandstone building with a Kelly green awning, the corrugated metal dented and rusting at the corner.

And blocking the sidewalk, two of those orange rubber traffic control thingies, strung with yellow CRIME SCENE tape.

She'd never liked Lucas, even before he attacked Janine. She'd been ticked at Holly for inviting him to the lodge that weekend, only grasping later that her sister had invited Lucas because she knew he'd bring Jeremy, the sweet, nerdy guy Holly had the hots for. The guy Sarah had chatted with a few times but never seriously considered until that weekend, the guy she married a year later. She'd been prepared for the possibility that Lucas would hear she was in town and seek her out to offer his condolences. She'd been prepared for that, for the awkward conversation.

But she had not been prepared for news of his death. His murder. For yellow tape screaming at the townspeople that no amount of baskets filled with nasturtiums and verbena and sweet potato vines would keep them safe.

No one, no town, is ever prepared for that.

4

"Sorry, love," the waitress at the Blue Spruce said as she refilled Sarah's coffee. Turned out the hipster coffeehouse slash wine bar she remembered, on the ground floor of the old Lake Hotel, had closed. That left the Spruce, the sugar in the same dispensers on the same Formica tables as when her parents had brought them here for waffles after church or they'd crammed too many girls into a booth for Cokes and a shared order of fries on Friday afternoons after school, the same faded color prints of elk and Bighorn sheep staring down at her from the same plastic frames.

"Didn't mean to keep you waiting," the woman continued, "but the crime scene crew from Missoula just left. Ate everything in sight. Hope you weren't wanting any sausage this morning."

"Uh, no, thanks. Coffee and toast. Whole wheat?"

"Yup. Coupla eggs, bacon? We make the best hash browns in three counties. You could use a few extra calories, you don't mind me saying."

How could she mind, put that way? Plus, it was true. "Sure. Over easy. Thanks." Before Sarah could ask the waitress what she'd heard about the crime, the woman was gone.

"Sarah? Sarah McCaskill? Is that you?"

Sarah set the glossy brown mug on the table. Not who she wanted to see her first day back. They were the same age—did she look that old, too? God knows, some days she felt it.

"Becca. Yes, it's me." Sarah slid out of the booth and the two women gave each other a half hug punctuated by air kisses. Then, not because she wanted to but because it was polite, "Join me?"

"No, no." Becca waved away the invitation with a plump hand. "I tried to slide in there, they'd need the Jaws of Life to pry me out, especially after breakfast. There's a stool at the counter with my name on it. No, I just spotted you on my way back from the ladies' and wanted to say hello."

A silence fell between them.

"Well," Becca said, her voice breathy, her full face growing blank. "Can't let my pancakes get cold. Or that coffee of yours. We'll catch up another time."

"Yes, let's," Sarah said, but the other woman had already turned away.

Seated again, Sarah cradled the warm mug. She'd encountered too many of these uncomfortable silences in the last seventeen days—eighteen, now—to count. People didn't understand that all you needed was for them to acknowledge your loss. Even if all they said was "I heard about your husband—I'm so sorry," or "you must be heartbroken." She'd settle for "I don't know what to say," but people didn't even say that.

She picked up her phone. Started a text to her mother. Put it down, unfinished, and sipped her coffee. What did it say, that it was easier to accept mothering from the waitress she'd never met than from her own mother?

It said that her mother knew what she was going through, and the stranger didn't. Her mother would ask how she was feeling, was she sleeping, when had she last eaten, and had she talked to the kids? Even though Peggy talked to the kids at least once a week—well, to Abby, anyway. Noah, not so much. It was hard, sometimes, to remember that the questions came from love and concern.

If only she had answers.

"Careful—hot," the waitress said and Sarah raised her hands. What had she been thinking, ordering so much food? She remembered telling the kids, the kitchen counter covered with muffins and salads people had brought when they heard the news, that they needed to eat. Both had given her that "you're crazy" look kids learned before they learned their ABCs. But then Noah had said "You, too, Mom," and his tenderness had nearly crushed her.

Did anything smell as good as bacon and potatoes still sizzling from the grill? She picked up her fork.

Twenty minutes later, Janine slid into the booth and nodded at the empty plate. "I guess the food's good." The waitress appeared, coffee pot in one hand, an empty mug in the other. "Desperately, yes. And buttered white toast, please?"

"You got it, doll."

Janine tugged off her scrunchie, shook her hair loose, then drew it back again, all while glancing around. "Hasn't changed much. Smells better, though."

Sarah leaned forward, her voice low. "Everything's okay, right? I mean, not okay, but you're in the clear."

"I'm not under arrest, but that's not the same as not under suspicion," Janine replied, in an equally low tone. "Leo's a nice guy, but he's got a murder and no suspects."

"Oh, honey," the waitress said as she set Janine's plate of toast on the table. "When it comes to Lucas Erickson, this town is full of suspects."

"Deb!" the white-haired man at the nearest table interjected. "How can you say that?"

"Why shouldn't she say it?" his wife asked. "It's what everyone's thinking."

"Not a fan, I take it?" Sarah asked the waitress. *Deb.*

"The son of a bitch represented my ex in our divorce," Deb explained. "I know darn well Lucas helped him hide assets from me. Now he's living the good life, with a brand-new pontoon boat and a shiny red truck to pull it with. Candy-apple red. And I'm working here. Not that I don't enjoy it, but you understand."

She did. She hadn't been away from Montana so long that she didn't understand the dangers of men who drove candy-apple red pickups.

"I heard they took some woman in for questioning," the woman at the table said. "From Missoula, but I guess she used to live here."

Janine froze at the words, a piece of toast halfway to her mouth. Fortunately, Deb had her back to them, busy refilling the gossipy couple's coffee.

Sarah grabbed her bag and fished inside. Dropped cash on the table and stood. "Thanks, Deb. You were right about the hash browns. Sorry we've got to run." She managed to position herself so Janine could slide out and head for the door without being seen. "Bye now," she called over her shoulder.

Outside, Sarah led Janine down the sidewalk, away from the Spruce's plate glass windows.

"No one in this town will ever believe me," Janine said.

"Don't say that. Those people don't know anything. They don't know who you are. And you heard them—nobody liked Lucas." Although he must have had friends in high places—or thought he did—if he planned a run for Congress. And money, though you'd never guess that from the exterior of his office.

Questions, questions, questions, as Jeremy would have said.

"Leo's deputy told me about an electronics repair shop a block off Main. After we see if they can fix your phone, we'll find you some clothes," Sarah said. She hitched her bag up on her shoulder. "Come on."

"Sarah," Janine said. "Get real. I can't afford anything in this town."

"I'll buy you—"

"No. I don't want to owe you."

Friends back in Seattle had told her she needed a project to take her mind off her loss. She'd managed to not tell them to go jump in the lake. Her mother wanted her to make the lodge her project. Washing windows, ironing lace curtains, and pulling birds' nests out of gutters might be exactly the therapy she needed. Counting sets of china and making lists of paintings and knickknacks. It would go quickly, and might almost be fun, with help.

"Make you a deal. Give me a hand cleaning up the lodge, and we'll trade work for whatever you need. If you can stay for a few days. Did Leo tell you not to leave town?"

"No. Nic said he can't say that, that it's tantamount to an arrest, even if TV cops say it all the time. But I'm not going to leave yet. Not before she gets here."

Sarah had almost forgotten about Nic, making the long drive across the state. Maybe she'd been wrong; maybe Janine did need a lawyer.

"Deal?" She held out a hand.

Janine's features softened. "Okay. But we're shopping the sale racks."

No one recognized either of them as they picked out shirts and pants at the sporting goods store, and found sandals and tennis shoes to replace the rubber clogs that were part of Janine's kitchen work uniform. Everyone was as friendly as Deb the waitress and the couple in the café, and no one gave them a second glance at the grocery store, where they picked up new tea and sugar, cat food, and cleaning supplies, among other things. Sarah could almost feel Janine's anxiety ease.

The SUV loaded, Sarah dashed into the pharmacy for a notebook and tiny stickers. And a measuring tape—there had to be one somewhere in the lodge, but you could never find things like that when you needed them.

One more stop. Why was it so hard?

Because she hated to admit that at forty-seven, she needed her mother.

A few minutes later, they rounded the curve at the end of the lake and there, at the corner of Lake and First, its three-sided turret a beacon, sat the Wedding Cake. That had been her name for her grandparents' pink Victorian when she and Holly were kids and walked here every afternoon from the squat two-bedroom starter house on the other side of Main, their mother pushing Connor in the stroller. Before Grandpa Tom and Grandma Mary, often called Mary Mac because she'd traded one Irish surname for another, moved to the lodge full-time and gave the house in town to the young family.

The frothy old frame house hadn't been pink in ages. After Mary Mac died, Peggy confessed she'd always hated the pink and repainted it a dusty dark blue, the white gingerbread cream. Though it had been odd at first to see such a dramatic change, the blue and cream were striking. Almost as if the house should have been those colors all along.

Through the multi-paned windows of her bedroom on the second floor, Sarah had been able to see much of Bitterroot Lake and the mountains ringing the valley. Her view hadn't quite stretched to the lodge, though on a clear day she could see the point that separated McCaskill land from the Hoyt property to the east, and the beginnings of the gravel beach. Idyllic, even when life itself had not been a fairy tale. Her mother had converted the room into her studio years ago.

No driveways on this stretch of Lake Street; garages opened on the alley. Sarah drove past the house, made a U-turn, and pulled up in front. On either side of the walkway that split the compact front yard, clumps of daffodils bloomed and peonies sent up their fringed red stalks. Last year's leaves hadn't been raked from the shrubs around the foundation, and the window boxes that usually burst with geraniums and lobelia hadn't been planted yet. They climbed the broad wooden steps and Sarah grabbed the brass doorknob. Locked.

Tried the door again. Why did you always do that? As if the result might be different the second time.

"Mom?" She peered through the oval glass in the door, then the sidelight window. Dark.

"Try the back," Janine suggested. "Or call her."

As they picked their way over the stepping-stones on the east side of the house, Sarah thumbed her phone. The faint ring from inside was her only answer. She tried her mother's cell. No response.

The back door was locked, too. So was the garage, too dark to tell if her mother's car was tucked inside.

The seed of dread that had been planted in her gut with Jeremy's diagnosis sent up another shoot.

"She must be out running errands," she told Janine, hoping it was true. It had to be true. "She's taking pictures of the light or leaves or scenes she wants to paint."

"She'll call when she sees she missed you," Janine assured her.

Back in the car, back on the North Shore highway, she wanted to ask Janine about her interview, but held back. She didn't want to cross another invisible line, like when she'd offered to buy Janine some decent clothes. In Seattle, she and Jeremy had gradually come to live in a bubble, most of their friends well-off, if not downright wealthy. Fortunes built on tech, as theirs was.

If Lucas had meant to run for office, chances were he'd have hit Jeremy up for a campaign contribution sooner or later. *Hey, old buddy, haven't seen you in decades, but I hear you struck it rich. How 'bout it?*

She did not want to think about Lucas Erickson or his plans. Or who had hated him enough to fire a bullet into his chest.

They drove by an old farm that was now an alpaca ranch at the foot of the wooded hills. Another had been subdivided into five- and ten-acre parcels, growing trendy homes instead of wheat or potatoes. Janine spotted a foal in a pasture and they shared a smile at the sight of the long-legged baby. Lynx Mountain and Porcupine Ridge rose high above them, the hillside covered with Arrowleaf Balsamroot, her favorite wildflower. The further west, the lower the tree line. Spruce, fir, and pine, the occasional cedar. Birch, aspen, vine maple. Familiar territory, a road Sarah had known all her life, from her family's regular treks between town and lodge.

And yet, like all roads taken, in places it felt unrecognizable.

The two-lane highway wound between a series of ponds surrounded by the scarlet shoots of ceanothus, better known as elk bush, and golden shrubs whose name she could never recall. They passed the wildlife viewing area and neared the Hoyt land. The old ice house and homestead shack weren't visible from the road, her memory of them complicated.

"Stop," Janine said. "Pull over up there." She pointed to a turnout leading to an unused two-track.

The moment Sarah put the rig in park, Janine hopped out. Sarah followed her twenty yards back down the highway to a freshly painted white metal cross atop a red metal post. Crosses like these dotted Montana roads, erected at the site of each traffic fatality. Some became shrines, tended by the families of the dead, decorated for holidays or with mementos. Some appeared neglected, just the bare cross rusted by weather and time—marking a forgotten soul or a traveler who died far from home. Though the crosses honored the dead, the main reason for them was to remind drivers to slow down, take care, arrive alive.

Someone had wound silver and maroon ribbons around this post, and attached a key chain adorned with a tiny grizzly bear.

"Recent," Janine said, crouching to stroke the little bear in a maroon sweater emblazoned UM. The school colors, the school mascot. "Since the last rain."

In the last two days, then.

Then Sarah saw a second key chain, dangling one of those clear acrylic rectangles intended to hold a photograph. She reached out for a closer look.

At a face long gone, a face forever twenty-two. The face of Michael Brown.

5

A familiar dark-red sedan sat in the circular drive in front of the lodge. Sarah parked the rented SUV behind it. What was she supposed to feel right now? She had no idea. That was the thing about grief that no one told you: you would not know what to feel. You would crave comfort, and resist it. You would be angry, devastated, heartbroken, uncertain—even, God help you, relieved. You'd be anxious, terrified. Impatient, needy, worried, betrayed. Sometimes all at once, or so it seemed, your heart flipping through the dictionary searching for the right word for the moment.

The mudroom screen door opened and a woman emerged, drying her hands on a white dish towel.

Sarah blinked, unsure whether she was seeing her mother or the ghost of her grandmother. Her eyes, her mind, playing tricks on her again. The two women had looked nothing alike—they were mother- and daughter-in-law, not blood relations. But that was where their grandmother had always stood to greet them.

Had her mother, who was only seventy-two—or was it seventy-three?—aged that much since the funeral? Slighter, smaller, more gray in her long, dark blond hair, the skin around her eyes and mouth drawn.

Or had the whole world changed when she wasn't watching?

She flung open her door and dashed across the driveway, the gravel crunching underfoot. Who held each other more tightly? She couldn't tell. It didn't matter. It had been three years since her father, JP, died. When she'd found herself dreaming of him, night after night, in the weeks before Jeremy's death, her therapist said that was typical. That the fear of coming losses often unearthed old ones.

She took a step back, studying her mother's face. There it was, that dread, that fear, mingled with the love and worry in the familiar hazel eyes.

"Leo said you were here." Peggy's voice hovered on the knife edge between hurt and understanding.

"I'm sorry, Mom. I wanted—I guess I wanted a night here alone first, to figure out whether this was going to work. And then—" She gestured toward Janine, a few feet away, a shopping bag in hand. "Mom, you remember Janine Chapman. Janine Nielsen, from high school. My old roommate."

"I know Janine," Peggy said, as she extended an arm. "She came to my show in Missoula a few weeks ago. I didn't expect to see you again so soon."

The show had been in early April. Jeremy had been too ill; Sarah hadn't dared risk leaving him to fly over, even for a couple of days, but Peggy had sent pictures and a video clip from the opening. Landscapes and portraits, like the ones that hung in the house in Seattle.

Neither she nor Janine had mentioned running into each other.

"But what are you doing in Deer Park?" Peggy asked Janine, releasing her from the one-armed embrace.

"Let's get the groceries unloaded," Sarah said. "Then we can talk."

"I hope you bought cat food," Peggy said. "He's been jabbering at me since I got here, and I may not know cats, but I know what that means. Where did he come from, anyway?" She didn't wait for an answer, and Janine followed her inside.

Sarah bent to pick up the white cotton dish towel her mother had dropped. *Tuesday*, it read in neat black stitches beneath the outline of a little Dutch girl in a pink and blue skirt, yellow braids flying as she leapt across the corner of the towel, the arms of a windmill behind her. Mary Mac had embroidered set after set of these towels. If her grandmother wasn't in her sewing room working on a quilt, she'd been sitting in the oak rocker facing the lake, or on the deck under the deep overhang, handwork in her lap. Most of it she'd given away. Trust her mother to dig out the right day of the week.

"No point putting anything in the cupboards until we've wiped them out," Peggy said a few minutes later as Sarah set the last bag of groceries on the kitchen counter. "This whole place is full of dust and cobwebs. I didn't realize until . . ."

"Until what, Mom?" It wasn't like her mother to leave a job unfinished.

Peggy sank against the counter, the rag in her hand dripping on to the floor. "Sometimes, it's just too much."

The size of the place? The grime? The memories? Sarah took the wet rag and wrung it into the sink.

Abby would be home for the summer in a few weeks, Noah a week or two later. She'd told them, before they went back to school, that she wanted them to come to the lake with her to spread some of Jeremy's ashes, but they hadn't made firm plans. So much up in the air.

A spasm of anger tore through her chest. At Jeremy, at the cancer. It wasn't right to blame him; she knew that. But sometimes she did.

The kettle whistled, bringing Sarah back to the present. She rummaged in a grocery bag for the tea they'd bought—Earl Grey, permanently linked to the lodge in her memory—then plopped bags in the white ironstone mugs and Janine filled them.

"I can't believe all this dust." Sarah dug for a box of tissues before taking her seat.

"I can't believe you didn't tell me you were coming," Peggy said as Sarah blew her nose. "I'd have picked you up at the train and taken you home. To a clean house and a clean bed."

This, this is why I didn't tell you. "You don't drive at night, Mom."

"I'd have asked your brother to take me."

"Connor's busy, Mom. He already took time away from the business to come to the funeral." McCaskill Land and Lumber, the family business for more than a hundred years. "He didn't need to be traipsing all the way into Whitefish last night to pick me up."

"Of course he came to your husband's funeral, and he would have driven me to the station."

"Besides," Janine said, "if she hadn't come to the lodge, I don't know what I'd have done."

Peggy turned to her. "And what *are* you doing here, dear?"

Janine flicked her dark eyes toward Sarah, who set down her tea and cleared her throat.

"Mom, you heard about Lucas Erickson, right? That he was killed, sometime yesterday afternoon."

"Yes, it's tragic. But what . . ."

Sarah poked her tongue over her bottom lip and exhaled. "Janine found him."

For a long moment, the only sound was the cat, scrabbling in the bowl of dry food they'd set in the corner.

"I didn't kill him, Peggy," Janine said. "I swear. After I found him, I came out here. To think. Make a plan. Then Sarah showed up."

"That's why you called Leo," Peggy said to her daughter, "and why you were in town this morning. Becca Smalley told her mother she saw you at the Blue Spruce, and her mother mentioned it to me when she stopped by to return a book. That's when I dropped everything and came out here."

What had her father always said about small towns? Everyone knows everything about you, whether it's true or not. People you don't know, know you. And his warning when they were teenagers, testing their wings: someone will see everything you do.

"We went in to give statements," Sarah said. "And pick up a few things. We stopped by the house, but you'd already left."

"I still don't understand why you came up here," Peggy said to Janine. "And why would anyone think you killed Lucas Erickson? Ohhh. But—but that was twenty-five years ago."

The crash had made headlines. A small town now, despite its discovery by tourists and wealthy snowbirds, Deer Park had been almost claustrophobic back then. The McCaskills were well known, and the death of a guest at their lake house was big news. Michael Brown had been a star on the basketball court and people up here were Griz fans. And Lucas had grown up in Whitefish, the next town over.

The assault, though, had been kept quiet. After Janine decided not to press charges, what would have been the point? They'd all expected that Lucas would be charged with negligent homicide, along with other charges for the injuries to Jeremy, and pay his debt to society. They'd all been shocked when nothing happened. Sarah had told her parents about the assault—she'd never asked what Janine told her mother—and if Peggy and JP thought it a mistake not to pursue Lucas in court, they'd never said so.

But she hadn't told them the part that kept up her up at night.

"I've never understood," Sarah said, "why Lucas settled in Deer Park. Wouldn't it have bothered him? To remember what he did here, to be stared at, whispered about?"

"I never heard anyone say a thing," Peggy replied. "Maybe when he and Misty first moved here—five years? More? It was all so long ago. And people understand. Accidents happen."

Sarah felt Janine's eyes boring into her.

"Misty," she said. "Should I know Misty?"

"Misty Calhoun. Calhoun Sporting Goods. She was a year behind your sister, I think."

"Ohmygosh, we stopped there this morning."

"She took over when her father died—expanded the Deer Park store and opened one in Whitefish. That's where she moved when she and Lucas got divorced last year."

"The wife's always a suspect," Sarah said, "at least on TV. Double that for ex-wives."

Peggy put a hand on Janine's arm. "No matter what he did, finding him must have been terrible. You poor thing. I'm glad you and Sarah ran into each other. Stay here as long as you want. Treat the lodge like your home."

Janine didn't say anything about running from the scene, or forcing her way into the cabin. She didn't mention the letter Lucas had sent her, or Leo's suspicions. So Sarah bit her tongue.

The cat rubbed against her leg. "You like that food? Or were you so hungry you'd eat anything?" She ran a hand down the cat's back, the spine and ribs too close to the surface, and the cat twitched. "We'll fatten you up."

"I can't imagine where he came from," Peggy said. "Ask around. Or call the vet, or the animal shelter. He might be lost."

"She. Janine found her sitting on the front porch last night. And ask who? There are no neighbors out here."

Peggy waved a hand vaguely but Janine interrupted before she could answer.

"When I called the bakery this morning, I promised to check in later and let my boss know when I'd be back. Mind if I borrow your phone?"

Sarah took her phone out of her pocket and handed it over. Janine left through the mudroom.

"I'm trying to understand," Peggy said. "I really am."

"When you figure it out, let me know." Sarah pushed back her chair and stood. At the stove, she picked up the kettle, then put it down without refilling her mug. She stared at the burners and the red kettle, not seeing anything, then spoke, her back to her mother. "I'm sorry. I don't know what's gotten into me lately."

"You're allowed to be off-center, honey. It happens to all of us."

"This might sound odd, but is there a group of volunteers that decorates the roadside crosses?"

"The American Legion puts them up. Every few years, you see a crew out sanding and repainting, straightening posts the snowplows bent. But decorating, no. That's up to the family. Why?"

"The cross on the highway, by the marsh," Sarah said. "Michael Brown's cross. Someone's tied fresh ribbon to it, hung a little UM grizzly. And now Lucas . . ."

Peggy pressed her hands together in prayer position, held them to her lips. "I didn't even notice. I was so worried about you. Do you think there's a connection?"

"I don't know what to think. About Lucas. About Janine being here. She called Nic—Nicole, who's on her way from Billings, for God's sake. That's more than four hundred miles. Why does she need a lawyer? Why is this all coming up now? Just when Jeremy . . ." She couldn't say it. Sometimes she could say her husband died; at other times, the words wouldn't form, as if her brain were refusing to admit reality. And she had no patience for the euphemisms—passed, lost. But right now, she had lost all words.

"Do you think I did it?" Janine asked from the doorway. "Tell me now. If you think I shot Lucas, tell me now and I'll go. I'll be out of your life for good."

"No!" Sarah said. "Janine, no! Why would you think—I thought you went—"

"I wasn't sure how far I'd have to go to get a signal, so I decided to drive and came back for my keys. Why is it that Lucas Erickson can come back to the town where he tried to rape me and drove so recklessly he killed his own roommate and he gets a free pass, like he did all those years ago? And I—I didn't do anything, not then and not now. But you wonder, don't you? You know me, and you wonder. Because of my mother."

The accusation stung the air. After a long moment, Peggy broke the silence.

"You are not your mother," she said, the firmness of her tone surprising Sarah.

"So you both keep reminding me," Janine replied. "Why don't I believe you?"

Sarah had completely forgotten about the cat until she heard a sharp yowl followed by a short yip. All three women looked to the little furball, sitting on the floor, swatting at something none of them could see.

I know the feeling, kitty-cat. I know the feeling.

6

This time, Janine let the screen door slam behind her.

"Wonder if she'll come back," Peggy said.

"Hope so. She's got my phone." Sarah dumped her cold tea down the drain. The pipes gurgled, unaccustomed to use. "You don't mean to wash every dish in every cabinet right now, do you?"

"At the risk of making generations of McCaskill women roll over in their graves, no. We'll wash up what you'll need for now, then get to the nitty-gritty when we have more time."

"It's a plan. I'll start making an inventory then."

Windows, counters, the oven and stove. They washed one cabinet's worth of dishes, a mix of Great Northern Railway designs. She smiled at a plate in the mountains and wildflowers pattern that had always been her favorite. Then they cleared another cabinet for a makeshift pantry. Gave the linoleum floor a good sweep. Sarah poked the broom into a corner cobweb, the threads stiff and sticky, and sent the spiders a silent apology.

"At this rate," she said mid-afternoon, "even a lick and a promise will take days."

"Your grandmother always said you should start cleaning at the top of the house and work your way down. Your great-grandmother, too." Peggy rinsed her washrag and wrung it out. "But Caro had live-in servants, and Mary Mac hired household help."

Three full stories and a cellar, linked by a narrow back staircase tucked behind the kitchen and a grand staircase that opened into the entry, the walls log, the ceilings tongue-and-groove. Plus the cabins and the carriage house, with its upstairs apartment. When her father and uncle, Leo's dad, were kids in the 1950s and '60s, the entire clan had summered here, even relatives who lived in town. Each family had its own cabin, the grandparents and strays sleeping in the lodge. By the time Sarah, Holly, and Connor came along, the extended family had dispersed. It had mainly been the three of them, along with Leo and his brother, who spent summers here, swimming in the lake and jumping off the long dock built in the steamboat era. Exploring in the woods. And on rainy days, playing board games or hide-and-seek, though she'd often taken refuge in the carriage house to read or play with the old dollhouse.

"I'll tackle a bathroom, if you want to finish up here," Sarah said.

"What about bedrooms? There's only two couches, and you'll need a place for Nicole. Besides, those couches aren't very comfortable." Peggy wriggled, as though the mere thought of a night on them made her back hurt.

"We'll manage," she said, and kissed the top of her mother's head. "But not without a bathroom."

She decided on the second-floor bath, since it had a tub and shower. She'd used it this morning, grateful that the claw-foot tub had never been replaced. In her design work, she'd witnessed too many of the hideous things people did to classic homes in the name of modernization. Hard water had trickled down from the faucet, forming a line of rust and a blue-green ring around the drain, but that was the only visible damage.

She knelt to scrub the porcelain, and through the thin fabric of her leggings felt the black-and-white hex floor tiles making tiny indentations in the tender skin below her knee caps. An hour later, tub and toilet too old and worn to sparkle but clean enough, the walls and wainscoting wiped down, the lights, the wavy mirror, and the classic white cabinets washed, she extended one leg, then the other, unkinking her joints. Plucked at her T-shirt where it stuck to her skin and ran her fingers through her hair, damp at the roots. Picked up her bucket of cleaning supplies and damp rags, but instead of heading back down, as she'd intended, she set the bucket on the floor outside her grandmother's sewing room and went upstairs.

The third-floor rooms were shaped by the gables and the steep pitch of the roof line. At the far end were the servants' rooms, a small bath between them. In her childhood, these had been the boys' bunk rooms, but they were empty now. Where had the furniture gone?

In the middle, overlooking the lake, was a large space her grandmother had called the ballroom and her grandfather the billiard room. The heavy oak billiard table with its woven leather pockets stood at one end. But what had happened to the poker tables and the marvelous velvet couches that once sat along the walls, waiting for dancers to rest their feet?

She paused, half-hearing a waltz play from the old cabinet Victrola that had stood in the corner. She'd coerced the other kids into holding pretend parties in the grand space, dancing with Leo, as the two eldest, and pairing Holly with his younger brother, who hadn't protested too much. Connor had hopped around the older kids until he got too tired, or bored.

Her mother hadn't mentioned clearing this space. Must have been a while ago, though, judging from the dust on the light fixtures and a cobweb in the door frame.

On her way back to the stairs, she peeked into the storeroom at the far end. Empty, the extra furniture, trunks, and odds and ends gone.

Curious.

Back on the second floor, she steeled herself at the door of the girls' room, where she and Holly had slept.

It was virtually untouched. Three iron bed frames, each a different design, separated by pine nightstands. A quilt lay folded over the end of each twin mattress, an old crate or a flat-top trunk at the foot. Hers had been the Flying Geese, Holly's a classic Starflower.

Untouched by a dustcloth too. She sneezed and closed the door behind her. Grabbed her cleaning supplies and gripped the pine banister as she descended to the main floor. In those same pretend dance days, she'd preened her way down the grand staircase, swishing imaginary skirts and flirting with phantom beaux, the belle of the ball that wasn't.

A sweet memory.

To her surprise, her mother wasn't washing windows or banishing cobwebs from corners. Instead, Peggy sat on one of the lumpy leather couches, staring out at the lake. Or whatever it was she saw.

Sarah set her bucket down and sat next to her mother. Flecks of green and red paint dotted her mother's nails and knuckles.

"After your grandmother died," Peggy said, "your father and I talked about moving out here. He wanted to live on the lake and wake up to this view. I'm sorry I disappointed him by saying no."

"Why did you?" Sarah had been busy with two small children then, and not paying a lot of attention.

"It just—it just didn't feel right. I never could explain."

"Well, sure. It was your mother-in-law's house."

"No. I adored Mary Mac. And I do love the place. It was almost as if—oh, never mind. Too hard to explain." Peggy started to get up but Sarah pulled her back.

"Try, Mom."

"It was as though the house wanted something from me that I couldn't give it. See? Now you think I'm nuts."

No, she didn't. Not at all.

Peggy stood. "But I know what the house wants right now. It wants a good cleaning."

* * *

They decided to wait on the windows until the sun wasn't shining directly on them, and moved up to the second floor, to her grandparents' bedroom. After all these years, it still held faint scents of cedar and lavender. A milk glass lamp sat on a simple oak dresser with cut-glass knobs, and Peggy switched it on. "This lamp is one of my favorite pieces in the entire house."

"Speaking of which, where's all the stuff from the third floor?"

"Don't you remember?" Peggy asked. "Brooke had visions of turning this into a luxury rental. They started clearing, but didn't get very far—Connor got too busy with work."

"Oh, right. I completely forgot." Her memory had become a sieve, another casualty of Jeremy's illness. Not a bad idea. Except that she hated it. Strangers in their house.

"By the way, your brother has something to discuss with you."

"That sounds ominous." Connor hadn't mentioned anything in Seattle. He and Brooke, a bubbly brunette who barely reached his shoulder, had brought the kids out for the funeral, but it had been a quick trip, so the kids didn't miss much school. Not much time to talk.

"No, no. Nothing to worry about."

A phrase guaranteed to make her worry. But Connor was rock solid. Always had been. She regretted that they weren't closer, mainly because of the age difference—he'd only been twelve when she left for college.

"I always felt like I was sleeping in a tree house when we stayed out here," she said. "That's the feeling I was after when we built our house. Watch out for falling spiders." She ran the yellow-headed dust mop around the coving where the walls and ceiling met, then both women picked up dustcloths.

A few minutes later, Peggy straightened. "So why is Janine here? Neither of you wanted to tell me."

And Sarah didn't want to talk about it now.

"It has to do with Lucas, doesn't it?" Peggy continued. "With whatever happened the day of the accident."

"You know what happened, Mom. He attacked her." Sarah started dusting the head of the sleigh bed she'd always loved. She'd searched all over for a king-sized version that didn't scream "new," and finally had one custom-made. After Jeremy's funeral, she'd crawled into it, seeking comfort. Instead, it felt cold and foreign, no longer hers. She'd crept down the hall and slipped into bed with Abby, the two of them holding each other through the long, sleepless night.

"I always felt terrible that I wasn't a better friend to Sue," Peggy said.

Sarah stopped dusting. "Janine's mom? You weren't friends at all. Were you?"

"I know, everyone thought she deserved what she got. And no denying, she had problems, long before . . ." Peggy waved her hand, as if to wave away the memory of what Sue Nielsen had done. "But when she was sober, she was nice. And funny."

Sarah sat on the edge of the bed. "How did you know her?"

"Pie, of course."

"What?"

"We bonded over pie. I used to treat myself to a piece now and then, at the Spruce, when I was feeling the need for a little sweetness. Sue was a terrific waitress, and we had some great conversations."

This was a side of her mother she'd never seen.

"You can tell, sometimes," Peggy continued, "when someone needs a friend. So I stopped by more often."

"For pie."

"Or just coffee and a chat. To keep an eye on her. You and Holly were off in Missoula, and so was Janine. Connor was in high school, busy with sports and girls and who knows what else."

"But then . . ."

"But then, we had staffing changes at the school and I picked up more hours. Something had to give."

"Pie."

"You graduated and moved out to Seattle. And you know what happened."

She knew. But why had she never known that Peggy felt guilty over Sue Nielsen's fall—or plunge—off the wagon and into hell?

Guilt, the legacy that keeps on giving.

They finished in silence, then moved to the sewing room. Part of the fun of hide-and-seek games in the lodge had been dashing out the door that opened onto the balcony, then disappearing around the corner and sneaking back in through her grandparents' bedroom.

Sarah was dusting the gold-framed pictures on top of the bookcase when they heard a car approach. Peggy went to the window and pushed the lace curtain aside, as Sarah had done this morning when Leo arrived. Had that really just been this morning?

"Well, that's a relief. You won't need to buy a new phone."

"I better go talk to her."

Downstairs, Janine stood by the windows, arms crossed, staring out at the lake. At the sound of Sarah's footsteps, she spoke. "I didn't run off with your phone."

"I didn't think you had. Janine, I know you didn't kill Lucas. I know you only went to see him because . . ." Sarah interrupted herself, aware of Peggy coming up behind her.

"Because of the letter," Janine said.

"Letter? What letter?" Peggy asked. "Why did you go see him?"

"I know," Sarah said. "Everyone who knows you knows you couldn't have hurt him. Even though he hurt you. Even though he threatened you."

"What are you talking about?" Peggy said. "What letter?"

"I drove into town." Janine sank into the nearest chair, a peeled pine armchair, the back a dark cordovan leather, the seat cushion reupholstered with a vintage Pendleton blanket. "Drove down every street we lived on, my mother and I. Past every run-down hovel, though most of them are gone now, replaced with cute little houses. Town is very cute now."

That could have been a compliment or a put-down.

"Funny, isn't it?" Janine continued. "When I think of Deer Park, I don't think of those places. I think of the lodge and the lake. Despite what happened with Lucas. This is a good place."

"I am so sorry. When the wreck happened on the highway, we lost each other, too. I hate that."

Janine clenched her jaw and nodded. "But would you and Jeremy have gotten together, if it hadn't been for—everything?"

"I think so. It would have been different, though. Can we make things different now?"

"Depends on your cousin, doesn't it?"

"Leo?" Peggy said. "Would someone please tell me what's going on?"

Sarah had almost forgotten her mother. "Sit," she said, and her mother sat. Sarah explained about the letter. Their theory that Lucas feared Janine would resurface and derail his campaign for whatever office he'd planned to seek. The gruesome discovery that led her to take refuge at the lodge.

As Sarah spoke, the cat jumped up next to her, and she stroked the thin back.

Peggy's face paled. "But that's all in the past. Janine, I hate that he never paid for what he did to you, but it was all a long time ago."

"What about what he did to the boys?" Sarah demanded. "To Jeremy, and to Michael Brown."

"It was an accident," Peggy said, voice rising, glancing from Sarah to Janine and back.

Sarah studied her hands, not trusting herself to speak.

"I get that men with flawed histories can still live decent lives," Janine said. "Even without deliberately making amends. But what I don't get, why I came up here, is why threaten me to keep me quiet?"

"Right," Sarah said. "Once you try to silence someone, the threat becomes the bigger story. People—voters, donors—would assume the worst, no matter how much he denied the attack or repeated his claim that you let it drop."

"Where there's smoke, there's fire," Peggy said.

"I didn't let it drop," Janine protested. "The sheriff—"

"I know, I know." No point digging it all up and picking through it all again. Not now. Later, if they had to. If she had to, to clear her own conscience.

"Now I see why you asked about the cross," Peggy said after a long moment. And to Janine, "and why you feared being compared to your mother. No one here remembers any of that. It was far too long ago."

Janine's lips parted, her brows dipping slightly. Sarah shared her disbelief. When your mother went to jail for shooting a man, it wouldn't be hard for people to believe you'd do the same.

She shifted her gaze to the cold waters outside.

Why was the past rushing forward now?

7

Roots had broken through the forest floor. Snowberry and mahonia, the tiny yellow flowers about to open, had narrowed the path, forcing Sarah to wriggle through the branches while ducking her head and pushing aside maple vines and usnea. Old man's beard, the gray-green lichen that dangled at exactly the wrong height. She'd followed the path along the lake past the cabins, then up into the woods, where it had become little more than a deer trail.

There was a metaphor in there, she knew, but she didn't have the patience to dig for it right now.

After their conversation about the letter, Peggy had suggested a cup of tea. Earl Grey cures all ills. Not a bad theory, in ordinary times. But things had not been ordinary in a long time, and they were showing no sign of improving. When Sarah put on her jacket and her white tennis shoes and said she needed a walk, Peggy had said she might as well leave, too. She'd laid a hand on Sarah's cheek, her eyes moist, and Sarah had felt like an ungrateful child, wallowing in her internal muck. But she hadn't said "don't go."

The trail widened, opening up as it gained elevation, and she pounded forward, onward, upward, the warmth of the late afternoon sun filtering through the fir and pines, the spruce and birch, releasing the soft scent of spring.

A good half mile from the lodge, she stopped and bent over, the heels of her hands digging into the tops of her thighs as she worked to catch her breath. Pushing the air out, pulling it in, unable to tell the difference between the physical pain and the emotional.

Finally, she straightened. In the spring, when she was a kid, her father and uncle had sharpened the saws and clippers and cleared fallen trees from the trails around the lodge. This overlook had gotten extra attention, a special place. A sense of elation spread through her as the warmth returned to her skin. Around her were more shades of green than she could name, new growth at the tips of the boughs, sunlight dappling the forest floor. Across Bitterroot Lake, though, the forests grew so thick and dark that the hillsides appeared nearly black. It was a matter of perspective, another metaphor she chose to ignore. Roofs clustered in small clearings, closer and more dense as they neared town. The church camp across from Whitetail Lodge was still in use, unlike many of the small camps that had once dotted western Montana's lakeshores, and in a few weeks, the sounds of children would drift across the water and campfires would dot the shoreline in the evening.

Above her, a birch bough waved in the wind. When she and Jeremy were first married, they'd driven over every summer for two or three weeks. Then the children came, Noah, and two years later Abby, and she'd relished the days at the lodge with them and the rest of the family. But Jeremy's business began to take more of his time, and though she and the kids sometimes stayed when he went back to Seattle, she hadn't liked being apart. As the kids got older, their summers filled with soccer camp and music camp and time with their friends. They'd been lucky to squeeze in a week in Montana, and to visit every other Christmas. The kids hadn't been here since her father died three years ago; last summer, she'd come alone. Her cousins didn't use the place much. Holly stayed in town when she visited. That left Connor, too busy to use the place much.

Maybe it was time.

She sat on the giant rock outcropping, too spent to cry.

The landscape where you grew up shaped you. Maybe you didn't need to own it, or visit often. Maybe it always lived inside you.

She had a friend in Seattle, the mother of one of Abby's besties, whose dad had been in the army. Every two or three years, they'd moved. She'd lived in Seattle for twenty years, half of it in the same house, but still felt she didn't truly belong anywhere. Because she wasn't from anywhere.

Sarah dearly loved their house in Seattle. Their dream house, near Lake Washington, roomy but not crazy-big. She'd been careful to make sure it reflected Jeremy as much as her, with plenty of light and calming spaces. It was a true home, and she belonged to it as much as it belonged to them. Or to her, now.

But at the moment, she was like her friend. She belonged nowhere.

Get over yourself, girl. So your husband died. It's not the end of the world. Even though it feels that way.

The world was still out there, spinning on its merry way. People were still going to work, to school, to lunch. Going about their daily lives.

Sending threatening letters and getting killed.

This endless rumination wasn't getting her anywhere. Although that was the point of wandering in the woods, wasn't it?

She pushed herself off the rock and continued up the trail. Soon it would fork, one branch heading toward the old horse barns, the other leading up to McCaskill Lane and the highway.

A few feet later, she stopped. Was someone watching her?

Ugh. Seeing things again. The woods were empty except for a handful of chattering squirrels and one young doe who'd sprinted away.

And a raven, who cawed. She raised her head, shielding her eyes as she searched, finally spotting the big black bird high in a lodgepole pine. "I suppose you've got an opinion, too. Everyone else does."

He said nothing.

At the fork, she angled toward the highway, pulling her phone out of her pocket to check the signal. Two bars, bouncing up and down. Texts and voice mails landed in her inbox as she walked, their pings and chimes merging with the whiz of traffic, the sounds of so-called civilization.

Any other time, she might enjoy being unreachable, but not right now. She needed to be able to check on the kids. To respond to her friends. Call her therapist.

The trail dipped, then climbed back up. At the fork, she stopped, out of breath, her legs shaking. *Was she that out of shape?* She'd given up walking with the neighborhood women a couple of months ago, not wanting to leave Jeremy alone, though the home health aide would happily have adjusted her schedule to allow Sarah to get out. Mainly, she hadn't wanted to answer questions about him every time she left the house. And she'd lost her ability to chat about insignificant things.

Her walking buddies had all come to the service and reception, but she hadn't tied on her walking shoes and rejoined them.

The white walking shoes that now bore dark smudges. What had she been thinking?

She leaned against a tree, grateful to see four bars on her phone. Grateful to see texts from both kids. Abby, on the way back to the dorm after turning in the paper that had been due the day of Jeremy's funeral, the deadline extended. *His exams are easy—I should get an A*, the text read. *Brownie sundae tonight!*

The family tradition to celebrate wrapping up a big project.

Good job! Sarah replied. *You've earned a treat!* The reply was almost instant. *Wish I could tell Dad. Miss you—love you!* She choked back a sob, then thumbed *Me, too. XO3.* Love and kisses, to the power of three, another family tradition.

She scrolled past texts from friends and paused on one from her therapist. A single word: *Breathe.*

In, out, her breath uneven, gradually becoming steadier. Her head cleared, the dizziness lifting. The technique didn't always work, but often enough to try.

Next, a text from Noah, with a quick update on a favorite class. His grades were as good as his sister's, but he didn't express the anxiety over them that she did. Then he wrote, *Good to be home.*

"Home," she said out loud. "You went home? But I'm here. Why didn't you tell me?"

And it hit her. He didn't mean their house in Seattle. He meant school, on the other side of the country.

Had she lost him too?

*　*　*

Sarah had almost talked herself out of detouring down the trail to the horse barns and the old homestead when the glint of sunlight on metal caught her eye. The road, such as it was, ran only between the cluster of old buildings at the top of the Hoyt property and McCaskill Lane. No one should be up here.

She ducked into the woods, inside the tree line. A short distance ahead, she spotted a small blue car, an older model, parked just this side of the horse stalls, the driver's door open. A thin, red-haired woman held a pair of binoculars to her eyes. Sarah glanced in the direction the woman was looking, expecting to see an owl or a pileated woodpecker. Nothing.

She took a step onto the road. "Are you lost? Can I help you find something?"

The woman jerked her head toward Sarah, dropping her hands, obviously startled. "Oh, gosh, no. I didn't see you."

That was obvious.

"I just—I was driving by on the highway, and I thought I'd pop down here and see if I could find some wildflowers for my mother. She's been in the hospital, in Deer Park, and she's always loved spring wildflowers—"

"I'm sorry," Sarah said. "I hope she's okay."

The woman's eyes widened and she exhaled. "More or less. But thanks."

"It's early, but if you head back that way"—Sarah gestured—"past the horse barns and the old ice house, you might find some pussy willows around the ponds." She turned back to the woman in time to see her toss the binoculars onto the passenger seat and reach one foot into the car. Her shoes were clean; she'd obviously just begun her hunt and gotten distracted by something in the trees.

"Good luck," Sarah called and raised a hand as the woman settled into the driver's seat and closed her door. "I hope your mother gets well soon."

She watched as the woman turned the car around and drove off, a soft billow of dust in her wake.

Strange, she thought. But then, strange things happened in the woods.

*   *   *

The first thing that struck her when she walked through the front door of the lodge was the smell. Clean. Not Lemon Pledge or Windex, chemical imitations of fresh air, but the real thing. The mildly astringent scent of wood that had been scrubbed, of vinegar spray, and a hint of lavender.

Then she spotted the cat, sitting a few feet away. The cat blinked but didn't make a sound.

"Dinner in minutes, I promise." She toed off her shoes, pushing them to the wall with one foot, and hung her jacket on a wrought-iron coat hook. Worked her fingers over her mid-back and the sensation, not quite an ache, that had never left her for more than a few hours the last few weeks.

Someone—Peggy or Janine—had cleaned the tiny half-bath under the stairs. She stood at the white pedestal sink and splashed cold water on her face. Ran her fingers through her hair to work out the tangles. The built-in mirror was original to the house, the silvering lightly foxed in one corner. She couldn't blame her splotchy skin or the shadows under her hazel eyes on the glass, darn it.

Out in the hall, the cat hadn't moved a whisker.

"Come on, then." She headed for the swinging doors that led to the kitchen, each with a small window servants could peer through to check whether the family was ready for the next course. Silently, on little cat feet, as the poet said of fog, the cat followed, then scooted past her.

"You faker." Both food and water bowl were nearly full. "You just wanted attention." She crouched beside the cat and scratched behind her ears, then rubbed the soft fur beneath her chin.

She uncorked the chardonnay she'd planned to drink last night. A collection of mismatched glasses gathered over the years filled half a kitchen cupboard. "No," she told the cat. "We're going to do this right." Though she hadn't begun the formal inventory, she knew where her grandmother's wedding china and glassware were kept, in the built-ins that lined one dining room wall. They'd used the pieces on holidays and special occasions, the gold-rimmed white dishes and the ruby crystal with its delicate gold filigree. Back through the swinging doors they went, she and her feline shadow.

But the glass-front cabinet was empty. Not a wine glass or a dinner plate in sight. No champagne saucers. No decanter or serving bowls.

"Where did it go?" she asked the cat, busy licking a foot.

In the kitchen, Sarah rinsed a glass printed with the Chateau Ste. Michelle logo, a souvenir from a wine tour they'd taken her parents on years ago. Poured and took a sip, the tang of fruit and flowers filling her mouth. Carried the glass outside.

How funny was it, to be five hundred miles from home drinking wine made not ten miles from home?

It was a moment Jeremy would have noticed, acknowledging it with a slight lift of the glass and a wink.

Her therapist had said those moments would hit her hard for a while, but that gradually the pain would ease. Everyone said that—don't make any drastic changes for a year, don't dwell on the past, blah blah blah. But remembering and dwelling weren't the same. She didn't want to forget Jeremy's laugh, or the way he always said "look at you" when she came downstairs in the morning. How he took his coffee, with cream and honey, not sugar. Forgetting the details would be like losing him all over again. Besides, those moments were part of her life, too.

She raised her face, eyes closed, and let the spring sun kiss her.

Was she crazy to think she was supposed to be here right now? That the lodge needed her?

She didn't know what to think anymore.

Lucas. So much promise destroyed by his pride and stupidity. His life upended. Michael dead. Jeremy had not been one for regrets or second-guessing himself—he'd left that to her—but it had always bothered her, that they hadn't been able to stop Lucas from attacking Janine or from tearing away in the red convertible.

Now they were all gone, those beautiful young men from that beautiful day on these shores, twenty-five years ago.

Leaving her to face the sad, sucky fact that life went on. Kids finished papers, studied for exams, made summer plans. Of course the kids would fledge. That was the point of raising kids. They left the nest. But did it have to be right now?

Sarah heard a sound and cocked her head. Heard Janine calling indistinctly. Letting her know Nic was driving down the lane?

One last swallow, then she headed inside, setting her glass on the walnut table next to her grandmother's rocker, the table's barley-twist legs dust-free thanks to Peggy. Now she could hear tires crunching on the gravel and Janine calling out hello. A car door closing.

Then, a second door? Had Nic brought her family? Tempe must be fourteen or fifteen by now, but she would be in school. Or was it just the sound of the back door as Nic got out an overnight bag?

Then Sarah heard the voices.

She watched from the doorway as Janine released Nic from a hug and turned to greet the other woman. Not a teenager at all. It was her sister. It was Holly.

What the hell was she doing here?

8

An invisible band tightened around Sarah's chest, squeezing out all the air. Bad enough that when they'd gathered at the house after Jeremy's funeral, she'd overheard Holly on the phone saying "so much for her perfect life." Meaning *her*, Sarah. Meaning the cracks in their relationship had become gaps too wide to bridge.

Now Holly was here, not fifteen feet away, glaring at her. But in her own fury and confusion, she couldn't read her sister's eyes.

Maybe she never could. Maybe she never had understood her only sister.

"What are you doing here?"

"I called her," Nic said. "She caught the first flight."

"But why? This isn't bridge. We didn't need a fourth."

"I want a chance to explain," Holly said.

"I don't want your explanation," Sarah snapped. "Mom asked me to help her with the lodge. We don't need you."

Holly's fair skin paled and her neck stiffened. She was being cruel, Sarah knew. And she didn't give a damn.

"I came because of this." Holly pulled an envelope from her brown leather bag and held it out.

And Sarah's very bad feeling got even worse.

*   *   *

"It has to have come from him," Janine said a few minutes later. "From Lucas. No one else knows everything that happened."

Outside the four of them, a point that hung heavily in the air over the dining room table, swirling like the cigar smoke of a hundred years ago. The letter lay on the table. Cups of tea and coffee and glasses of wine sat, untouched. That one of them could have done something so awful, so hurtful, was impossible.

Or was it? Sarah shuddered involuntarily, and she drew her wine glass closer. It gave no comfort, the smell, the thought of drinking it turning her stomach sour.

"Plus it doesn't make any sense," Nic said. She sat across from Sarah, her back to the view. "The letter says 'only you know the truth.' That can only be one person, not two. Not both Holly and Janine."

"He didn't expect us to talk to each other," Holly said. "But how could he have known . . ." She let the words trail off, the question unfinished, its import clear.

"You mean, how could he have known we aren't close any-more?" Nic asked. "Not like we were, anyway. He could only know if he'd talked to one of us." Her piercing blue eyes rested on each of them in turn, but no one flinched.

Could Lucas have heard the truth from someone else? Jeremy might have told him, innocently enough, that "the girls" had drifted apart. That would have been years ago, though—he hadn't talked to Lucas in ages. He'd reached out to a lot of people from the past as he got sicker—she'd find

66

him in a T-shirt and flannel pajama bottoms, on his phone, his dog-eared address book on the table next to him, dialing away. Well, not dialing. The address book was hilariously retro, when you thought about it, for a tech guy. He hadn't been a Bill Gates or Steve Jobs tech guy, whose name and products everyone knew, though his banking apps and pay-roll accounting software touched a lot of lives. But Lucas? No, she couldn't imagine Jeremy making that call. He'd known how she felt.

But then, she couldn't have imagined anything that had happened in the last few months.

"You ever run into him?" Holly asked Nic. "Professionally?"

"I haven't talked to Lucas Erickson since law school," Nic replied. She'd grown up in Billings, in the eastern end of the state, and had gone back there after graduation. "Other than seeing him across the room at a seminar or two, our paths never crossed. Not that I minded."

A movement caught Sarah's eye. Janine had stiffened, her jaw tight, her shoulders rigid.

"How did you know he lived in Deer Park?" Sarah asked.

"I googled him," Janine said sharply, but a flush crept up her cheeks.

"What? You saw him, didn't you? Recently, I mean. Did you at least tell Leo?" Not waiting for an answer, she swiveled her attention from Janine to Holly and back. "We have to tell Leo. About your letter and about—I can't believe you saw him and you never said. You sat right here and you never said."

"It was more than a year ago." Janine's voice held a note of irritation. "I'd delivered an order of desserts to a restaurant downtown and when I walked out, there he was. Standing on the sidewalk, in a suit, talking to someone. It was near the court—I assumed he came down for some legal thing."

"Did you talk about—what happened?" Holly asked. "About any of us?"

"We didn't talk at all. I just stood there and he—" She clenched her jaw and swallowed hard. "He recognized me right away, I could tell, and he had this look on his face. A sneer, like he thought he had some kind of power over me. Then he just walked away, like I wasn't worth acknowledging."

"He didn't threaten you?" Nic's tone was probing but careful.

Slowly, Janine shook her head.

Unbelievable. This was all so unbelievable. Sarah scanned the letter again. *Unless* . . . She sat back and folded her arms, hands gripping her elbows. "Unless there's something else only you two knew. You two, and Lucas."

"No," Janine snapped. "I told you everything that happened. How he got me into the cabin. What he did, what I said. How he wouldn't stop and I finally got away and ran. You saw me, all of you. And I told the sheriff everything, fat lot of good it did me."

"But the letter," Nic said, "is suggesting there's something you didn't say."

"There isn't," Janine said, leaning forward, biting off the words. "There isn't. We told them everything."

No, they hadn't, Sarah knew, but it wasn't Janine keeping the secret. Secrets, plural. Did Nic and Janine know Holly had invited the boys to the lake so she could cozy up to Jeremy? Did they know how much Holly hated her, envied everything she had? Not that her sister didn't have a good life, with a great job and a trendy urban condo. *Let it go,* her therapist had said. *He didn't reciprocate, never even knew. If you want a relationship with her, you have to let it go.* The memory of the admonition started the stupid song playing in her head. Abby had been eleven or twelve when *Frozen* came out, too old to put on her favorite princess dress when they went to the movie theater, but not too old for a tiara. Sarah had worn one, too, borrowed for the occasion. Abby's tiara sat on a shelf in her bedroom, not part of the ridiculously large wardrobe she'd taken to college. The image of that tiara, shining into the silence in the house in Seattle, tore at Sarah's heart.

At this rate, she would have no heart left, the muscles and arteries ripped to shreds for the birds to pick.

Deep breaths, her therapist would say. She inhaled, heard how thin and ragged her breath was, how short the exhale. *Focus. In, out, in, out.*

As for the rest—well, Holly knew part and Jeremy had known part. But no one had known it all, not even her therapist. And she sure as hell wasn't going to say anything now.

"Sarah? Sarah." The sound of her name brought her back to the room, to Nic pressing a hand on her arm.

"It's okay. I'm okay." She shook Nic off, tried to shake off their concern. She was tired of everyone's concern, at the same time that she craved it. What a mess she was.

"Okay," Nic echoed, not sounding convinced. "The question is, what does the letter writer want? Or what *did* he want, if it was Lucas?"

"You don't seriously think it wasn't him?" Holly said.

Nic held out both hands. "I'm saying we'll never get to the bottom of this if we don't consider every possibility. We can't start with a conclusion and get anywhere."

Across the table, Janine closed her eyes. Though she was forty-seven, she looked like a teenager right now, younger than Abby, and scared as hell. Sarah ached to comfort her. But that wouldn't help them get at the truth, would it?

Janine opened her eyes, exhaling heavily. "Okay. Every possibility, right? No matter how unlikely. No matter what other—issues it might create."

All for one and one for all, Sarah thought. She stifled the urge to squirm. Any movement more substantial than the flicker of an eyelash and the fragile peace would shatter.

Janine took another deep breath before speaking. "What if the letter isn't referring to the wreck? What if it's referring to my mother?"

"Oh, God," Sarah said. "But what would that have to do with Lucas?"

"Or with me?" Holly asked.

"Nothing, as far as I know. But you said"—Janine glanced at Nic—"every possibility."

"Go on."

"That was the year my mother died. Sarah had already moved to Seattle when the shooting happened," Janine said, "but you two, you were my rock. I'm not sure I'd have made it through without you."

"Yes, you would have," Nic said. "You'd have found the strength."

The bare facts were brutal. Sue Nielsen had fought with her boyfriend and kicked him out. He'd come back later to get his stuff but she'd been drunk and mistook him for a burglar. She'd shot and killed him. The hard life had ruined her health, and later that fall, in jail awaiting trial, she'd developed pneumonia. The end had been mercifully quick. Sarah was focused on her new job and interior design classes, and on helping Jeremy get back on his feet, literally, though she'd have come home if there'd been a service. But Janine had decided against it. No one would come, she'd told Sarah, except out of pity, and she was probably right.

"I never told anyone that my mother called me," Janine said. "After the fight, but before he came back. I was too ashamed to admit that I didn't take the time to listen to her."

They were silent, making sure they listened now, as she told the story. Finally, Sarah spoke. "I'm so sorry. But would it really have made a difference?"

"Maybe," Janine said. "Maybe it would have."

If not then, if not that, some other tragedy would have struck. Sue Nielsen had been a magnet for bad luck and bad choices. But Sarah could see how Janine might have blamed herself, especially after the attack and the crash, and spun out of control. Hadn't she married Roger Chapman, a poor choice of her own, not long after her mother's death?

"I don't see how that could be connected to the letter," Nic said. "Since Holly got one, too. Do you?"

But no one did.

As if by unspoken agreement, they all stood, Holly heading for the powder room, Nic and Janine for the kitchen. Sarah took her phone out to the deck, the display alight but the bars flat.

Must be some kind of gadget that would solve the problem. She'd ask the repair guy when they picked up Janine's phone. Though overgrown as the trees around here were, she'd probably need to call NASA.

Who would ever have imagined she'd give an eyetooth for a landline?

What a mess they all were. Blaming themselves for the past, for what they hadn't done. Except Nic, who'd called when Jeremy died, and made a generous donation to hospice in his name.

But when Sarah had asked about Kim, Nic's wife, and their daughter, Nic had said they were fine without elaborating.

Were they fine? Not fine? Should Sarah have asked more questions? Nic had never been one to avoid difficult conversations. But she'd seen too often in the last two and a half weeks that death silenced people. They worried about saying the wrong thing, so they said nothing, which made her feel even worse. Like the thing ripping her apart wasn't worth mentioning.

She and Nic had been so open with each other back in college. Though the last half hour had made painfully obvious that the relationships between the four of them had shifted. The other three still seemed close, while Sarah, once the ring-leader, had become the outsider.

What was she going to do about that?

Or about her kids. Or her mother and the lodge.

And the letter. They had to call Leo. She could not lose sight of one simple fact: Lucas Erickson was dead, and Janine was the obvious suspect. Although surely there were others—an a-hole like that had to have rubbed plenty of people the wrong way, starting with his ex-wife. What leads was Leo pursuing? Who was he talking to? She knew squat about murder investigations, but she did remember the investigation into the car wreck. The road had been closed for hours while sheriff's deputies and highway patrolmen took pictures from every angle and measured barely visible marks on the road, all while Jeremy's once-beautiful red car had sat, impossibly crumpled, tangled with the body of the dead moose. Peggy and JP had come out. Mary Mac, thank goodness, had been traveling with friends, though the news deeply upset her when she returned. The sheriff—Sarah didn't remember his name—had insisted on interviewing the girls alone. He hadn't told her he wouldn't pursue the assault charges; no, he had never been that blatant. But she'd understood the message, and she'd gone along.

Once when Noah was four or five, he'd been playing with a set of toy cars and smashed the red one into a dump truck with a gleeful little-boy shrill and Jeremy had nearly lost it. She'd managed to drag him out of the room, where Noah couldn't see him, and the boy had never known there was a problem, but the man. Oh, the man. Jeremy had gone sheet-white, sitting on the edge of their bed with his elbows on his knees, his head in his hands.

When she thought about that terrible day twenty-five years ago, it was the sounds she remembered most. But if she closed her eyes and peered into her memory, it was all there. And the clearest image, the one she could still see in living color, hear, smell, touch as if it were unfolding in front of her right now was when the EMT jumped into the back of the ambulance and pulled the door shut behind him, and his partner flicked on the lights and drove off, rushing Jeremy to the hospital. Had she honestly, truly known in that moment that she and Jeremy were meant to be together, that he had to survive so they could build a future?

Yes, she had.

"Oh, Jeremy," she said out loud, her hands steepled against her lips. "What am I going to do?"

WEDNESDAY

Nineteen Days

9

The wind worked at the corners of the shutters on the front windows, picking them up and slapping them down. Picking them up and slapping them down. Pick, slap. Pick, slap. Slap, slap, slap.

Sarah struggled to sit up, the wool blanket slipping on the leather couch. Too dark to see the clock on the fireplace mantel, so she grabbed her phone, good for something. Half past twelve. That made it Wednesday, nineteen days since Jeremy's death.

She'd have sworn she hadn't slept a wink, if not for the dream. Even with her eyes open, she could picture the woman running along the lakeshore, silhouetted against the night sky, a bit of moon, a tree whipping in the wind. Who was it? Surely not herself—she was watching the dream unfurl. And the woman was light-haired. Or, in the way of dreams, had she been both watcher and watched?

No sign of the cat. She unwound the blanket and stood, then made her way quietly through the dark to the powder room. Holly had taken the other couch. Nic and Janine were sleeping in the cabin where Janine had holed up that first night—ever the Girl Scout, Nic had brought sleeping bags. More cleaning tomorrow. The dust clung to these old logs as if it wouldn't have a life without them. *Where did dust go when you wiped it up?* She remembered Abby asking her that once while the cleaning woman was working, the two adults having no answer and trying not to laugh.

Finished, she turned off the light before opening the door, and was surprised to see a soft light glowing in the tiny windows of the kitchen doors. She hadn't noticed it a few minutes ago. She picked her way around the furniture and across the room, then pushed open one swinging door.

In the light coming from over the stove, she saw Holly sitting at the table, long legs outstretched, one hand resting on the Formica table next to a half-empty glass of red wine. The other hand cradled the cat, who raised her head, spotted the newcomer, and lowered it.

"At least one of us can sleep," Sarah said, nodding at the cat. She gestured to the wine. "Leave any for me?" Her stomach growled. Janine's mac and cheese dinner had smelled great, but Sarah had only taken a few bites, pushing it around on her plate.

She poured a glass and found the leftover pasta in the fridge. Scooped a mound onto an ironstone plate—this one bore the familiar green and gray mountain scene, with the Rocky Mountain goat silhouette—and sat across from her sister.

"Oh, give me that." Holly snatched the plate and stuck it in the microwave. The motor whirred and Sarah took a long sip of the cab, letting the jammy red wine roll over her tongue and slide down the back of her throat.

Beep. Holly popped open the oven, made a "yeow—hot!" noise, and set the plate in front of her. "Just because you look like death warmed over doesn't mean you can't warm up your dinner."

"Do I look that bad? And thanks. For the nuke job, I mean. Is it safe? Those are old dishes."

"Oh, who cares? It's one dinner. As long as it doesn't set the house on fire, you'll be fine. And to answer your question, yes. You look that bad." Holly gathered her gray plaid wool robe around her and sat. "Not that I blame you."

A gust rattled the mullioned windows and sent a scattering of pine cones across the metal roof.

"Nic shouldn't have—" Holly said at the same as Sarah said "I'm glad Nic—"

They stopped. Sarah spoke first. "I'm glad she called you. That's so like her. And I'm sorry I snapped when you got here."

"You're allowed," Holly said. "You've been through hell and I have been a lousy sister."

Sarah picked up her fork. "Goes both ways." Another gust. She put a bite in her mouth, listening. "How's work?"

"It's okay." Holly took another sip.

"I thought you liked your job."

"Liked. Past tense. Let's not talk about it tonight."

Sarah worked a piece of pasta loose from a tooth with her tongue and eyed her sister over the rim of the wine glass. She was about to get smart-alecky and ask what Holly did want to talk about when a loud crack stopped her.

"Holy crap. What was that?"

"Tree splitting. Let's hope it didn't hit the house." Sarah opened the door to the deck, holding tightly as another gust tugged at it. "I don't see anything out here." She shut the door firmly, then checked the front. "Nothing there either. Stove clock's blinking. Power must have gone out."

"For about the third time tonight. I tried resetting it, but it wouldn't stay reset. Electronics never work right here."

She'd forgotten. It had driven Jeremy nuts.

"So Janine found the cat when she got here?" Holly continued, working one silky ear with her fingers. "We should ask around."

"Ask who? The nearest neighbor is George Hoyt and his house is half a mile away. Besides, I don't figure George for an indoor cat. A mouser in the barn, maybe."

"If she isn't lost, someone may have taken her out to the country and dumped her. Crazy that people do that, but you know it happens. Anyway, she needs a name. What's that Egyptian cat goddess? The name of the cat in the house behind us in town."

"Bastet."

"That's right. You always were better at history than me," Holly replied and Sarah glanced up sharply. An innocent comment or a barb, a swipe at her tendency to hold on to the past? She couldn't tell. "It'll be nice for you to have the company when we leave."

"I'm not staying long," Sarah said. "Oh. You mean Mom has other plans for me? What has she said to you?" Her fingers tightened on the stem of the glass.

"Nothing. Well, she asked what I thought about suggesting you come here for a while."

"To help her clean. Decide whether to sell."

"Oh, no. No, she thought you and Abby might spend the summer here. It always was your happy place. The whole family loved it, but you most of all."

Had she misunderstood her mother's intentions for the house? Certainly possible; she'd misunderstood a lot of things lately.

But if Peggy imagined Abby might spend the summer here, she hadn't told Sarah.

She pushed away the plate, not quite empty. Holly pushed it back. She couldn't eat another bite, or sit here any longer, or let other people tell her what to do. She just couldn't.

No, she was not going to feel guilty just because her sister felt bad. She hadn't hurt anyone; she hadn't done anything wrong.

Her wine glass was empty. Fine. Eating and drinking this late at night wasn't good for her anyway. Outside, the wind had given way to rain, pounding against the logs and windows. As a child, she'd loved the rain. Now, it scared her.

"You don't have any idea why Lucas sent you the letter?" she asked. "You and Janine."

"No."

But there were too many secrets, too many silences between them for the words to be convincing. "Let's go back to bed. Mom will be here at the crack of dawn, snapping her dust rag at us."

"You go."

What was bothering her sister? Had it been Holly she'd seen in the dream, her hair lit up by the moonlight, running with the wind as it whipped the trees?

The thought kept Sarah awake for hours.

* * *

Something tickled Sarah's cheek.

Two green-gold eyes stared at her, inches away.

"You little sneak," she said. While she'd been sleeping, the cat had wormed its way under the blanket and Sarah had instinctively wrapped her arm around it. *Her.* Abby's cat used to do the same thing.

She freed her fingers from the blanket and stroked the soft black-coffee fur.

Coffee. That's what she smelled. And something baking. Happy smells in her happy place. She tightened her grip on the cat and sat up. Outside, the lake glistened as if last night's storm had blown all worry away and left the world shiny and smooth.

Why hadn't her mother hired professional cleaners? Even just for the windows. She could afford it. She didn't need Sarah here for free labor. Trying to keep her close and busy. Fine. She'd inventory the furniture and artwork and figure out where Mary Mac's glassware had gone.

And what to do about the cat. *Bastet.* She buried her face in the soft fur. Thank God the dream that woke her had not returned when she came back to bed after her late-night snack.

No sign of her sister, not even a rumpled blanket. Had Holly gone for a run?

She put her feet on the floor. *What was that?* Glanced down. Shivered, despite the blanket wrapped around her, the warm cat in her arms.

The first time Jeremy left her a penny on the floor, she hadn't known it was from him. The coin had been on the rug in the upstairs guestroom where she'd been sleeping, or not sleeping, the night he died. Sarah didn't think she'd dropped it—she kept her purse downstairs. Only the housekeeper had been in the room—she'd come to the house, unscheduled, when she'd heard the news, knowing Sarah would be overrun with visitors the next few days. Just to "tidy up," she'd said. But it was unlike her to drop something and leave it, even something as inconsequential as a penny.

The second time, last week, Sarah had been alone. The kids had gone back to school, her family had all gone home. Jeremy's mother had dropped by, but they'd sat in the breakfast nook, nursing coffee and grief. There was no way her mother-in-law had dropped three pennies on the rug in Sarah's second-floor closet.

She'd heard stories. Pennies from Heaven. Feathers. Sightings of a special bird or butterfly. She'd overheard a woman in a coffee house tell a friend that her late husband often left a light on for her when she was out late and had forgotten. Creepy or comforting? Could go either way.

But what was Jeremy doing here? And what was he trying to tell her?

"Why couldn't you pick a butterfly, Jeremy? Who doesn't love butterflies?"

The cat in her arms, Sarah shuffled to the kitchen. As she neared the door, the sounds of conversation leaked out, low and furtive. She pushed it open with her hip and the conversation stopped. Were those guilty looks on the faces of her sister and their old friends? Had they been talking about her?

"What smells so good?"

"Scones," Janine replied, shoving her chair away from the table and standing, though there was no need. A fourth chair sat empty, and the plate of scones held plenty. "I've been getting up at three to bake for so long, I wouldn't know what else to do."

The cuckoo clock above the deep white farmhouse sink said midnight, or noon. Dead battery? The stove clock flashed two forty-one. So no one else had been able to set it correctly, either. "What time is it?"

"Seven thirty," Holly said. "We didn't want to wake you."

She was still in her robe, not running clothes. Had she even been to bed?

Sarah set the cat on the floor and refilled the food and water bowls.

"Anybody take a look at the storm damage?" From their blank faces, clearly not.

They were up to something, but she didn't have the bandwidth to guess what it might be. One foot in front of the other, her therapist had said. Decide what has to be done, do it, and let everything else wait. Like the bag from the mortuary filled with condolence cards she'd hauled in that first night and left next to the couch, untouched, unread.

At the front door, she shoved one foot into her shoe, but the other balked. She bent to untie the laces and slip it on. She was still wearing her pajamas—faded black yoga pants and an old sweatshirt of Jeremy's she'd started wearing when he got too sick for her to share the bed and she'd moved into the guest room. She intended to sleep in his shirt until it fell off her. She grabbed a jacket from the coat rack. A blue fleece. Nic's, she guessed, from the roominess. The shortest of the four of them, sturdy but not fat, Nic always dressed like she thought she was bigger than she was.

The skies were clear, the air chilly for May, and she huddled into the jacket, her pants too thin for warmth. It was the calm after the storm, one of those glorious mountain mornings that make you think you'd imagined all the wind and the rain. Though the cones and branches littering the gravel drive said the gusts and torrents had been very real.

Her head and heart said so, too.

She bent to pick up a knobby branch from a larch. Tossed it to the edge of the lawn. Beneath it lay a cedar shake, split down the middle, a hole at the edge where it had torn away from the nail. More shakes lay scattered amid the blowdown. They'd been cut decades ago at her family's mill. Did they still make them?

Careful of the debris, she stepped backwards for a better view of the lodge roof. One bare patch, a few shakes still waiting for the next big wind to finish the job, but no other damage visible from here.

The carriage house roof looked no worse than it had yesterday, but a gap had opened between the gable and the side of the building, a birch bough lying awkwardly across the roof.

How had the other buildings on the property weathered the storm? The cabins, and the small McCaskill horse barn on the trail where she'd seen the woman looking for wildflowers yesterday. She'd better check. It had been years since she'd ridden. Neither of the kids had been interested, and eventually she'd given it up. Maybe now . . .

"Oww." She dropped the broken shake. A splinter had driven its way into the soft flesh at the base of her thumb. She pried it out with her fingernails, then pressed the spot.

A movement on the east end of the lodge caught her attention. A squirrel. A squirrel running down a tree that stood at an angle trees didn't take naturally.

Squeezing her hand against the sharp pain, she picked her way down the drive to that end of the lodge.

Where she saw the explanation for the loud crack she and Holly had heard last night. The top of an old spruce had sheared off and hit the roof, then slid down and struck the second-floor balcony. The decking had pulled away from the house, and the pine rail dangled loose. She pressed her hands into her face.

The sound of an engine broke into her fuzzy brain. A pickup came into view, the engine loud, the muffler rattling.

George Hoyt? Was he seriously still driving that old Chevy, its exterior a patchwork of rust, primer gray, and the original olive green? It had been past its prime when she was a kid. So had George, or so her younger self had thought. Now, as the truck slowed and the man behind the wheel rolled down the window, she guessed him to be north of eighty.

"Sarah McCaskill," he said. "Aren't you a sight for sore eyes?"

"George, you need glasses." She leaned in the open window and kissed the grizzled cheek. "What are you doing out so early? And what brings you down here?"

"Early? You've gone soft in your city ways. When you were a kid, you and your sister would have ridden those horses of yours up to the ridge or out to Granite Chapel and be halfway back to the barn by now. That blood on your cheek?"

She touched her face, then glanced at her palm and held it up. "Splinter. Roof shake." A black-and-white dog sat on the seat next to the old man. "Hey, Shep. Good dog. It is Shep, isn't it?"

"I forget whether he's Shep the eighth or Shep the ninth, but at least I never forget his name." George grinned, then his well-lined face turned somber. "I heard about your husband. Stinks. You gotta wonder sometimes what the Big Guy upstairs is thinking."

"Thanks. My nephew thinks God needed a technical consultant, to keep track of everyone's good deeds and bad."

George snorted. "Then your man's got his work cut out for him. That was some storm last night. Gusts up to forty, I heard. How'd the old girl fare?"

Took her a moment to realize he meant the lodge, not her. "Not so good. Crunched gable on the carriage house, and you can see that spruce tore the balcony off the east end. I haven't been upstairs yet to check for damage inside."

He got out and together they surveyed the damaged balcony, Shep beside them.

"Looks bad," the old man said.

"I've got to call the insurance agent, and my mother. But cell service is iffy down here, and the landline's disconnected. Guess I'll be going into town later."

"You be careful who you hire," George cautioned. "Lotsa builders think they can do anything. Throw up trophy homes, sell 'em to rich fools who pat themselves on the back for being eco-friendly while they drive them big SUVs and race their speedboats up and down the lake. Folks who don't know a thing about the history of this town and don't care. Spend two mill building a place you visit six weeks a year? It ain't right. A house wants to be lived in."

"It's not for us to judge, is it, George? Their lives, their money. Besides, wealthy families have always built their retreats and vacation homes. The lodge started out as a summer camp for a railroad executive and his family, before my great-grand-parents bought it." Why it had been sold, she'd never known. Financial trouble, or the original owners discovered that keeping a summer home was more work than they wanted. Their loss; her family's gain.

"You be careful," George said as if she hadn't spoken. "Not just anybody can work on a jewel like this."

"Thanks. Long as I'm outside, I guess I'll hike up and see how much blowdown we have in the woods."

"Hop in. Shep and I'll help."

In her pajamas and a borrowed jacket. Her city friends would be appalled. She followed George back to the truck. The passenger door stuck and she reached across the seat to open it from the inside. She grabbed the roof strap and pulled herself in.

George shifted to make room for the dog between them, and his worn denim jacket slipped open, revealing the holstered gun on his hip. Another sight she'd gotten out of the habit of seeing. Without a word, he tugged his jacket over the gun and continued down the narrow lane to the cabins. Small branches littered the ground, and a tree had bent the edge of one metal roof, but the cabins appeared otherwise unharmed.

Then they drove the property, George squeezing the pickup down narrow lanes and up half-abandoned logging roads on both sides of the highway. Several times, Sarah hopped down to drag branches out of their way. Twice, they had to back up, the road blocked. No storm damage at the horse barn, thank goodness, although barn was a fancy word for the two-stall shed her father and grandfather had built when she and Holly got serious about riding. In the distance, she could make out the roofs of the larger Hoyt horse barn and the ice house.

"Looks like you've got some merchantable timber down on your place, too. Call my brother to clean it up for you."

George grunted. "Wouldn't want to trouble a busy man like him for a few sticks."

"He's gonna bring a crew out here anyway. He'd be happy to help."

The old man pressed his lips together. "I'll manage."

Pride? A reluctance to admit he wasn't as young, or capable, as he used to be?

Back at the lodge, George stopped the truck to let her out.

"Appreciate you coming over to check on us," she said as she climbed out.

"Shoulda stopped to see you Sunday when you got here. I thought I saw headlights."

"Monday. I took the train and rented a car in Whitefish."

"No," he said. "Sunday. When I came back from town. I been taking my granddaughter to the Blue Spruce for Sunday supper since she was ten years old. Now she brings her own daughter. White SUV, but smaller. Not one of them monsters the summer folk drive."

Sarah's rented SUV was smallish and charcoal gray. Janine's van was white, a popular color right now. Was George mistaken? Had he seen someone else down here?

Had her childhood friend lied?

10

The cat was sitting on the front porch.

"Ohhh, fudge. I forgot to ask George about you." She rubbed the magic spot on the top of the cat's forehead with her thumb, and heard a satisfied purr in response. "Or have you decided you're mine now, since I fed you?"

First, she checked Grandpa Tom's office, at the southeast corner of the house, off the main room. No broken windows and no visible damage to the log walls or the twelve-foot tongue-and-groove ceiling.

Upstairs, in the master bedroom, she scanned the walls, then knelt to inspect the chinking on the lower logs. Were those cracks new? Impossible to tell. She dusted off her knees and opened one of the French doors leading to the balcony. A-okay.

The oak door connecting the bedroom to the sewing room stood open. At some point, probably in the 1950s, a small closet between the rooms had been converted to a bathroom, though the white porcelain fixtures and hex floor tiles were a good match for the other baths. Nothing amiss.

But in the sewing room, everything was amiss. The exterior door had popped open, though the glass hadn't broken, and cones and needles lay strewn across the Persian rug. She picked her way through the debris and peered outside. The spruce she'd seen from below lay across the broken railing, the top branches snagged on the eave, the soffit and fascia splintered. A strong woodland must stung her nostrils. Whitetail Lodge was a treasure, and not just to her family. If George was right and there were more pretenders these days than real craftsmen, would they be able to get the damage repaired?

Every time she pushed the door shut, it resisted. What could she find to hold it? Chair, no. Table, no. What about the oak bookcase, only thirty inches high but heavy? First she had to clear a few things. A ceramic meadowlark, the state bird. A lopsided clay cup, the name "Connor" scratched in the bottom. She set them on the library table her grandmother had used for cutting fabric. Stacked the framed photos she'd dusted yesterday and put them on the table, too.

She took hold of the end of the bookcase and began wiggling backwards, toward the damaged door. The bookcase barely moved, so she grabbed a few fat, heavy volumes from the bottom shelf. As she tugged, one slipped from her grasp and slid to the floor, flopping open. She groaned, hoping she hadn't damaged the fragile spine.

"Oh, my gosh. I haven't seen this in ages." A scrapbook from the construction of the lodge, filled with photos and newspaper clippings. It could be useful to her inventory. She set it aside.

Relieved of the extra weight, the bookcase moved more easily, and a few minutes later she had it in position. Not perfect—daylight leaked in through a narrow gap between door and frame. But it would do for now.

She picked up the top photo in the stack on the table. An eight-by-ten in a gold-toned frame showed Mary McGinty in front of the altar at Sacred Heart Church, the train of her long white dress draped artfully down the steps. She'd been young, only twenty, in 1946 when she married Tom McCaskill, ten years older and probably ten inches taller—what would have been called a fresh-faced girl, with freckles and reddish-brown hair, though that was Sarah's memory coloring the black-and-white photo. In her arms lay a bouquet of roses and ferns. Sarah had been married in that same church, and her own wedding album held a similar photo, though she'd had no veil or train. She'd loved her dress, creamy white satin with a wide sweetheart neckline, beaded bodice, and flowing skirt. Still in a box in her closet in Seattle.

Next, in a matching frame, was a photo of her great-grandparents, Cornelius and Caroline McCaskill, who'd bought Whitetail Lodge not long after it was built. Caro wore a lovely tea-length dress with a draped neckline. She'd been a handsome woman with full lips and an impressive head of hair. Sarah had always been told she had the McCaskill eyes—kind eyes, people said. This was where they had come from. Though she was not looking at the world kindly these days. Con had been a tall, broad-shouldered man in a dark suit. McCaskill men were tall—her father, Leo, and her brother, Con's namesake. Noah, too, though he had Jeremy's features.

"I'll get it fixed," she promised. "As soon as I can. But the place needs—"

"Sarah? Where are you?" Her sister's voice interrupted her. "Oh, my God. What happened?"

She explained. "I'll clean up in here, then go call Mom. She's going to be sick about this, but—" Holly chimed in and they repeated Peggy's mantra. "It could have been worse."

"Where is the woman, anyway? I thought for sure she'd be here at the crack of dawn, chasing us around with a broom and a vacuum."

"No clue," Holly said. "I came up to tell you we're headed into town. I'll swing by the house and let Mom know about the damage."

"Ask her to call the insurance agent, would you? I don't even know who it is."

"Sure. After I give Leo the letter from Lucas."

"Do you think . . ." She couldn't finish the question, the thought too awful, but her sister's face said she knew what Sarah couldn't say.

"That Janine killed him? No. That they might try to pin it on her? Yes. And it's our job to be there for her if they do." Holly turned and bounded down the stairs. Sarah followed slowly, her hand on the railing.

George had seen a white SUV in their driveway, but Sunday, not Monday. Janine drove a white van. George could have mistaken the vehicle, but not the day. If he'd been meeting his granddaughter at the Spruce every Sunday for twenty-five years, then he darned well knew what day it had been.

But Janine had had no reason to come up to Deer Park until she got the letter, on Monday. And she'd still been wearing her work clothes when Sarah found her.

No. Both George and Janine could be telling the truth. George had seen someone else in a white SUV, driving down the road to the lodge. Who?

No matter. It didn't mean anything.

*　*　*

By the time she'd changed out of her pajamas and went to find the broom to sweep upstairs, Holly and Janine were in the kitchen, ready to leave.

91

Nic came in, glancing around for something. "Have you seen my jacket? I'm sure I hung it in the entry last night, but now I can't find it."

"Oh, geez. I wore it when I went out on the property. It's filthy now—sorry. Take mine and I'll wash yours while you're in town."

"Good, thanks. It's an all-purpose errand trip. Buy a signal booster. Pick up Janine's phone. Convince the sheriff she had nothing to do with the murder."

"You could come," Holly said, the invitation clearly an afterthought. "We could squeeze you into Nic's car."

"No. Thanks. I've got work to do here," she replied. "Hey, would you call Connor, too? We've got some trees down— nothing urgent, but I doubt there's a working chain saw out here, if I did dare to use one. But we'll need to get some tarps up pretty quick."

"Sure. Surprised he didn't come out as soon as Mom told him you were here. He's been worried."

So they'd been talking about her, the whole family. That was good, she supposed. But the thought of people feeling sorry for her made her twitch.

"With this storm and thousands of acres to manage, he'll be crazy-busy. This is nothing. Get the roof and balcony covered and we'll be fine. You go. Don't worry about me."

A few minutes later, she was alone. Another thing she hadn't understood about grief was that one minute she was ter- rified of being alone, and the very next she wanted nothing more. Depended, in part, on how pushy the other person was. Were they continually asking if she was okay, did she need anything? She was not okay, damn it. She needed Jeremy. And if you couldn't bring him back, and no one could, then just shut the fuck up.

But she couldn't say that. Except to Holly, who didn't hover, but certainly not to her mother. Peggy had suffered her own losses when JP died, but being widowed at seventy was a whole different thing from being widowed at forty-seven. Though seventy was too young, too, wasn't it?

And where was her mother, anyway?

Gad. She'd told Nic teenagers were a handful. Turns out middle-aged adults could be mood-swing wrecks, too.

Get a grip.

She gathered up Nic's fleece and a few other things and headed to the cellar, flashlight in hand. Surveyed the pipes before loading the washer—the last thing they needed was a flood.

No broken windows. A decade's worth of cobwebs between the joists and a faint whiff of mouse, but nothing out of the ordinary.

Back on the first floor, she found a broom, then checked the doors and windows. None had blown open or been cracked by debris. They were mostly original, except for a window or two that had been replaced over the years. They ought to all be replaced, but double-paned, insulated upgrades would cost a small fortune. Add in the sagging roof and the loose gutters, and now the storm damage. Make that a sizable fortune.

In the sewing room, she swept up the storm litter. Among the rubble lay a long, curved cone from a white pine. When she was a kid, they'd gathered cones in late summer and Peggy and other teachers had used them for school craft projects—pine cone reindeer and hedgehogs, owls and elves. They'd dipped a few in wax to use as fire starters, stashed in giant baskets next to the fireplaces. Whenever she'd found a white pine cone with all its scales intact, a rare thing, she'd saved it and tucked it on a shelf in her bedroom—her treasure shelf.

They could spend Christmas at the lodge this year. If she managed to get it clean by then. If they kept it.

Keep moving, girl. She set the cone on the top step and made a quick circuit of the upper floors. Satisfied, she returned to the main floor and headed outside. The wind had not budged the heavy log tables and chairs, but serious sweeping was required. She walked down the stone steps to the lawn.

An object lay on the grass and she bent to pick it up. A nest woven of pine needles and grasses, a fragment of speckled shell stuck inside. The sight snagged her breath and she let out a strangled sob, her worry, she knew, even more for her own chicks than for the unhatched baby bird.

11

Sarah crossed the driveway to the carriage house and slid open the double doors. Specks of dust swam in the beams of sunlight.

This time of year, it stayed light until well after nine. Her bet: George had spotted a sightseer hoping for a surreptitious peek at the historic lodge. In the off-season, as long as the roads were passable, no one minded.

So why had he mentioned it?

Holy crap. In the twilight and her hurry the other night, she had not noticed. Peggy had said the carriage house needed to be cleaned out, but—whoa.

How had they ever accumulated so much junk? Tires and tools, skis and snowshoes, paddles and life jackets. An old band saw and drill press—her dad's? He'd taken up woodworking after he retired, working in an unused corner of the lumber company shop. What were his tools doing here?

And that old wooden canoe. They ought to haul it out. Toss it in the water, see if it was sound.

She picked her way around a roll of field fence to the work-bench, where wrenches and hacksaws and tools she could barely identify hung from hooks on the pegboard mounted to the wall. Another wall held odds and ends of tack—ropes and leads, bits and guards, cinches and straps.

Back home, her saddle and bridles hung in the storage room Jeremy had insisted they build in the garage, too good to get rid of. Too much a part of who she thought herself to be.

Maybe she would take up riding again. There were stables in Kenmore and Woodinville, or out at North Bend, where a horse could be rented for a few hours. Once she got the feel for it again—got her seat back, as horse people would say—there were miles of woodland trails to explore.

"Look what you started," she said out loud to Con and Caro. "Four generations of pack rats."

She wound her way through the piles to the staircase at the rear, glancing in the open crates as she went. Flipped the switch. Nothing happened. She aimed the flashlight beam upward, where thick cobwebs ran from the milk glass light fixture to the ceiling. A burned-out bulb. Finally, something she could fix.

Thick dust coated the steps. The floor creaked as she stepped onto the landing. This had been the caretaker's apartment, fur-nished but unoccupied when she was a kid. Being allowed to play out here had been a treat, and she'd felt so grown up when her grandmother had finally deemed her old enough, and responsible enough.

The oak door was heavy and paneled, twin to the doors in the lodge. The brass knob—oval, with a domed top—fit neatly in her hand, despite the dampness in her palm. She turned it, but it didn't budge. Rattled it back and forth and finally heard a slow groan as the bolt moved and the door opened.

She stepped across the threshold, head cocked. Quiet, the air stale. The living room was crammed with furniture, some upended, much of it draped with sheets. The beds and dressers from the boys' bunk room, no doubt, and the ballroom couches. The kitchen was compact and efficient, meant for someone who took most of their meals in the lodge. Dust covered every surface. The mullioned window panes were caked with grime. She rubbed at one with the ball of her hand, creating a sticky swirl.

"Well, I didn't come up here to clean," she said out loud. "Just checking out the job."

Where was the dollhouse? When she and Holly were children, it had sat on a low oval coffee table in front of the sofa. One summer visit, Jeremy and JP had carried it, oh so tenderly, into the lodge and set it up for Abby in a corner of the living room. She'd begged to take it home, but it never would have fit in their car, so they'd bought her one of her own. Sure enough, she'd outgrown dolls, dollhouses, and princess dresses not long after. Who'd built the replica of the Victorian, Sarah had no idea. A gift for Sarah Beth, Grandpa Tom's little sister, it had been tucked away when she died, until the next Sarah Elizabeth McCaskill came along. Though she'd been both thrilled and terrified to share a name with a girl who'd died, playing with her namesake's dollhouse had been pure joy.

When friends saw Peggy's paintings of the lodge and the Victorian that hung in Sarah's entry, they assumed those houses had sparked her love of decorating. But she traced her passion to the dollhouse. To the hours she'd sat on the floor here in the apartment, moving furniture around in the tiny rooms or cutting tiny pictures from magazines to tuck into the tiny frames that fit in slots on the walls. She'd been given a box of tiny plastic dolls, but they'd never appealed to her.

People. Too much trouble, then and now. Digging up old conflicts, getting themselves killed.

Moving all this furniture out here had been a major chore. Many pieces were genuine antiques. Should she hire a crew and move them back?

Don't be ridiculous. You're here to help your mother make decisions, not redecorate. When they finished cleaning the lodge, she'd tackle this place—she couldn't work in all this dust. Then she'd make a list and start figuring out what it all might be worth—the green Roseville pottery and pink Depression glass visible through the windows of the mahogany breakfront, the calendar art, the tools downstairs.

Between the bathroom and bedroom stood a bird's-eye maple armoire, the inset oval mirrors on the doors almost as grimy as the windows. The doors opened at the touch of her hand on the glass knobs, the scent from the cedar shelves mingling with lavender from the tiny sachets her grandmother had tucked in every drawer and closet to keep bugs away. One good whiff and it was as if Mary Mac were standing next to her.

For a moment, she couldn't breathe. Could. Not. Breathe.

Then her grandmother's words filled her ears, consoling her after some girlhood slight or an argument with her sister. *It will be all right, Sally. I know you can't imagine that now, but I promise, it will be all right.*

A sense of calm overtook her. Maybe it was the lavender. Maybe she was going crazy. She sure as hell wasn't going to tell anyone about the voices, or the dreams. But they were soothing, reassuring, in a way, even if they were weird-ass crazy.

Quilts filled the wardrobe shelves. Though she'd given away dozens in her lifetime, Mary Mac had left almost as many behind. Sarah ran her fingers down the stack, naming the patterns. Irish Chain. Double Wedding Ring. Bear Paw and Dresden Plate. A colorful Spider Web like the one Abby had taken to college. Noah's pick had been a flannel Log Cabin.

She could stand here and admire these quilts for hours, but that wasn't getting anything done.

Did her mother really want to clean out the lodge and all the buildings? To scatter and sell the family history?

Once again, she felt irritated by her mother's absence. Peggy had practically insisted Sarah come to the lodge, then all but disappeared.

She closed the wardrobe doors. In the bedroom, she flicked the switch. The overhead light came on, dimmed by the dust in the etched glass fixture.

Stacks of cardboard boxes and wooden crates filled the room. The linens and lamps and knickknacks from the upper floor? The dishes and stemware she couldn't find last night?

Time for that search later. Her attention was drawn, like a magnet to the North Pole, to the top of the cabinet Victrola. There stood her quarry: the dollhouse. The sense of magic it had given her forty years ago came flooding back. Three stories, rose pink with white trim and deep mauve accents, the scalloped edges of the tiny black shingles on the roof dusty but distinct. Lace curtains hung in the windows, the three-sided turret as mysterious as ever.

A shadow moved and she jumped. "Oh, Bastet. You scared the—what are those doing there?"

On the floor, next to the cat's paw, lay three shiny pennies.

"What are you trying to tell me, Jeremy?" She looked around as she spoke, as if her husband might be hiding behind a stack of crates or perched on an old cane-seat chair.

She slipped the pennies into the pocket in the waistband of her black pants.

A small thud startled her and she glanced around, spotting Bastet's bright eyes in the dim room. The cat had jumped onto a domed-top trunk against the far wall, next to a stack of leather suitcases.

The McCaskills weren't packrats. They were hoarders.

She didn't remember the trunk. Whose it was or what it held, she had no idea. She set Bastet on the floor, where the cat immediately began licking a paw and washing her face.

Sarah undid the two large brass buckles on the front of the trunk and pushed the lid with the heels of her hands. It didn't budge. She groped at the ends of the trunk for more buckles, finding only thick leather handles. She gave the tongue another tug, then tried again.

The lid remained firmly shut.

She shone the flashlight on the front of the trunk and craned her neck, spying a small brass keyhole she hadn't noticed earlier. It couldn't be hard to pick an old lock like that, could it? Unless the key was around here somewhere.

But what was so valuable that it had been locked away for decades?

She carried the cat out of the apartment and closed the door, then made her way down the unlit staircase. The windows on the ground floor level were as filthy as the ones upstairs, and she played the flashlight beam across the rows of tools. No keys. Had her mind been playing tricks on her?

Not for the first time. When, she wondered, would be the last?

12

"Squat." Nic spat out the word and dropped a white paper bag on the table outside where Sarah sat, facing the lake. "They told me squat."

"Care to be more specific?" Sarah asked.

"I should have ignored the letter," Janine said, taking the seat across from Nic. No sign of Holly. "Then none of this would have happened."

"Well, you wouldn't have broken your phone, but Lucas would still be dead," Nic said. "And you'd still be a suspect, unless you had an alibi. Which, bottom line, you don't."

Lucas. Still stirring up trouble from the grave. Metaphorically speaking.

"Would she?" Sarah closed the notebook in front of her, the start of a list of repairs and other projects. "Be a suspect, I mean. She never filed an official report against Lucas, so even if they dug that deep in his background, they wouldn't find a link."

"Somebody had to know," Nic said. "His wife, his partner, his therapist."

Sarah and Janine snorted in unison, almost as if they'd rehearsed.

Nic threw up her hands. "I'm being theoretical here. He has to have told someone. No one keeps a secret like that his whole life."

"What was there to tell?" Janine opened her own white paper bag. "He never thought he did anything wrong."

When it came to Janine, maybe, but the rest? The wreck?

"Well, they know now. The price of honesty." Nic made a noise like an unhappy horse. "The prosecutor was in trial today, so no chance for a meeting. I called a friend to ask about her—turns out she beat Lucas for the job a couple of years ago, handily. Rumor is, he never got over it and took every opportunity to slam her. But from what I hear, she's fair. She won't let his behavior affect her prosecution."

"Did you see Leo?" Sarah asked.

"Spent most of an hour with him." Nic peered inside her paper bag.

"And?"

Nic raised her head and bit her lip. "Preliminary autopsy results confirm the cause of death was the gunshot. Manner, Leo wouldn't say, but it's gotta be homicide."

Sarah shuddered. Ugly word. An ugly death she didn't wish on anyone.

"Apparently Lucas was known to keep a gun in the office," Nic continued, "but it isn't there now. No sign of it in his house or car. Good chance the killer used his own gun on him and took it with him."

Or her.

"Leo won't find anything to connect the shooting to me," Janine said. "I know how it looks, but I didn't kill him."

"There's reasonable doubt, right?" Sarah said. "Don't they have to show no reasonable doubt before they can charge her? I forget how that works."

"To charge her, all they need is probable cause to believe she committed the crime. Then, at trial, they have to show proof beyond a reasonable doubt."

The words hung in the air, meaning nothing, meaning everything.

"So, what next?" Sarah asked.

"Meet with the prosecutor," Nic replied. "Talk to people who knew Lucas. My guess is they'll release the body in a day or two. His mother is widowed. Lives out of state with his sister."

Lucas Erickson had a mother. Everyone did, but she hadn't given his any thought. Poor woman.

"They're on their way up," Nic continued. "The ex-wife is taking charge of funeral arrangements. Two kids—boys. Middle-schoolers."

He had kids. There would be a funeral. She should go.

God help me. She couldn't go to another funeral, not now. No one would expect that of her. Hardly anyone in Deer Park had any inkling she'd ever known Lucas Erickson.

The back door squeaked open and footsteps crossed the deck. Holly set a bag and a can of pop in front of her. "We got you lunch."

"I'm not hungry. But thanks."

"Suit yourself." Holly took the fourth spot and carefully tore her bag to make a place mat, kept from blowing away by her Mountain Dew can. Sarah watched as her sister set the pickle at three o'clock, the white envelope of seasoned fries at nine o'clock, and a small plastic cup of ice cream at twelve o'clock, the paper-wrapped wooden spoon on top, crosswise and perfectly straight. The burger Holly positioned in the center, the white paper wrapper held by a toothpick with a frilly plastic end that also held a radish. She pulled out the toothpick and the wrapper flapped open. The smell sent Sarah back in time to high school summers, taking orders at the Burger Depot window.

Holly raised the toothpick and opened her mouth, then stopped. "What?"

"You are so weird," Sarah said.

"I'm a creature of habit."

"Which is why we all knew you were going to do that the moment you sat down," Janine said. "Do you rearrange the table when you go out to dinner?"

Holly glowered. Pulled the radish off the toothpick with her teeth, then set the pick on the bag-turned-place mat, behind the ice cream cup.

"If the Burger Depot's open, summer's not far behind," Sarah said. "What did Leo say about the letter?"

"Not much." Holly reached for her pop. "Our cousin's gone closed-mouth on us."

"They wouldn't confirm whether they think Lucas sent the letter to Janine," Nic said, "but the fact that Holly got one too makes it more probable than not. In my opinion, anyway. The trick will be to convince them that the letter didn't have anything to do with his death."

"You threaten somebody, in writing, and end up dead," Sarah said. "It's gotta be connected."

"I didn't kill him," Janine said, her tone insistent.

"And I have an alibi," Holly added.

"I know, I know." Sarah raised her hands. "I'm not accusing either of you. It's just—who? Why?"

"Who and why are inextricably linked," Nic said. "And that's what makes the letter interesting. But they're looking at every possibility for the shooter. The ex-wife, opposing counsel, disgruntled clients. A burglar, though the secretary claims nothing is missing."

Except the gun. "What about the former law partner?"

"Dan Fleming. We met on a case eons ago. I'm hoping to connect with him this week. Find out what happened to their partnership, see if he can shed any light on the case."

The smells finally got to her and Sarah slid the burger and fries out of her bag. Offered the radish to Holly, who wrinkled her nose. Radish first, then pickle, then burger and fries. Certain things remained predictable. Sarah unwrapped her burger and took the first bite. It wouldn't win culinary prizes, but it was exactly what she'd been craving.

"What am I going to do about my phone?" Janine said.

"Isn't it fixed?" Sarah waved a hand in front of her mouth. "I'm sure he said two days."

"When he thought all it needed was a new screen," Janine replied. "Now he thinks it might need a different part, which will take at least three days to get here. If that's what it needs."

"Where's it coming from? China?"

"Spokane. Same diff."

Two hundred and fifty miles. And several thousand light years.

"No big deal," Holly said. "Get a new one."

"I bake cakes for a living. I can't afford a new phone. Now with all this . . ." Janine threw up her hands.

All this? What did she mean? The letters, the murder? What did that have to do with buying a new phone, unless she expected to need every penny for a lawyer. Not Nic, who focused on family law and gay rights and Sarah wasn't sure what else, but who would never ask an old friend to pay her. No, Janine feared needing money for a criminal defense lawyer.

She wouldn't be charged with murder. She couldn't be charged. "Janine, it'll be okay. Not right away, but it will be okay."

"Says you." Janine's curls swung in her face and she shoved them out of the way. "You and your perfect life."

All the warmth went out of the sunshine. "You mean the life that just fell apart? When my husband died?"

"Sarah, I am so sorry," Janine said, her voice breaking. "I didn't mean that. It's the stress talking. But at least you don't have to worry about money."

Small comfort at the moment. "I know. Thanks."

"Cheer up, Janine," Holly said. "None of our phones work out here."

Janine stuck out her tongue.

"We got a booster for the cell signal," Holly told Sarah. "The guy said it plugs into the jack for the landline. Easy as pie."

"Assuming he knows which end is up," Janine said.

"No help on the landline, though," Holly continued. "Mom was on her way out, so I called the phone company, but they wouldn't talk to me, since I'm not the account holder. At least the insurance agent was helpful. And Connor will swing by as soon as he gets a chance."

"Pray it doesn't rain before then." Sarah glanced to the west, the sky clear and cloudless. But the weather changed quickly in the mountains. "Where was Mom going?"

"No idea." Holly plucked a fry from the bag. "We walk in. She's all friendly. I say I want to see what she's working on—she must be deep into it if she's not out here riding herd—and all of a sudden she's got some place to be."

"That is crazy."

"Oh, by the way," Nic said, "Leo was very interested when we showed him pictures of the roadside cross."

Holly held out her phone, and Sarah took it, though she'd seen the memorial herself. Scrolled through the pictures rapidly. Stopped and swiped the other way. Tapped the screen, then spread two fingers to zoom in on the photo. Showed it to Janine. "That gold charm, with the basketball sitting on top of the letters UM. That wasn't there yesterday, was it?"

Janine leaned in, frowning. "But who in Deer Park knew Michael Brown?"

"Good question, although there are plenty of college basketball fans up here, and he was a hot shot."

"Twenty-five years ago. Who would remember him now?"

"I wondered if it was Lucas, but obviously not, if new things are being added to the shrine," Sarah said. "We could share that photo on Insta or Facebook and see what we find out."

"Leo's already on it," Nic said. "I can't imagine how it might be connected to the murder, but you never know."

"Could be totally innocent. Griz fan with a long memory," Holly said. "Found a photo of him online and printed it out. Though why now, after all these years?"

Sarah picked up her pop can. "A sports fan that attentive, that obsessed, is probably male. I've always assumed it was women who decorated roadside crosses."

"Tempe took drivers' ed last fall," Nic said. "The teacher made them work in teams and research newspaper stories about roadside fatalities. They had to visit the cross, take pictures, and give a report in class."

"That's cruel," Holly said.

"And there's a judge in Billings who makes that part of the sentence after a DUI," Nic continued. "Leo said nothing like that goes on up here, but I think he liked the idea."

"While you three were in town, I went up to the carriage house apartment," Sarah said. "No interior damage, thank goodness. That's where all the stuff from the third floor is. And the dollhouse."

"I loved that old dollhouse," Holly said. "But not half as much as you did."

"None of you have gone out there?" Sarah asked, though there had been no footprints on the dusty steps. No's, all around. "So how do you suppose these got on the bedroom floor?" She fished the three pennies out of her pants pocket.

"They look brand-new." Janine plucked one out of Sarah's palm and held it up. "It's dated this year."

If you've got something to say, Jeremy, just tell me.

* * *

Below the highway, Sarah pulled off McCaskill Lane onto the trail leading to the horse barn, then further east to the Hoyt place. She passed the weathered building, its stalls holding nothing but horses' dreams, and kept going. In her bag, her phone pinged, but she ignored it.

She ignored the boundary between Hoyt and McCaskill land, too, certain George wouldn't mind. She slipped her foot off the brake, then pressed the gas gently, steering the rig between the high spots and the muddy potholes frost heave left behind. Clearly, the road hadn't been used much in the current century.

Ahead loomed the Hoyt barn, where George had kept his stock. Never much interested in managing the timberland he'd inherited, he'd turned to outfitting once he sold the sawmill. He'd run several crews of guides and hands, using horses and mules to carry guests into the backcountry to hunt or fish. The stock were long sold off and the barn looked lonely. The rails of the old corral had splintered and collapsed in the middle, like a shallow V, the posts leaning, as though they'd lost the will to stand up for themselves. Hints of wild brush and grasses greened the ground on either side of the road, but inside the corral, the dirt held only the faintest greenish sheen, as if all the hooves over all the years had pounded too hard even for weeds to take hold.

An illusion. Weeds were the sturdiest plants around. "A weed is just a plant in the wrong place," her grandmother had liked to say.

"Bloom where you're planted," proclaimed a poster Abby had hung on her bedroom wall.

The world is full of such contradictory advice.

Clearly if she were going to take up riding again, it would not be here.

Beyond the corral lay the first pond, the road dipping below it, then moving on to the next, each pond ringed in last year's cattails, a red-winged blackbird perched on one. No wildflowers, and the pussy willows hadn't opened yet. Maybe the woman in the blue car had found some forsythia in bloom, or a wild fruit tree by the side of the road.

She kept going. Above the largest pond stood the old ice house. Two stories, deeply weathered, the cupola on top tilted slightly, and something inside her seemed to heat up, freeze, and melt again.

The barn road was a wreck. Her front tire hit the edge of a pothole, the SUV swerving sharply to the right. The vehicle bounced and she swore and jerked it back. If she weren't careful, the soft dirt along the edge could grab her tires and pull her off into the narrow drainage ditch.

Steady, Sarah. Don't get stuck up here. Even if her cell worked, she did not want to get stuck up here.

The spring that fed the old homestead had turned the meadow green already, and the pond shimmered in shades of chilly blue. A pair of mergansers swam effortlessly on the far side. A hundred years ago, ice had been cut here for the railroad and townspeople. She parked beside the ice house, near where the road teed into Hoyt Lane. Over a small rise to the east, she saw the chimney of the house where George's mother had lived when Sarah was a kid.

She swung her car door open, testing the ground with one tennis shoe, then the other. Took a deep breath. Took one step, a second and a third, bypassing the ice house until she stood in front of the homestead shack. No picturesque logs here. Rough lumber but well-built—it was still standing, after all—that had been whitewashed once, so long ago it was nearly impossible to tell.

A creeper clung to the door frame, last year's leaves dry and brown, and they rustled in the soft breeze. The upper half of the door stood open, the screen torn in one corner. A squirrel or a racoon? A tree branch tossed by the wind?

She stretched out a hand, then pulled it back. She didn't need to go inside. She didn't *want* to go inside.

Jeremy would not be waiting for her.

13

When she reached the North Shore Road, she jammed her foot on the brake and slammed her fist into the steering wheel, the impact vibrating up her hand.

"God *damn* you, Lucas Erickson." It wasn't rational, blaming the man for his own death, for his death interfering with her grief.

But very little made sense anymore, and she saw no point pretending that it did.

She turned toward town. Her destination was her mother's house, her mission—what? No family was perfect. No one got everything they wanted from the people closest to them. But was it expecting too much to think that after inviting her home, only nineteen days after her husband's death, that her mother would be eager to help her at the lodge? To comfort and console her?

No, it was not too much. And her mother's absence was unlike her. So what was going on?

In town, she turned left off Lake Street. Passed the post office and made a right. The crime scene tape that had surrounded the law office was down, and a woman stood in the entrance, about to open the door.

Sarah parked and quickly crossed the sidewalk. "Hello," she called. "I was hoping to catch someone here. I'm so sorry—"

"The office is closed," the woman said, glancing over her shoulder, then stopping, her mouth open.

Sarah was equally startled. It was the woman she'd seen yesterday, searching for wildflowers.

The other woman recovered first. "Are you here for the files?"

Sarah's turn to be puzzled.

"For the lumber company," the woman added. "You are a McCaskill, aren't you?"

How did she know who Sarah was? And what files? Did Lucas do legal work for the company? No reason Connor shouldn't have hired him, and no reason she should have known. But the thought didn't sit well.

"No," she said. "I mean, yes, that's my family. I'm Sarah McCaskill Carter. My brother runs the business. I—I went to college with Lucas, and I stopped by to offer my condolences."

The door was open now and the woman held it, stepping back for Sarah to enter.

"I'm Renee Harper." Now that they were face-to-face, Sarah could see that the other woman appeared to be a few years older, sharp-eyed, hair colored a shade of red that didn't match her skin tone. And too thin, her black-and-white striped blouse loose on her frame, the skin around her eyes drawn. "Secretary, bookkeeper, mail clerk. You name it."

Sarah matched the woman's wry smile and stepped inside. A pleasant space, despite the dingy exterior and the mingled smells of paper dust and bleach. A curved counter hid the reception desk. In the small waiting area, chocolate brown leather chairs faced a couch that sat beneath a giant topo map of the lake. To the right, a door stood open, but the space beyond was empty. The ex-partner's office, she presumed.

What had Janine said about the body? On the floor near the entry. She instinctively shuffled her feet and looked down. Had she been standing where a man died?

"Farther back," Renee said, answering her unspoken question. "Before you get to the conference room."

"I'm so terribly sorry," Sarah said, surprised to find that it was true. She wasn't ready to give up being angry with Lucas for what he'd done to Janine, Michael, and Jeremy. To all of them. But her anger felt almost extraneous at the moment. Like a burden she'd carried for so long that suddenly meant nothing.

"Sheriff took most of our equipment." Renee gestured toward her desk, where a monitor and cords sat, untethered, and an empty space on the back counter appeared to have held a printer. "Why, I have no idea."

Sarah tightened her lips.

"He left the files," Renee continued, "but I'm not allowed to return them to the clients yet. Not until they've combed them for clues, I guess. Although I can make copies if the client needs anything."

"I'll let my brother know," Sarah said.

"At least they let me reconstruct a client list, so I could help Dan notify people. Daniel Fleming." The secretary gestured to the front window, the black-and-gold letters backwards from this angle. "They dissolved the partnership a couple of months ago, but we hadn't changed the sign yet."

"Oh." Sarah wanted to ask how the two men had gotten along, why they broke up the partnership, whether Lucas had seriously been considering a run for office, and a million other things a casual acquaintance from college should not be asking the secretary of a murdered man.

The woman's skin paled, her jaw tightening. Anger, or fear? Her hands went to her face. "I can't believe this. I cannot believe this."

Renee Harper's response was hard to read. Had she been in love with her boss? If not that, then something equally problematic. Or just struggling with the horror of it all.

"You found him. That must have been dreadful." Sarah's mind's eye flashed on Jeremy, lying in their bed, his lifeless hand in hers.

"I'd gone to the post office," Renee said. "I ran into Becca Smalley. Chattiest woman in town."

Except when you're newly widowed and she can't wait to get away because death might be contagious.

"She's always going on about nothing," Renee continued. "If I hadn't been gone so long, maybe I could have . . ."

"Or maybe you'd have been hurt, too."

"The moment I got back, I knew right away something was wrong. I could smell it." She shuddered. "Now all I can smell is the bleach or whatever it is they used to clean up. The place reeks."

"It stings the nostrils, for sure. Why don't we get out of here—grab some coffee at the Spruce?"

"No. No, thanks," Renee said. "I just came in to get some personal things."

"Then I won't keep you," Sarah said. "Unless you could use some help."

The secretary's brow wrinkled and she lowered her chin, then replied, her voice husky. "Thanks. That's very kind of you."

Renee directed her to the storage room by the back door for a box, and on her way down the hall, Sarah tried to open herself to the space. To sense what it held. Conflict, beyond the murder? Hard to tell. Hard surfaces, like the conference room's glass wall and the porcelain tile floors, didn't pick up emotion the way rugs and carpet did. Bookcases filled with law books lined the hallway. Wasn't most legal research done online these days? But she knew from her design work that people often held on to the things that symbolized their trade and their past, especially if they'd invested a lot of time or money acquiring them.

Across the hall sat the classic lawyer's office. A large desk, stained a dark cherry and highly polished, dominated the room. A brass lamp with a creamy white pleated shade sat on one corner, a matching credenza behind it. A black leather desk chair and two client chairs. A Persian rug. No computer, as Renee had said. A wall full of diplomas and certificates interspersed with photos. Age aside, Lucas had looked much the same as the young man she remembered. One of those men whose features were too strong to be considered handsome, the jaw too firm, the eyes too intense, but he had been—what? Not imposing. That suggested a big man, and he wasn't that—he stood several inches shorter than the man he was shaking hands with in the first photo, the current governor. Other photos showed Lucas in small groups of smiling men and women in suits. He stood out. *Compelling.* That was the word.

And then she spotted the snapshot behind the desk, at the end of a row of family photos, school portraits, shots of two boys in sports uniforms. She had never seen this picture before, but knew it in an instant. He'd handed her his camera and she'd taken the picture of Michael, Jeremy, and Lucas on the lawn below the lodge, the lake sparkling behind them, the day before everything changed.

She turned and fled.

At the end of the hallway, she found the restroom. Shut herself inside and leaned against the door until her breath steadied. Had he kept that photo to remind himself of what had happened? Of what he'd done?

Had she misjudged the man?

The tissue box was empty. She opened the cabinet beneath the sink and found a fresh box. Blew her nose and fluffed her hair, then grabbed two empty bankers' boxes from the storeroom. Glanced out the rear door, then faced the hallway. Took a step forward, then another. The front and back doors were offset, but once a person got about five feet inside, he or she could have seen someone come in the front.

Whose presence had Janine sensed? Had the killer been close enough to identify her? Anyone else—a deliveryman, say, or a client coming in the back—would have called out at the sight of a body on the floor and a woman bent over him. Would not have hesitated, would have rushed forward, frightened but determined to help, at the very least to call 911.

Would not have been skulking around.

She stopped. Renee was watching her.

"Popped into the restroom," she said. Lifted the boxes. "You always need more boxes than you think."

The woman glared at her, as if Sarah hadn't been speaking English.

"Yes," she finally said, turning back to her desk. "Yes. You want to help, you can box those up." She pointed to a stack of picture frames.

Sarah glanced casually at the photos as she packed. A younger Renee with a small girl on her lap, and another she guessed to be the girl's senior portrait. A narrow black frame held a certificate from a legal assistant training program.

"What will happen to this office?" she asked. "And what will you do? Work for Fleming?"

"His office is in Whitefish, and I can't make that drive every day."

"Oh, so he left Deer Park?" The box was full and she set it on the floor. "Why did they dissolve the partnership?"

Renee's eyebrows rose. "He and Misty, Lucas's ex-wife."

"Oh-h-h." They would have warranted a close look anyway, wouldn't they, the victim's former partner and his former wife, but if they were together . . . No wonder Leo had refused to give Nic any specifics about other suspects.

"I heard," Sarah continued, "that Lucas was considering a run for office."

"Everybody wants to know about that." Renee wrapped a small ceramic robin in a crumpled piece of newspaper and placed it in the other box. "All I know is he talked with a few people. If he had any plans, he didn't tell me."

"You knew him. What do you think happened?"

"No idea."

"Misty? Fleming? An angry client or an ex-employee?" The woman jerked back, as if Sarah had slapped her. "I'm sorry. I've upset you."

"No, no. It's important to talk about it, even if you didn't like him any more than the rest of us did." She held up a hand. "It's true. I see it on your face. Lucas was a difficult man."

The woman's insight was rather breathtaking, as was her willingness to speak so bluntly to a near-stranger. But that didn't answer Sarah's question.

Dislike was easy; murder was hard. Wasn't it? Either it happened in an instant, a snapping, or the killer nurtured the anger, the resentment, the unrelenting hatred for a long time, tending it, polishing it, until it became a reason to kill.

Could Janine have done that?

Please, God, don't let it be Janine. Because if it had been . . . Because if it had been Janine, then she was to blame, too.

*   *   *

So much had changed. So much was going to change. Such a relief that the Blue Spruce never changed.

Sarah took a seat at the counter and ordered coffee and huckleberry-peach pie. When she'd last had a slice of real live, honest-to-goodness pie, she could not recall. You could get pie in Seattle, of course. In Fremont, a shop served nothing but pie, and a diner in Lake City served killer coconut cream. The last time she'd taken a visitor downtown, to Pike Place Market, they'd seen crepes and donuts, fancy cheesecake, fresh croissants, and fruit-filled piroshky topped with sweet whipped cream. But pie? Not one slice.

And huckleberries? Fat chance.

Besides, if you were going to drink coffee and eat pie in a Montana café in the middle of the afternoon in the middle of the week, you ought to sit at the counter.

She laid her phone next to her napkin. Cradled the steaming brown mug in both hands and closed her eyes. She needed this.

Outside the law office, she'd loaded the box of pictures into the trunk of Renee Harper's blue car. Emotion virtually swirled around the woman—sorrow, fear, anxiety about her own future? And maybe, or maybe this was Sarah projecting, a twinge of guilt over not having liked Lucas Erickson better when he was alive.

Then Renee had driven off and Sarah had walked down the block, past the quilt shop and the locksmith. She strolled down the alley behind the law office. She could see the post office from here. It shouldn't have taken Renee more than ten minutes to walk out the back door, drop off the mail, and return. But running into Becca Smalley had thrown her off schedule.

Janine had been inside only a minute or two. According to Nic, no one in the nearby shops or offices had seen her. They hadn't seen anything suspicious.

But until Janine was formally cleared, they'd all be on edge.

The coffee had cooled enough that it didn't scald the roof of her mouth, like it had the other day. Which came first, the broken marriage or the broken partnership? Had there been arguments over betrayal, or money?

She did not envy Leo the task of wading through that cesspool. Jeremy had once had two senior managers who'd been best friends until one man's flirtation with the other's wife, also an employee, turned into an affair, and the fallout had been ugly. Ultimately, all three had left, taking with them knowledge and experience nearly impossible to replace, and leaving a sense of distrust that lingered for months.

But, murder?

"Here you go, Miss Sarah," Deb said as she set a white plate in front of her. *Pie, oh pie, we love pie*, the chorus in her head sang at the sight of the flaky, golden crust, deep purple goo oozing out between the strips of lattice. "The family favorite. Your mom loves it, and Leo always orders a slice when he comes in. I haven't seen him lately. Murder on his menu."

Figured she'd know who Sarah was without an introduction—a waitress's role in a small town. A movement at the other end of the counter caught her attention. A short, fiftyish woman with dark skin and close-cropped hair, tugging on a sage green blazer.

A Black woman. Okay, so Deer Park had changed.

Deb waved at the departing customer. Sarah picked up her fork and cut the first bite. Before it reached her mouth, Deb called out. "Crust first. I win."

Mouth full, Sarah let her eyes ask what that was about.

"Some people take a bite of the crust first and work their way across." Deb mimed the action with her hand. "Other people start at the tip and work their way to the crust."

"Does it mean something? And what do you win?"

"Not a thing, and not a thing." Deb flashed her a grin. "Just café nonsense." She topped off Sarah's coffee and moved down the counter.

Sarah rested the fork on the plate and picked up her coffee. How could she possibly eat another bite, knowing she might have prevented all this? If she hadn't dragged Jeremy out on the long ride. Hadn't suggested they rest a bit at the homestead shack by the pond after they unsaddled the horses, since he wasn't an experienced rider. Hadn't said yes, when Jeremy's eyes and hands asked.

Hadn't listened when Holly insisted her dream meant nothing, hadn't persuaded Janine to move on.

She picked up her phone. Distracted herself, replying to texts from Abby and the house sitter, listening to a voice mail from a friend. Saw the reminder for tomorrow's phone appointment with her therapist. What would the woman say, if she knew what Sarah was thinking? "Are you perhaps imagining yourself a tad too powerful? Forgetting that other people made choices to act as they did?"

Lucas sent those letters. He'd wanted to make sure Janine and Holly kept their mouths shut. To keep the past in the past, making sure no one brought up rumors that he'd once attacked a girl out at Whitetail Lodge. The good old boy sheriff had retired years ago. He was probably long dead. Had any deputies on scene heard Janine's accusations? Had Misty Erickson or Dan Fleming dug up the truth, and tried to use it against him?

None of that had anything to do with her. It was Lucas's actions, not hers, that had started this long ugly chain.

But whose actions had ended it?

14

The pickup in front of her, pulling a boat on a trailer, signaled for the turn off Lake Street into the marina, and Sarah stopped behind him. Glanced over at the historic Lake Hotel, a FOR RENT sign plastered across the closed café. Why had it closed? Good food, great location. Fabulous views. The summer before her father died, she and Jeremy had motored down the lake one sunny afternoon and met Peggy and JP for a drink and a bite on the stone patio.

Loud rock she couldn't identify blared from the truck's open window. Deb the waitress's ex with his shiny new toys bought with hidden assets? The driver was waiting for a young woman pushing a stroller to cross the street. About a quarter of the docks were full, a mix of power boats and sailboats. That would change big-time this weekend, if the weather held. Yes, town was quiet in the off-season but with only the Spruce and the bowling alley for competition, surely this was a great spot for a decent café.

A few minutes later, she parked in front of her parents' house. Her mother's house. Glanced up at her corner room, as she always did. Lights were on, and a figure moved in and out of view. Her mother was home, working in the studio.

Bag on her shoulder and a go-box with a slice of pie for her mother in hand, she marched up to the door. Peggy wouldn't hear her, might not have noticed her pull up outside.

Locked, again.

No need to check behind the downspout for the spare key. Instead, she circled around the house, passing under the old rose arbor, the canes beginning to turn green, to the back yard. Cones and branches littered the grass and deck, along with tiny yellow blossoms from the forsythia and pink petals from the neighbor's flowering crab. Considering last night's wind, it was good that her mother hadn't gotten out the deck furniture yet, or filled the huge terra cotta pots stacked under the eave.

She didn't bother knocking. Inside, she set her bag and the pie on the kitchen counter, next to a used coffee cup. Her mother had never been one of those artists who lost track of time or forgot to eat, likely because she'd snuck painting between work and family for so long. It hadn't become her focus until she retired from teaching. After JP's death, she'd stopped painting for a while, brushing off her kids' concern. Now, Sarah understood. If her mother had found the spark again, good, even if that kept her from paying attention to other things.

One foot on the bottom step, Sarah glanced into the living room with its high ceilings and tall windows, the decor a quirky mix of new and old, her father's bronze urn on the fireplace mantel. What was that line from the poem, about arriving home and recognizing the place for the first time? This hadn't been her home, the place where she lived, for a long time, and neither had the lodge, long her second home, but her heart would always recognize them both.

She started up the staircase. The wall had been covered with family portraits when she was growing up, but now held only one painting, a large oil Peggy had done of Bitterroot Lake. At the landing, where the staircase turned, she called out. "Hey, Mom, it's me." The smell of paint mingled with the raw odor of brush cleaner.

"Sarah!" came her mother's voice from the studio. A rustling sound. A door closed and footsteps followed. Then Peggy stood at the top of the stairs, eyes bright, cheeks flushed.

"I didn't hear you come in." She smiled broadly, almost breathless.

"Caught up in your painting. Show me." Sarah took another step.

"Oh, no." Peggy wrapped her hand around the newel post. "No. It's—they're not in any shape for eyes other than mine."

"Oh. Okay. When you're ready." That was new; her mother had never hesitated to show work in progress, even soliciting opinions. She started back down, Peggy behind her. "I stopped at the Spruce. Brought you pie."

"Huckleberry-peach? Perfect—I'll have it for dinner."

One of the many secrets of adult living was that you actually could eat pie for dinner, or breakfast, contrary to what your parents had told you when you were growing up. Contrary to what you'd told your own children.

In the kitchen, Sarah opened the fridge to tuck the pie box inside. Cream, a jar of strawberry jam, and a jar of pickles. Two bottles of mustard, a bag of sliced salami, and half a loaf of cinnamon-raisin bread.

"Come out to the lodge for dinner. No cleaning, I promise. I'll run you back into town later. You can help Holly and me make a plan." She filled the pot with water and poured it into the coffee maker. Not that she needed any more caffeine. She needed the ritual. "There's so much to do in the lodge, and the carriage house is worse. Where do you keep your coffee?"

"Hmm? Umm. Freezer." Peggy was sitting on a stool at the kitchen counter, chin resting on the back of her hand.

"Earth to Mom," Sarah said as she opened the freezer and took out a bag of ground beans. "You're a million miles away."

"Nooo. I'm right here." Peggy blinked. "What were you saying?"

"I was saying, we need to make a plan. I'm not sure how long either of us can stay, so we need to identify the most important projects and get as much done as we can." Sarah scooped coffee into the filter basket, slid it into place, and pushed the button.

"Oh, honey. Tonight? I wish I could but—the painting. I'm—I'm at a delicate spot, and I need to get it right." She gestured with both hands, fingers close together, not quite touching.

"Okay. Sure. Tomorrow, then. I'm not going to stand in the way of art."

What wasn't her mother telling her? Was it about her health? The lodge, or Holly? She opened her mouth to ask, then closed it. Took two mugs from the cabinet—at least they were where she expected them to be. Nothing else was as she expected.

Deep calming breaths, she could hear her therapist say. Was it nuts to hear the voice of a woman five hundred miles away in her head? Only if she listened, she told herself.

In, out. In, out. In, ouuut. You don't know if there's a problem. You don't know if she's sick. And you've dealt with worse.

Ohhh god, oh god oh god. In, out.

She got the cream and found a spoon. Poured the coffee and carried the cups around to the other side of the counter.

"Finish the painting, or at least, this delicate spot. Then come out tomorrow and spend the day with us."

"Thank you, dear," Peggy said, though whether for the coffee or the reprieve, Sarah couldn't tell.

"By the way, George Hoyt stopped by this morning."

Peggy raised her eyes quickly. "What did he want?"

"Nothing. Just making sure we were okay after the storm. I'd already walked part of the property, but we drove up and down most of the logging roads. Holly called Connor and he'll send someone out to clear them and throw some tarps up." She filled in the sketchy picture that was all Holly had had time to give their mother.

"Your father always called major windstorms a lumberman's dream and nightmare, rolled into one."

"Speaking of Dad, he'd be shocked to see all the junk in the carriage house. There's barely enough room for two cars."

Peggy lowered her cup. "Connor decided they needed your father's shop space as part of the expansion, so he moved the tools and equipment out there."

"What expansion?"

"Your brother works too hard," her mother went on, ignoring Sarah's question. "That company's a big responsibility. Too much for one man to shoulder."

"Connor's a big man. Broad shoulders."

"I am speaking metaphorically." Peggy gave her a sidelong glower, then picked up her cup.

"Ohhh-kay." She'd ask Connor about the expansion when she saw him. "It would be a lot easier to inventory the lodge if they hadn't started packing it up. That was a lot of work for nothing."

"Well, it seemed like a good idea at the time," Peggy said. "But he's too busy now, and I can't decide whether to put everything back, call an auction house, or what."

"Sounds like we all need to sit down together and talk things over." Everyone said you shouldn't make a major decision like selling your house for the first year after your spouse died, but that didn't apply to family property, did it? It couldn't. She couldn't ask everyone else to put this off until she was ready. With three siblings, someone's life would always be in flux. And Peggy was getting older, and what if she was sick? Sarah added that to her mental list for this hypothetical conversation. "While Holly and I are in town. And we should probably include Leo. I know you and Dad bought his parents out years ago, but we've always let him use the place. Although he's got a full plate, too."

"Why is Holly here?" Peggy asked.

Sarah's breath stopped.

"To support Janine?" Peggy continued. "They've stayed fairly close, I know. Unlike you. And—well, she came right out."

There it was again, the hint of something about her sister that no one was telling her.

"Nic called her. You remember the letter Lucas Erickson sent Janine?"

"Of course I remember. Sarah, what is this about?"

"Your guess is as good as mine, Mom. He sent Holly one, too."

*   *   *

The car behind her honked. Deer Park only had one stoplight and it had turned green while she was daydreaming.

The horn beeped a second time and she resisted the urge to flip off the other driver as she accelerated through the intersection. So much for the quiet, small-town life.

Not fair, she told herself as she steered the SUV into the shopping center lot. The rules of the road were a mutual agreement. You went when it was your turn, you stopped when it wasn't. You drove close to the speed limit, you stayed in your lane, and you turned down your brights when traffic was approaching.

If only the rest of life were that fair, and that simple. It wasn't. It never had been. Her husband was nineteen days dead. And she hated when people reminded her, as Janine had at lunch, that she didn't have to worry about money.

Did they think she didn't know that? Did they think she wasn't grateful that at least money wasn't part of her worries?

Did they think she wouldn't trade all the millions for more time with a happy, healthy husband?

At least Janine hadn't invoked the other phrases she detested. "He's in a better place," or "God has his reasons."

No way out but through. A saying from her therapist or another one of Abby's posters?

She sighed, then grabbed her purse and stepped out of the car. Straightened her back and pretended she felt better. *Fake it till you feel it.*

Shit. She was full of cheap wisdom today.

Weird to go from bright daylight to brighter fluorescents. Weirder still to walk in the grocery store and hear her name. She turned to see a slender woman with short, highlighted hair, wind-whipped like her skin.

"Sarah," the woman repeated, her voice rich with emotion, and set her shopping basket on the floor, then extended her arms. "How good to see you."

"Mrs. Holtz. Hello."

"It's Pam," the woman said. "I stopped being Mrs. Holtz when I retired. Forty-two years in the classroom—can you imagine? I don't know how I did it."

Sarah took in the woman's close-fitting neon yellow jacket, the tight black pants that ended just below the knee, the cleated shoes. The bike helmet in the shopping basket.

"You biked to the grocery store?"

"Stopped in on my way home. Ted and I do a training ride a few afternoons a week. And I walk with your mother." The longtime high school English teacher, one of Sarah's favorites, turned somber. "Sarah, we were devastated by the news about Jeremy. I'm sorry we couldn't make it out for the funeral."

"Thank you." Were the simple words enough? She hoped so. "I'm staying at the lodge."

"Ahh," Pam Holtz said. She picked up her basket. "I wondered. We just rode out to Granite Chapel and back and when we passed the lodge, I had the sense of it coming to life."

"Pam, do you know"—it felt like betrayal to ask, but she had to. "Is my mother sick? Ill? I can understand her not telling me so soon after, but . . ."

"No, she's not. And yes, she would tell me, and yes, I would tell you. My guess is she's got a painting stuck in her head. You can count on it."

She was counting on it. Desperately.

A movement caught the older woman's attention and she gave a small smile, one hand raised. Renee Harper returned the greeting and turned her cart down the closest aisle.

"Another former student," she said. "Renee Taunton. Harper, I think, now. Smart as a whip. But then there was that business over the scholarship." She shook her head, remembering.

"I met her this afternoon," Sarah said, not mentioning the encounter in the woods. "At Lucas Erickson's office. I didn't realize she was a local girl." What scholarship business? There had been no diploma in the frames she packed up this afternoon.

"Came home a couple of years ago to take care of her mother. Judith Taunton would try the patience of a saint under any circumstances, and now . . ." Pam shook her head. "I've gotta run. Ted had a few more miles in him, so he rode out to the cemetery. He'll be waiting for me on our deck with a cheese plate and a glass of chardonnay. As soon as I get there, with the cheese and wine." She laughed, then touched her fingertips to Sarah's arm. "Let's make time for a real catch-up while you're here. You and your mother and I can take a nice, long walk."

"It's a date," Sarah said, and leaned in to kiss the air next to her old teacher's cheek.

Though the entire conversation had lasted three minutes, five tops, Sarah realized as she watched Pam Holtz click-clack her way to the express lane that it was the first time in the two days she'd been back in Deer Park that she'd actually felt welcome here.

* * *

They were good for wine, thanks to the case Holly had bought, but Pam Holtz had inspired a cheese binge. Not quite the selection Sarah was used to, but she'd made some tasty finds. Cheese, light bulbs, and cat treats safely stashed in the back seat, she punched in her brother's cell number.

"Sis!" the deep voice said a moment later. "You're back in God's Country."

"And hoping to see you. I'm in town—can I swing by the mill?"

He made a grunting sound. "I'm still in the woods. I'm gonna miss soccer practice, for sure. Just hope I get home in time for pizza night with the kids."

Cleaning up storm damage. She should have known. "Oh. Right. Sure. Mom said you wanted to talk to me."

A heavy silence. "Another time. In person."

"Okay, sure," she repeated. What that was about, she couldn't imagine. "Maybe when you come out to the lodge. Give Brooke and the kids my love." Call over, she headed out of town, thinking not of Connor but of Pam Holtz. The ride to Granite Chapel and back had to be twenty-two miles. She couldn't do that at forty-seven, let alone seventy-whatever.

Dang. She should have asked Pam about the roadside memorial. The woman knew everyone and everything going on in Deer Park.

Was Pam right and Peggy was just preoccupied with her art?

Would she ever find something she cared about that much?

She glanced in her rearview mirror. The same white car had been behind her since she'd left town. Was it following her?

"Oh, give up the paranoia, Sarah. The world does not revolve around you."

The car was close now—close enough to glimpse the driver's face. The Black woman she'd seen in the Blue Spruce.

She passed a few roads and driveways—the houses were closer together this close to town. The names on the mailboxes were unfamiliar.

As she neared the memorial, she slowed, debating whether to stop. Was it selfish to drive on, promising to stop another day? Her therapist would say no, that she had to take care of herself first. Only then could she take care of anyone else.

She wanted to be *home*. In Seattle, in the sanctuary she'd created for her family. But the place had felt so big, so empty, after Jeremy's death. After the visitors left and the kids went back to school. Tragedy affected a house. That made sense. If you could change the mood in a room by swapping a vibrant but faded plum on the walls for a calming sage, by switching out the flooring or the artwork, why wouldn't death change the place, too? Wasn't a house meant to hold the full range of a life, to contain and support the people it held? You lived inside the space, you changed it, it changed you.

She wasn't ready for all this change.

When she slowed to turn onto McCaskill Lane, the white car was no longer behind her. The woman must live out here, but where? Next chance, she'd introduce herself. If she stuck around.

15

"Oh, shit. You scared me half to death." Holly stopped short on the threshold of Grandpa Tom's office. "What are you doing, just standing there?"

"Just—standing here," Sarah echoed. She'd been listening to the lodge, to the hum of it, the low underlying noises you didn't notice until they stopped. When she and Janine walked in the other night, the place had been spooky-still, only the old refrigerator muttering to itself. Now, though they'd barely dented the dust that caked every surface, Pam Holtz was right. The lodge was coming back to life.

"Whatever Janine's making, it smells great." She held up the grocery bag. "I may not be the cook she is, but I excel at buying cheese to go with your wine."

"I like how you think, big sister. We will not go thirsty or hungry in this joint." Then Holly dropped the good cheer. "I was missing Grandpa, so I decided to clean his office."

This morning, she'd been focused on checking for damage. Now, Sarah gazed at the shelves, grateful that Connor and Brooke hadn't touched this room. The photos and objects told the history of the logging business in the valley. Scaling tools and calipers. A sepia-toned photo of two men in high-waisted pants and suspenders, feet in heavy work boots planted wide as they worked a crosscut saw. A yellowed newspaper shot of the last three-log load pulling into the mill.

Outside, the lake rippled. "Whenever anyone asked how Grandpa got any work done with a view like this, he got all mock-gruff and said 'discipline.'"

Holly joined her. "But Grandma always said the only work he got done here was the Sunday crossword."

They shared a smile. It felt good. The way it was supposed to.

Sarah took a step toward her sister. But before she could say a word, her foot touched something, no doubt a stray stone or a bit of cat food.

But no. In a straight line on the rug lay three bright copper pennies.

What game are you playing, Jeremy? Sarah asked her dead husband. *It's starting to scare me.*

She raised her head and met her sister's gaze. "What were you saying about wine?"

*   *   *

"Did he leave them for you or Holly?" Nic asked. They sat on the deck, in the same chairs they'd taken at lunch. A tray of cheese, crackers, and grapes sat in the middle of the table, beside a bottle of something white.

"Sarah, for sure," Holly said. "I'd just vacuumed."

"We all know you had a thing for him," Nic said. "That's why—"

"Right. It's all my fault," Holly snapped. "Blame me for everything bad that's happened in the last twenty-five years."

"Hol." Sarah stretched a hand across the table, though she couldn't quite reach her sister. "No one's blaming you."

"There was never anything between us. You know that, right?" Holly's voice took on a pleading tone. "It was a silly crush. I admit, when it was obvious, about two minutes after they got here, that Jeremy only had eyes for you, that he only came up here because of you, I was ticked. But I got over it. Especially after the crash. And he was a great brother-in-law."

"I know," Sarah said. "I know."

If they were dredging up the past, there was plenty of blame to go around. If you wanted to play the "what if?" game, all of them had done something to regret that weekend. Except Nic. Who wasn't a Deer Park girl. Who wasn't part of the family drama. Who, if she had any sense, was regretting being here right this minute.

Nic had driven halfway across the state to help Janine. But if she was irritated to find herself literally in the middle of a tense conversation between the two sisters, she betrayed no sign, intent on clearing Janine from suspicion.

But the pennies were only one of the mysteries brewing at Whitetail Lodge. What was up with her mother? Pam Holtz had assured Sarah that Peggy wasn't ill, but what if Peggy had kept the secret from her friends too? What did Connor want to talk about? And what was the deal with the letters, and the ribbons and mementos on the roadside cross?

She meant it when said she didn't blame Holly. If they were taking responsibility for their own actions, as she'd said of Lucas, then she had to take responsibility for what she'd done. Or not done. For not speaking up about the dream, and then not being there to protect Janine. Not speaking up for her. For going along with the sheriff who said Janine might want to be careful what she said, who she accused, considering whose daughter she was, that it might come back on her and she might not like the outcome.

If only . . .

She could practically hear Jeremy telling her the dangers of those two little words. The man had made a religion out of refusing to be dogged by regrets. And of all of them, he was the one who'd suffered the most from that weekend. Except for Michael.

"Look at us," she said, scanning the group. "Grown women, unnerved by pennies. We're together again, finally, in a place we love. Maybe Jeremy's just telling us to have fun."

"I'll drink to that," Holly said, raising her glass.

"You'll drink to anything," Nic said lightly.

Maybe she'd fooled them, Sarah thought as she lifted her glass. But she didn't believe her own words. Not for a minute.

*　*　*

"A normal mom would be out here supervising every sweep of the broom," Holly said when Nic and Janine had gone into the kitchen.

"You wouldn't want a normal mom," Sarah said. "If there were such a thing."

"You do a pretty decent impression of one." Holly's smile quickly faded. "She wouldn't let you see what she's working on either?"

"Couldn't slam the studio door fast enough."

"I've got a friend with her own gallery," Holly said. "In an artsy district, near downtown Minneapolis. She paints in a glass-walled studio in the corner. People watch her all day and she doesn't mind a bit."

"Mom never used to mind. Remember when we were kids? She did that series of Blackfeet portraits using the beaded gloves and moccasins Grandpa took in trade and let us play with them while she painted."

"So what's changed? What's different? Her or the painting?"

Sarah swirled her wine glass and didn't respond. The only answer was "everything."

Holly plucked a grape off its stem. "I crawled around in the carriage house this afternoon. How did one family ever accumulate so much stuff?"

"One dish at a time," Sarah replied, "for a hundred years. The first thing to do is make a plan. See what's here and set some priorities. Though even then . . . what a mess." She raised a hand, gesturing to include the carriage house, the attic, the cellar, but what she really meant was the silence and resentment that had crept in between them and become a habit they couldn't break. And the threat none of them had seen coming.

"Hol," she started as her sister raised her head and said "Sally . . ."

"You first," Holly said. "Age before beauty."

An old joke between sisters only a year apart who shared a strong resemblance. Though Sarah knew she was thinner now, her cheekbones and jaw more prominent. When she'd ordered the pie to go for her mother, Deb the waitress had insisted on boxing up her mostly uneaten piece, too. She'd forgotten it, on the front seat in her car.

"I don't want to sound like I'm blaming you," Sarah said, "but is there some other reason Lucas sent you that letter? Something you haven't mentioned?"

"No." Holly shook her head. "I swear, I don't know anything more than the rest of you do. Well, except . . ."

"Any sane person would absolve us both of guilt over that."

"That assumes we're sane."

The crack was meant as a joke, but Sarah felt no humor. Only heaviness. The same dark weight she'd felt that night, so long ago. "Most people would have done the same thing. Even if I had spoken up, said I'd dreamed something terrible was going to happen, we didn't know exactly what it was going to be."

"Yes," Holly said, earnestly. "You did. You knew Janine was in danger. It had to be from Lucas. And I told you it was just a dream, that it meant nothing. If I hadn't kept you from warning her . . ."

"Holly, stop. I decided for myself not to say anything. It's not your fault."

"You stop," Holly replied. "You feeling guilty is equally ridiculous. Neither of us is responsible for Lucas trying to force himself on her, or for racing off in Jeremy's car. And we sure as hell aren't responsible for his death now."

Sarah wanted to believe her. Oh, dear God, how she wanted to believe her.

* * *

After dinner, Sarah grabbed her jacket and snuck out the front door. The skies were still light, that turquoise-y blue with a hint of gold that you didn't see in Seattle. She could hear a power boat on the lake, a faint whirr of traffic up on the highway, and if she listened hard, birdsong. It wouldn't be full dark for another hour or so.

In Seattle, it never got truly dark or truly silent, except when the power went out. If her children were home, the silence would have been almost immediately broken by one of them wondering what was up and when would the power be back on. They weren't whiny kids. Just kids. They'd had fun on visits here, sure. They'd swum in the lake and gone sailing and canoeing, but they could do those things at home. Playing with the cousins and hiking the hillsides—that was fun, too. But not enough to draw them back to the lodge for more than a few days.

And with Connor immersed in work, Holly firmly entrenched in the city, their mother content in her studio in town, who was left to enjoy these evenings, when the birds were flitting from tree to tree, the colors turning to shadow?

Maybe it was time to turn Whitetail Lodge over to another family.

The gravel crunched under her feet as she started down the path. When she was a little girl on a sled, the gentle lawn had been scary-steep. Especially on the trek uphill.

"What do you think, Dad?" she said out loud. "Is it time to sell?"

Her father, God rest his soul, did not reply.

She'd reached the cabins, almost as ancient as the lodge. No doubt they needed repairs and updates, too—she hadn't gotten more than a glimpse into the cabin on the end two nights ago when she'd arrived and found Janine holed up inside.

Two nights.

If they sold, it would have to be "as is." It would take too much time and too much money to bring everything up to snuff. But they couldn't begin to think about putting the place on the market until the roof and balcony were fixed. That meant soffits and gutters and who knew what else. She hadn't come out here to spend hours with contractors and insurance adjusters. Log homes were great until they weren't.

Thank God Janine had taken refuge here. Thank God one of the cabins had a broken lock. If she hadn't . . . Sarah didn't want to think about what would have happened. About what her friend might have done in her despair. Although it would have been better had she gone straight to the sheriff. Called for help, reported what she'd seen and heard, given no one any reason to doubt her.

Not that she blamed Janine, not when her friend had told the truth all those years ago and gotten the clear message that she'd be better off if she kept quiet. And Sarah had been part of the problem.

She had put that day out of her mind on purpose, determined to be grateful that despite everything, Jeremy had survived. Determined to be grateful for the life they had made together. But since coming back to the lodge, she'd thought of little else.

Past the turn in the path, past the last cabin, a fence ran along the property line. Cedar rail, the wood bright and fragrant. When had that gone up?

She dropped down to the edge of the lake and sank onto the grass, the water lapping rhythmically at the shore. Holly didn't know everything. It wasn't just the dream. They'd said, she and Jeremy, that they ought to get back to the lodge, keep an eye on Lucas, but they hadn't meant it, too intent on each other. Sarah hadn't known then, didn't know now, if the old sheriff had truly believed Janine would be better off keeping quiet, or if he believed no harm, no foul, because Janine had fought Lucas off. He'd torn her clothes and forced his fingers inside her but she'd kept him from the rest. The sheriff hadn't said "boys will be boys." He hadn't said "now, honey, you don't want to ruin a man's reputation when you got no proof, do you?"

But when Sarah replayed his words in her mind, that's how it sounded.

The setting sun cast a soft, golden glow on the lake. She could hear the sheriff as clearly as if he were standing here right now. Could hear him telling Janine to think about it carefully. Take some time. Sleep on it—as if she'd be able to sleep. If she still wanted to press charges tomorrow, then come to his office and give a formal statement. Fill out a report. She'd have to see a doctor. She'd have to be prepared.

They'd known what that meant. The denials. The accusations that she'd led him on, then changed her mind. The local talk.

It was all inevitable.

Sarah closed her eyes. *Do you really want to have to go over it again and again?* the sheriff had asked. *Think about it. You'll have to testify.* To relive every moment, and though he hadn't said it, to be disbelieved.

In her mind, she heard shouts and laughter coming from the lake, from people who didn't have a clue about the tragedy unfolding. She heard distant boat motors, the dying moose up on the road. She heard the warning in the sheriff's words. Had he been a husband? A father? Had he known what he was asking? He'd been a sheriff a long time; surely he had known.

And she heard herself agreeing. Not right then; she'd been in shock. But later, in a quiet corner of the lodge, Sarah had wondered out loud if the sheriff didn't have a point. They were going to have to testify against Lucas for killing Michael and critically injuring Jeremy, and that would be hard enough. Better to focus on making sure he was punished, swiftly and severely.

How could she have been so naive? Janine had decided to keep quiet. The crash had been ruled an accident and Lucas was never charged. Even a slap on the wrist would have been more than he'd gotten for ending Michael's life and seriously changing Jeremy's. Thank God for the strength that had pulled Jeremy through. She'd known Janine wasn't that strong. Wasn't that strong now.

Now they were grown women.

Now she was a mother who worried about her daughter's safety.

Now she'd be outraged by the suggestion that a woman keep quiet. Wouldn't she? God, she hoped so. Had anything really changed in twenty-five years, after #MeToo and all the revelations about all the ways powerful men silenced powerless women?

That, all that. That's why she felt guilty. That's what Holly didn't know.

She paused. Was that a light, shining in the woods? She closed her eyes and opened them. Nothing.

Was she losing it, going a bit crazy, seeing things that weren't there? Finding pennies and seeing strange lights and thinking it meant something?

But Holly had seen the pennies too. George Hoyt—and there was nothing woo-woo about that man—had seen a car and lights on the lodge road and it hadn't been Janine. Who, then? A looky-loo, a lost driver, someone turning around?

The phone in her pocket buzzed, startling her, the signal so intermittent down here. She took it out and swiped and pushed. A text from Abby. What, what was wrong? *Love you, Mom!* the message said. The bars on her screen were bouncing up and down like her heart rate, but she had enough reception to reply. *Love you more!*

Under a wild juniper, crickets were beginning to peep. She tipped her head back, gazing up at the sky through a gap between the lodgepoles. Her dad used to make a game of dragging the three of them outside before bed to see who could find the first star. Connor was so much younger, he only won if Dad spotted a star before the girls did and pointed it out to him. She and Jeremy had played the same game with Noah and Abby.

She used to know the names of all the constellations, but now . . .

Now everything was different. The sun had set and the air had turned cool. She shivered and headed up the lakeshore, drawn by the comforting lights of the lodge.

Inside the front door, she hung up her jacket and kicked off her shoes. Tomorrow she'd give them a good scrub. In the living room, Holly sat on the floor at the end of a couch, the canvas bag from the mortuary next to her. Cards and letters surrounded her.

"What are you doing?" Sarah's hands clenched and heat shot through her. "Those are mine. Mine and my children's. You have no right—"

Then she noticed her sister's eyes, wide and afraid. She sensed rather than saw Nic standing a few feet away. Holly's hand shook as she held out a sheet of paper. A single sheet, just like the ones they'd seen before.

God damn you, Lucas Erickson. God damn you.

16

"I was coming back from the bathroom," Holly said, gesturing. "I tripped over the bag. I didn't see it, I swear. We were going to play Scrabble."

The board lay open on the game table in the corner. Sarah sank into a chair, the letter in her hand. The cat jumped into her lap, and she steadied the wiry little creature.

"I—I left it there," she said. "Friends, business acquaintances—they sent cards and notes, but I didn't have the heart to read them. I thought it might be easier here." Ha. The joke was on her.

The kitchen doors swung open with their rhythmic thump and Janine pushed through with her backside, a tray with glasses and a bottle of sparkling water in her hands. "Oh, you're back."

"I'm back," Sarah said. "To this." She lifted the letter, then dropped it on the table.

Holly scrambled to her feet. "I think we could all use something stronger."

"Don't you think you drink enough?" Nic asked.

Sarah's eyes slid to her sister. Fair question.

"Don't, Nic," Holly said, her voice sharp. "Not tonight." She walked to the buffet where a bottle of cabernet sat uncorked and held it out, a questioning look on her face. Sarah nodded and Holly poured two glasses, setting them on the table next to the mound of Scrabble tiles.

"It's identical to the others," Janine said. "The envelope, too."

"You found the envelope? Who was it addressed to?" Sarah demanded.

Nic picked a plain white business envelope off the floor and handed it to her, then slid the rest of the cards back into the canvas bag and tucked it out of the way.

It was addressed to her. Had whoever sent it known of Jeremy's death?

The familiar numbers and letters of her address in Seattle blurred. Vomit swelled in her throat and hit the back of her mouth. She swallowed instinctively, the hot, sour taste burning as it slid back down. But why? Why send her a letter like the ones he'd sent Holly and Janine? She hated to touch the foul envelope, but she couldn't read the postmark in the dim light.

"Why send me a letter?" she finally asked. "Did he know—about Jeremy, I mean? He might have heard through friends or the alumni network. Plenty of people did hear, obviously."

"He must have known," Nic said. "I wonder if that's why he decided to send the letters. He knew that with Jeremy gone, there was no reason for you not to speak out."

"What are you saying?"

"What if he thought Jeremy was the reason none of us ever talked about the assault? By the time we knew Jeremy would recover from the accident, it was too late to say 'oh, and by the way, this all happened because Lucas was pissed that Janine didn't want to have sex with him.'"

"He tried to rape me," Janine said.

"I know that. We all know that." Nic's hand shook as she poured herself a glass of wine. It was the first time she'd been snappish since she got here, though they'd given her plenty of reason. "What's different now is that Jeremy's gone."

"And the anniversary," Holly said. "The letters must be connected to the anniversary."

Twenty-five years next week.

"Why not send one to you?" Janine asked Nic.

"I'm tempted to feel slighted," Nic said wryly. "Seriously, I have no idea. Did he think I might report him to the bar association for misconduct? It doesn't add up."

"That brings us back to yesterday's question," Holly said. "Did he think we wouldn't tell each other about the letters? That we wouldn't tell you?"

Nic swirled the deep red wine. "I don't know. He left me out for a reason. But what?"

"Did he?" Janine asked. "Do we know that for sure? Maybe it was lost or stolen when your mailbox was smashed."

"What? What happened?" Sarah asked. The thing they hadn't told her—or one of the things, she realized as she looked from Nic, her jaw tense, to Janine, focused on their friend, and Holly. Holly, who met her gaze with an expression of acknowledgment and apology.

Nic exhaled. "Stuff—happens sometimes, when I've been in the news with a client. Usually a queer client, but sometimes it's because of the environmental activism. We're not in the phone book, but nobody's hard to find these days."

"So," Sarah prompted. "What happened?"

"Someone took a baseball bat to our mailbox a few days ago. A bunch of our neighbors fly Pride flags in support of us, and a few let Tempe paint rainbows on their mailbox flags when she painted ours last summer for Pride Day, but their boxes were untouched. Which suggests it might have been random, or because I was on the news last week, testifying against expanded wolf hunting. Part of the state's proposal to update the wolf management plan. We don't know. Kim was pretty shaken by it. I know it's not my fault, but it feels that way."

Sarah squeezed Nic's hand. "People are idiots sometimes. I'm sorry." She nodded at the letter on the table. "We have to tell Leo."

"And give him one more reason to think I killed Lucas," Janine said.

"We can't blame him for sniffing around your life," Nic said. "That's his job. The longer he takes, the more time we have to convince him he's wrong. But I'm still puzzled about the letters. Why anonymous? And they couldn't have been mailed at the same time, not if Sarah's arrived before she left Seattle on Sunday and Janine didn't get hers until Monday."

Sarah didn't care about that right now. She couldn't sit, not one more minute, not with all this adrenaline, this anger, this fury racing through her. Bad enough, fucking shitty enough, to lose her husband—though he wasn't lost; she knew exactly where he was. Dead, that's where he was. She had a tube of ashes in the zippered compartment inside her tote bag, the only place she'd felt safe carrying it on the train ride.

Bad enough, but then to have all this crap from the past rising up again . . .

"Lucas wanted to scare us. Intimidate us. Make sure we kept quiet." She pushed away from the table and stood. "Because we knew something that scared him. Something besides the assault. But what?"

"Doesn't matter," Holly said. "He's dead. He can't scare us anymore. He can't hurt us."

"He can. He did. Why?" She looked at each woman in turn, her sister, her oldest friends. "He tore us apart. We can't let him win."

They talked about her conversation with Renee Harper, about Nic's interviews with Lucas's neighbors, about Misty Calhoun Erickson. They dredged up every single reason the sheriff might cite to suspect Janine of murder. They drained the bottle and Holly opened another and even Nic had a second glass. But they came up with nothing.

While she'd been in town, the others had cleaned the girls' bunk room and started on the cabin Nic and Janine had claimed. Sarah dragged her suitcase up the stairs and set it on the trunk at the foot of her bed.

In the bathroom, she was afraid to look in the mirror.

Suck it up, Sarah. It can't be as bad as you think.

But it was. Her eyes were wild, her brows shaggy. Had she packed tweezers? Might be better off using pliers. Needle-nose—there had to be a pair on the workbench in the carriage house. *Gad.* She ran her fingers through her hair, rough with sweat and yesterday's hair spray. It didn't help. The circles under her eyes had grown steadily deeper and darker over the last six months, and they hadn't improved in the last nineteen days.

Should she stop counting? Probably. But not yet. Not until it stopped hurting.

"You need a project," her mother had said when she'd urged her to come to the lodge. Turned out Sarah herself was the project.

And what about solving a murder? Truth was, she didn't much care who shot Lucas Erickson. For all the grief he'd caused back then, and was causing now with his anonymous letters, he was better off dead.

"Oh, Sarah, how can you say that?" she asked the shadow in the mirror. "The man had children. A mother. A sister." That was reason enough to pray that Leo solved the murder soon.

Who cared now why he'd sent the letters? He had no more power over them. She rummaged in her cosmetics bag. "Yes!" she said when she found the tweezers, then started plucking. Washed her face, brushed her teeth, and turned out the light.

The dark, the night, the fear—she was done giving it power.

*　*　*

The scream woke her.

"Sarah, Sarah," her sister said, bare feet thumping on the floor between their twin beds. "It's okay, Sarah. I'm here."

Oh, God. She grabbed her throat, rubbing it between the vee of her thumb and fingers. That was *her* screaming. The mattress groaned and sagged with Holly's weight and Sarah bent forward, her sister's hand on her back.

Was someone else here? No. No, that had been in the dream. A young woman in a long white nightgown, her back to Sarah. Hurrying down the grand staircase, the thin white fabric fluttering behind her. Sarah squeezed her eyelids shut. The woman reached the main floor, her hand on the newel post, and glanced back, up the stairs. Sarah stared into the memory, the waves of terror flooding over her. Then the woman angled toward the French doors that opened onto the deck. That's when she'd heard the scream. Her own scream.

"Abby," she said, gasping. "Where's Abby? Where's Noah?"

"The kids are fine," Holly said. "It was just a dream."

Sarah ran her hands over her face, pressing the heels into her eyes, then rubbing them with her fingers. The images were gone; the screaming had stopped.

But the terror still lapped at her skin like the waves lapped the cobbled lakeshore.

She'd said there was nothing left to fear, with Lucas dead. Was she wrong? Was the fear just in her mind?

"You're freezing," Holly said, draping the thick cotton quilt around Sarah's shoulders.

"No," she said. "No. I have to see where she went." She pulled away, swinging her feet off the high mattress and onto the braided rug.

"Who?" Holly called after her. "Sarah, stop. There is no one."

In the hallway, Sarah gripped the rail with both hands, then rocked back and collapsed onto her heels.

"She was right here. I saw her. I saw her go down the stairs and out the door. I heard her scream."

Holly crouched beside her. "There's no one here but us."

"I—heard—her. I *saw* her."

"Who? Who did you see?"

Sarah raised her eyes to her sister's, so like her own. So like her daughter's.

"No one," she said. "It was no one. You were right. Nothing but a bad dream."

She couldn't tell her sister the truth. She had only caught a glimpse of the woman in the nightgown, the woman running toward the doors and out to the lake.

But while she didn't know the face, she recognized the terror.

THURSDAY

Twenty Days

17

This time when Sarah woke, it was to the sound of rain.

But why was she in Holly's bed? An arm's length away, in Sarah's bed, Holly was fast asleep, cocooned in the Flying Geese quilt, the cat tucked behind her bent knees. Sarah pushed herself up, leaned against the pillows, and began to tease the middle-of-the-night events out of the cobwebs in her mind.

The face. The screaming girl.

Her fingers plucked at her chest. The thick cotton of her sweatshirt, not the wispy white nightgown she half-expected to be wearing.

The three-legged clock on the nightstand said six fifteen.

The dream—the nightmare—had been so vivid. As though she herself had been that terrified, panic-stricken girl.

Her therapist said that people in dreams are often mirrors of ourselves, chosen by the subconscious mind to force us to focus on some aspect, some trait that the dream figure represents.

No question what that girl represented.

Déjà vu all over again, her mind alerting her to danger. Was it to her this time?

But why? And from whom?

Or was the danger from within, from her own emotions, as tangled as the bedcovers?

After the nightmare, after she'd rushed down the hall in search of the mysterious figure, Holly had led her back to bed and crawled in beside her, wrapping her arms around her. Like when they were kids and one of them needed comforting. But at some point, she'd woken and switched beds. Now alone in Sarah's bed, Holly uncurled and rolled onto her stomach, one arm under the pillow, legs bent as though she were running, or leaping.

The way Abby slept.

And the terror struck her again.

Abby's fine. She's fine, a voice inside her said.

How do you know that? You don't know that, another voice said. She can't reach you. She doesn't have a father to call.

Sarah rushed out of the bedroom to the landing and grabbed the rail, one hand to her chest. *Slow, slow, slow.* In and out, the way her therapist had told her to do when the panic attacks hit. Breathe slowly, try not to think, just focus on the breath.

In, out. In, out. Out of the corner of her eye, she saw the cat sitting in the bedroom doorway, watching her.

"Go on," she told the cat. "Janine's up. I smell coffee. She'll feed you."

The cat did not move.

In the bathroom, Sarah rested her hands on the cool white porcelain of the pedestal sink. "Sarah Elizabeth McCaskill Carter," she told the face in the mirror. "Get a grip. You are fine. Your daughter is fine."

The sharp, floral scent of the lavender soap calmed her as she washed her face. "You've got this. You've got this."

So easy to say in daylight. So hard to believe in the darkness.

*　*　*

But before she did anything else, she had to know whether the voices were right. Which voices to believe. Abby was an early riser, like Jeremy, who loved a morning run, also like him. And she needed to hear her daughter's voice.

She hiked up the lane, her bare feet slipping inside the tennis shoes, checking for reception every few hundred yards. The car would have been quicker, but she needed to move. When she got past the big bend, her phone pinged and her heart leapt. But it was just the morning check-in from the house sitter, followed by a text from a friend.

She touched the screen and watched the phone icon vibrate. Heard the almost imperceptible catch as the call was answered.

"Hi, Mom." Bright and shiny, her Abby. Nothing was wrong.

"Abby, honey. So good to hear your voice."

"Yours too, Mom. I'm out for a run with my roommate and the girls from down the hall." More former high school runners. Sarah and Jeremy had met them last fall at parents' weekend, slender, leggy colts like their daughter. "I gotta go, Mom. They're getting away from me. I'll text you later."

"Bye, honey," Sarah called into the silence.

Nothing was wrong.

Nothing was wrong.

"Ohmygosh, bacon," she said a few minutes later, the kitchen's linoleum floor chilly on her bare feet. "Second time this week. And coffee cake?"

"I am the Cake Lady," Janine said.

"Great name for a bakery. If you ever wanted to open your own." Sarah filled a heavy white mug with fresh coffee, then lifted it to her face. "Mmm. Cinnamon?"

"Now you sound like Holly," Janine said, her tone wary. "Talking about me opening my own business. Are you two conspiring?"

"Great minds think alike?"

"I don't have any money. I took this week off to stay up here and solve this problem, but I've got to get back to work. And if I have to pay a lawyer—"

"Janine, if you need money—"

"I don't want yours. Thank you, I don't mean to be ungrateful, but I don't want people feeling sorry for me." Her voice quivered.

Tread lightly.

"Where's Nic?" Sarah asked, glancing around reflexively the way you do when you mention someone, as if they might be hiding underneath a chair or behind the breadbox. Or might walk in any moment.

"She drove up to the highway to call Kim. To check in, and warn her to be on the lookout for a letter."

Her brain frazzled by the nightmare, Sarah had almost forgotten about the letter from Lucas tucked in with the condolence cards, and their speculation about why he hadn't sent one to Nic. If he hadn't.

"Then she was planning to go into town," Janine continued. "To take your letter to Leo's office and snoop around. Absolutely refused to let me go along. Said she wanted to track down people willing to talk freely about Lucas and she could find out a lot more without me. I get it, but that left me stewing in my own juices. So—coffee cake. You can't worry when you're baking."

"She doesn't know Deer Park like we do. Or like we think we do. She might see it more clearly." Sarah cut a piece and sat, Janine across from her. She took the first bite. "This is so good. No wonder your license plate says Cake Lady."

"Thanks. Zak gave me that."

"Sounds like a great kid. Sitting here with you, in my grandmother's kitchen, eating off the dishes with the mountains and the pink bitterroots—it's like you said. Magic."

She took another bite, then set her fork down. "Nic and Kim okay?"

"Yeah. But Nic's work puts her in the spotlight in a way that isn't always comfortable."

"Every marriage has its trade-offs and tensions. Comes with the territory."

Janine looked up sharply. "Not you two. Not you and Jeremy."

"Oh, yes, even us." She picked up her coffee. Although their trade-offs hadn't resulted in vandalism. "Especially when he was building the business and I was focused on the kids. The usual stuff. We worked through it."

"Of course you did. No big deal," Holly said. Sarah hadn't heard her sister come in. "The perfect couple. You even managed to go through a rough patch perfectly."

Sarah put the mug down heavily. "What's that supposed to mean?"

"You want us all to be such great friends again, who confide in each other and help each other out." Holly took a mug, twin to Sarah's, off the drying rack and poured herself coffee. Leaned against the counter, crossed one foot in front of the other, and took a sip.

Sarah glanced at Janine, watching the sisters warily, then turned her attention back to Holly. Not that she hadn't felt the silent stings of her sister's jealousy plenty of times, but why this, why now?

"Did you get up on the wrong side of the bed—or the wrong bed, since you were in mine—and decide to take it out on me?"

"You," Holly shot back. "You act like the lodge is yours, and resent me for being here. You don't know what's going on in our lives. What worries Nic. That Janine doesn't want to be bought off with guilt money, even if her legal fees would be pocket change to you, like the pennies your perfect husband leaves."

A slow burn crept up Sarah's spine.

The refrigerator hummed and the clock ticked.

"Ever since we've been here," she said slowly, "I've had the distinct impression that each of you had some secret you weren't telling me. I tried to convince myself you didn't want to add to my troubles. Since my perfect husband—who was pretty darned great—is dead. I knew I should appreciate your thoughtfulness, but instead it felt like you were pushing me away. Excluding me. Because apparently you think that I think I'm too good—too perfect—for you." She pushed her chair away from the table and stood. "Well, maybe I am."

*　*　*

Plop. Sarah crouched on the gravel beach below the lodge, rubbing two stones between her fingers. The beach at the wildlife refuge had the best skipping stones. These just plopped in the water and sank.

She heard soft footfalls on the gravel but didn't turn. Janine crouched beside her.

"I'm not going to tell you not to be angry," Janine said. "She was pretty nasty."

"She's right, though. You three talk, you keep up. I'm the one who pulled away."

"Yeah, well. She's got a lot on her mind. You know."

She shot Janine a sharp glance. "No, I don't know. How am I supposed to know? She doesn't tell me anything. She never came out when Jeremy was sick, not once."

"Did you invite her?"

"She knew she was welcome."

"That's not the same."

"She came out for the funeral and stayed at a hotel. We had room, even with both kids home, and Mom and Connor and his family there. Plenty of room, in my big, perfect house." Sarah dropped one of the stones into her left palm and threw the other into the lake. *Plop.*

"She lost her job a couple of months ago," Janine said. "She didn't want you to know."

"That's what she's been not telling me? What Mom's been not telling me? We all see she drinks too much. Is that why she lost it, or the other way around?"

"She applied to be director of the museum. So did one of the curators. The board chose him, and the first thing he did was fire her."

"Can he do that? Legally, I mean?"

"Apparently, yes." Janine tilted her head. "But it's not an easy job to replace."

Sarah let the last stone fall onto the beach and got to her feet. Holly had worked at museums and art centers for years, most recently as director of operations, more of a business position than an artistic one. Sarah had done time on boards herself, including the board of a children's art center, and thought Holly would make a great director. She was certainly good at telling people what to do.

"But why didn't she tell me?"

"I don't know." Janine slipped an arm around her and they walked up the slope a few feet and sat on the slate steps that led from the deck to the beach.

"Is she—I hate to ask this, but is she okay for money?"

"I think so. They gave her a good severance package."

They'd all kept their bad news, their hard times, from her. To keep from bothering her, from upsetting her, while she had so much going on. Didn't they know that keeping things from her made it worse?

How much of the distance and silence was her own fault?

And how did she fix it, now that she was on her own?

18

"C on!" Sarah stretched on tippy-toes to hug her little brother. "My favorite lumberjack!"

He pulled her close, but gingerly. Did he think she would break? Or was it the instinct of a man who towered over nearly everyone else? Connor McCaskill wasn't fat, not one bit—he was a McCaskill, after all, always on the move. But he was *big*. Tall. Muscular. And looking far more comfortable in his brown work pants and plaid flannel shirt than in the black suit he'd worn at the funeral. Everyone, everything had looked different that day.

"Good to see you home," he said.

"Good to be home," she said automatically. It was, finally, beginning to feel good, being back here. If only . . . She shook off the memory of the nightmare.

"Sorry I didn't make it out yesterday. Bad as things are on the north slope, the south shore's worse. We're contracted to manage the hillside behind the church camp and the storm practically clear-cut it. That's where I was when you called, helping the crews scope out the damage and make a plan."

"Did you get home in time for pizza night?" she asked. "How are the kids?" Olivia was eleven, Aidan nine, and they'd been somber and well-behaved on the visit to Seattle. Most of the time.

"Good. Eager to see you. So is Brooke."

"Great. We're in good shape here, mostly. But the roof—" She broke off at the sight of a second white pickup coming down the lane, the familiar logo stenciled on the side—a grove of evergreens encircled by black letters reading MCCASKILL LAND & LUMBER, DEER PARK, MONTANA. Who was at the wheel?

"Matt Kolsrud," Connor said, answering her unasked question. "We'll size up the damage, then I'll put him to work."

"Matt?" Her date to senior prom. She hadn't thought of him in years. "He works for you now?"

"Junior," Connor said, eyebrows raised in amusement.

"Ah. I should have known." The young man crossing the driveway did look like his father, or like his father had looked when they were teenagers, with the same loping gait and floppy brown hair. Introductions made, Connor suggested they inspect the structures first. "The roof fixes are easy, but if you're right and that ripped balcony damaged the log work, we might want to hire Matt's dad. He's a real craftsman."

They scouted out the exterior damage, then the two men followed Sarah up the steps to the lodge. Both stooped to untie their work boots and left them outside. Mud-spattered, mouths gaping now that they were empty—you almost could live in one, like the nursery rhyme said.

Young Matt's mouth gaped, too, when he saw the massive stone fireplace, the tall ceilings, the staircase with its peeled pine balustrade and the knotty newel post as intricate as any hand-carved woodwork. They traipsed upstairs behind Sarah in their stocking feet.

"The only damage I saw was in here." She led the way into the sewing room, where the men wrangled the bookcase away from the door. She held her breath when Connor inched his torso out onto the balcony, the decking at an awkward angle, Matt's hand on his belt. Then he wriggled back in and inspected the logs inside. Used the level on his phone, and frowned.

"That what's bothering you?" Matt pointed at a long horizontal crack a few inches above the floor, and Connor nodded.

"My guess, the way the doorjamb's tilted, and now this, is that when that spruce hit the balcony, these old logs couldn't absorb the force of the impact. They settle over time"—Connor directed his words to Sarah—"which adds to the stress on the chinking. In modern log construction, the chinking itself is flexible, so when the logs settle, it doesn't crack. But with old logs like this . . ."

"They've already settled, so they can't take another blow," she said. "They crack."

"Exactly. We can tuck-point the chinking, repacking it. Some cracks, that run through the joints, a guy might fill." Connor made a cross with his hands. "But if the log's split all the way through, then it's lost its strength. Water can seep in, cause rot. Not to mention bugs."

"What's the fix?"

"Worst case . . ." Connor stood. "Replace the log. And while we're at it, inspect the entire structure for rot, weak joints, other damage that's gone unnoticed for decades."

"Sounds like a major project," Sarah said.

"Matt senior can tell us more and give us a preliminary estimate." He turned to his employee. "I threw a couple of clean brown tarps in the back of my truck. Would you bring those in? Just drop them inside the front door. And my tool belt. Then set up the big ladder at the corner. I'll work from inside, you outside, and we'll get this balcony covered and keep the house dry."

"You got it, boss." The young man padded out.

Sarah watched as her brother scrutinized the door.

"This framing is shot," he said. "The jamb is splintered. You couldn't close the door because the hinges are bent. There's a guy in town, blacksmith, who can fix the gnarliest old hardware."

"We're going to have to talk about the lodge," she said. "The four of us. Make a plan."

He looked chagrined. "Brooke and I thought we had a plan, and Mom approved, but I just don't have time for anything extra right now. Hey, the kids have soccer games on Saturday. Whitefish against Deer Park, here. Mom's coming. You and Holly should come, too."

"Wouldn't miss it." She missed cheering on kids—Noah on the soccer field, Abby coming into view on the home stretch of a race. "So what's this expansion Mom mentioned? Is that what's taking up all your time? And why you needed more space at the mill?"

They heard the front door open and broke off to haul the tarps upstairs. She waited while Connor and Matt worked, quickly and efficiently, and within minutes, the northeast corner of the lodge was protected by shiny brown tarps, tacked and tied so the wind couldn't whip them up like sails.

"Good job," Connor called. "Why don't you take a break? Leave the ladder out so we can check the carriage house. I'll be out in a bit."

They headed for the kitchen. "Employees don't get to take inside breaks?" Sarah asked.

"I know the kid. He'd rather sit in the truck with his earbuds in. I'll call his dad, but it might be a few days before he can get out here."

"Good. Thanks. Oh, by the way, when I was in town yesterday, I stopped by Lucas Erickson's office and his secretary assumed I was there for the company files."

No point saying she wished he hadn't done business with Lucas. Whatever the business was, he'd be finding a new lawyer. She was about to ask if he knew what had their mother worried when the mudroom door opened.

"One cabin clean," Holly called. "I may have a future as a housekeeper. Lord knows there's plenty of work here. Connor!"

He had to know about the job loss, Sarah thought as her brother and sister hugged. And Holly had to know Janine had spilled the beans. They were all talking about her. They just weren't talking *to* her.

Coffee was poured and cake cut. Though Connor was the youngest—Holly had five years on him, Sarah six—next to the rest of them, he looked like a grownup sitting at the kiddie table for a pretend tea party.

"The edge of the roof is damaged on the middle cabin, and a couple of trees are leaning pretty badly," Holly said. "There's a tree down on the fence, though. Is that our responsibility or theirs? And why is there a fence, anyway? It looks new."

Connor put his fork down and gestured with the big hands that reminded Sarah of their dad's. "You know the rule. If the fence is on the property line, you find the halfway point. Everything on your right is your responsibility. Everything on their right is theirs."

"Even if they built the fence and you thought it was a dumb idea?"

"Even if," he agreed.

"I saw that fence earlier," Sarah said, "and I meant to ask George about it."

"When did you see George?" Connor sounded wary.

"Yesterday. He came down to check on the place while I was out picking up shingles. Helped me drag a few branches off the road, then drove me around to check out the damage."

"I don't know what George is up to." Connor stood. "I need to finish up here, then get back to the mill."

Meaning they'd have that talk later. But one more thing, before he left.

"While you're here," Sarah said, "would you take a look at the phone box? The cell signal down here is totally iffy, so Mom called the phone company to turn the landline back on. I think she did, anyway. She's kinda spacy right now. But we're still not getting a signal."

"Yeah, sure. Though I don't know that I can help."

A few minutes later, standing outside the lodge near the mudroom door, she peered over her brother's shoulder as he crouched in front of the green phone box. Handed her a tiny bird's nest that sat on top. Slipped a screwdriver blade underneath the door and pried it open.

Inside, in the bottom of the box, lay a bright, shiny copper penny.

*　*　*

They decided a mouse must have chewed through the wires. No other animal could have worked its way in. Why, what the pea-brain expected it could find to eat inside a plastic box filled with plastic-coated wires and metal switches, they could not imagine. The critter must have been sharp-toothed—the break was awfully neat—and he'd left nothing behind. But no other explanation made sense. Their search, in the carriage house and in the cellar, for wire to make a splice had come up empty. So Connor had gone to check on his young employee one more time, and she'd made the trek up to the highway in search of a phone signal, one more time.

She was getting tired of this.

It was time to go home. Time to get on with life, whatever that meant. She had board meetings and volunteer commitments and a house and friends. And the kids would be home soon. It wouldn't be the same, of course, but it would be good. She pictured kayaking with them on Lake Washington and wandering the farmers' market. Morning coffee in the bright kitchen, drinking in the wide-angle views, sleepy teenagers wrapping their arms around her neck, then sliding into the breakfast nook beside her and just hanging. Although Noah wasn't a teenager anymore.

In the kitchen, she set the tiny nest on the window sill beside the nest she'd picked up on the lawn and the pine cone from the sewing room. Grabbed her keys and strode to the carriage house.

She backed the rig out, then paused at the end of the circular driveway to watch the two men remove a badly leaning fir that might threaten a cabin if the winds turned wrong. Both men wore white hard hats bearing the company logo. Her brother held out a hand to stop her, but she was already stopped. She was a lumberman's daughter.

Matt made one last cut and Connor used the winch and cable in the back of the truck to land the tree softly without damaging the undergrowth or the soft earth. Then Connor waved her through. She waved back and slipped the rig in gear.

The rain had stopped, but water ran down the ruts in the road. Her tires slipped in the mud, sending the rear end sideways a few inches, and she shifted into low gear. Felt the front tires start to catch, then begin to slide backward. "Don't let me down now, car," she urged and the wheels spun, then caught solid ground. She fed the gas slowly and the wheels took hold, gliding forward.

At the top of the road, she stayed on McCaskill Lane but pulled over to the side. First call, her mother. No answer on the house line; voice mail on the cell. Peggy must be painting. She left a message saying Connor had been out and while the damage to the lodge was more extensive than she'd thought, he was sure it could be easily repaired. Not much of an exaggeration—he had been sure, calling Matt Kolsrud the elder a log home magician. Enough time and money, the man could do anything.

Next, the phone company, where a digitized voice told her to touch one for this and two for that and sent her in an endless loop until she finally touched zero and after a long silence in which she was sure the line had gone dead, she was told to wait. A small-town phone company should not need such a cumbersome system. When a human finally came on the line, Sarah gave her mother's name, remembering that they wouldn't talk to Holly, and answered the perfectly pleasant service rep's perfectly reasonable questions: the number, the address, and what could Mrs. McCaskill tell her about the damage? No service call on record, meaning Peggy had forgotten, as Sarah had begun to suspect. They'd try to get someone out Friday, but couldn't make any promises. Monday, more likely, or possibly Tuesday. Was there anything else she needed?

Oh, yes. There was so much more she needed than a working landline. A cell signal. A sister who didn't keep secrets. A friend who wasn't under suspicion for murder. A time turner so she could bring Jeremy back to life, get him to the doctor sooner so they could catch his cancer before it took off like the proverbial bat out of hell. Why were men so stubborn about going to the doctor? Would it have made any difference? The oncologist had been noncommittal on that point, not wanting, she supposed, to give them one more thing to beat themselves up about. Hadn't they always known the cancer might come back? Yes, but not for years. Decades. Not until they'd spent a good long life together, finished raising their kids, spoiled grandchildren, taken a cruise down the Danube, all those milestones you assumed you'd live to see.

Why were there bats in hell anyway?

"Thank you, no," she told the faceless woman in the phone company office. "You've been a big help."

The car windows had begun to fog, so she punched buttons on the dashboard. The vents opened and cold air smacked her in the face. She pushed more buttons, until the air began to warm and the fog to recede. Her mother refused to get a new car because the new models were more like mobile computers than cars. She'd rolled her eyes, but now she had to agree. Why was life so stinking complicated?

She cracked the window open. In the distance, she heard Matt's chainsaw. Glanced at the time. Her kids would be in class. *Don't call.* Don't become a stalker-mom. Texting was a godsend. Abby's first few weeks at school, she'd texted at least once every day, and the hour before bed had often been a text-fest, with pictures and sometimes a call. Then Jeremy's diagnosis had come and they hadn't told the kids, but when it became apparent that this time the cancer wasn't going to go away quietly like it had before, they'd shared the news. After that, both kids called and texted daily. The phone had been the glue that held her heart together.

And now? Now she was in the middle of the woods in the middle of nowhere with the bars on her screen flat as the proverbial pancakes.

But she'd talked to Abby this morning, so she sent both kids a quick text saying Uncle Connor was here checking on the storm damage, but everything was under control and he sent his love. The second she hit send, on a rare upward bounce of the signal, she wished she hadn't been so breezy. Been more caring, asking how they were doing, yadda yadda.

As if anybody, let alone a teenager or just-recently-former teenager, ever responded to mush like that.

Truth was, she didn't know how to take care of herself in this terrible time, let alone her kids.

Just be there, her therapist would say.

Easy to say, and hard to do. Where exactly was "there"?

Her phone buzzed with a flood of texts. Including a reminder of the call with her therapist at nine thirty. It was nine fifty-three.

Oops.

Could she claim she hadn't been able to get a line, which was half true? Pretend she'd spaced it out, though she'd seen the reminder yesterday? She sort of had, preoccupied with her brother's visit and the damage to the lodge.

Face-to-face, she wouldn't dare lie. Not that the woman would ever call BS or even flick an eyebrow in disappointment. But in-person contact kept her honest, if for no other reason than the unspoken question: what is going on that you feel the need to lie to me?

She punched CALL. Apologized. Told the therapist about the nightmare. The fear that the face of the mysterious woman was her own. The strange discoveries.

"It's not unreasonable to fear that your life is falling apart. It just did."

"And the pennies?"

"It's common. There is no rational explanation."

"Meaning it's all in my head."

"Good Lord, no. The pennies are real," the woman said, the delay in the signal giving her voice an other-worldly sound. "That we can't explain how they got there just means there are limits in our understanding."

"Ha. That's my life right now."

"People have gotten all kinds of reminders or signs from their loved ones who've passed on. Butterflies or dragonflies. Certain smells—perfume or aftershave. One client had a sister who was murdered by her husband. She sent clouds in the shape of angels."

"I don't think I could handle that."

"Me neither, but she found them reassuring. I have another client whose husband sends her the number eleven."

"Why? His lucky number for roulette? They were married on November eleventh, eleven years ago?"

"She has absolutely no idea."

Great. Just great. "Jeremy didn't have a thing for pennies. He didn't save them in a big jar and buy himself a present when he cashed them in. He didn't habitually find them on the street and consider them lucky. Pennies didn't mean anything to him."

"Do they mean something to you?"

Did they? Not that she knew.

"What if," the woman continued, "they're simply an indication that he's thinking of you? Hold that in your heart, see how it feels. Ask your dreams for an interpretation if you'd like."

She would not like. She would not like to dream again, not if it meant risking another sight of the terror on the young woman's face, or a midnight tumble down the grand staircase in her rush to catch the specter, to find out who she was. To save her.

"Hey, I'm sorry. I hate to cut things short, but we got started late and I can hear the grief support group arriving. Same time next week, by phone if you're still in Montana? Though you know you can call me any time. Any time. And think about joining the support group when you get home."

Not until they'd broken the connection did Sarah realize she hadn't told her therapist the scariest part. It wasn't the pennies from her dead husband. Pennies were nothing, compared to letters from a dead man she'd hated.

19

Back in the carriage house, she scanned the workbench. Stuck a needle-nose pliers, slightly rusty, in her pocket. You never knew when you'd need one, or where to find it when you did.

An old oil drum sat on the floor, full of detritus likely meant for the hide and steel company's next community recycling day. She glanced in a wooden tool box and a glint of brass caught her eye. A key? *Yes!* She hadn't been imagining things after all. Not this thing, anyway. She dug out a ring of keys in all shapes and finishes, even a black skeleton key. Several small keys could be the right size for a padlock or a trunk.

At the bottom of the steps, she pulled on the cord. *Shoot.* She'd forgotten to bring out a new bulb, or the flashlight.

No matter. She made her way up the stairs and into the apartment. They had a virtual antique store in here. Fingers crossed that Brooke remembered which box held the china and stemware.

In the bedroom, she gave the dollhouse a fond look, then turned her attention to the trunk. *In, out, in, out.* Yoga breathing had its uses in all kinds of situations. Her fingers shook as she fiddled for one of the smaller keys. She took another calming breath and bent close.

For the first time, she noticed a monogram on the brass plate beneath the lock. *CSE* in an elaborate script, the S larger than the initials of the first and middle names. This had been her great-grandmother's trunk before her marriage.

She tried the first key. Nothing. Found a second, the same size. No luck.

On the third try, something gave inside the mechanism. She waggled the key gently until she heard another movement. Lifted the latch. The lid was hinged, and she held her breath as she used both hands to raise it.

The scents of rose and cedar greeted her, along with the smell of old paper—slightly sweet, with a hint of must. And dust. She turned and sneezed into her elbow.

A cedar-lined tray rested on a narrow ledge. On the top of one compartment, cradled in tissue paper, lay three white roses tied together with sprigs of baby's breath by a pink ribbon. She set the paper aside gently, then lifted out a white satin dress with a lace collar. A child's dress.

Sarah Beth's.

The loss of her husband at forty-seven was killing her, but to lose a child . . .

Beneath the dress lay a small book, the edges of its white cardboard cover darkened with age, and in the center, the drawing of a baby, draped in a garland of flowers. *Baby's Days*, it read. Sarah laid the dress carefully across her lap and reached for the book. The first page showed a sleeping baby beneath the words "Record of Birth," and below, the particulars of Sarah Beth's arrival into this world. She turned the pages slowly, noting each milestone Caro had recorded—first steps, first words, first laugh. A height and weight chart. Black paper corners held small black-and-white photos onto the pages and Sarah squinted for a closer look. She'd seen photos of Sarah Beth on the gallery wall in the Victorian—as a baby in Caro's arms, as a toddler with her brothers, and in this very dress. The photos had come down years ago, and her mother set a few around the house, rotating the display. But seeing these pictures, in this lovingly detailed baby book, the little girl's dollhouse close by, broke her heart, because she knew that the rest of the pages— the school record, the list of friends, the markers of a full life— would always be blank.

She closed the book and gently returned it to the tray, refolded the dress, and laid the dried roses on top. The other compartment held two matching sailor outfits in different sizes. These she was sure she'd seen, in a photograph of her grandfather and his brother as young boys.

Beneath the tray were more albums and scrapbooks— leather-bound, cardboard, even handmade with thin wooden covers. Boxes crammed with bundles of letters tied with ribbon, so full the lids no longer fit. She pried a bundle out just far enough to read the handwriting. From Cornelius McCaskill to Miss Caroline Sullivan, Butte, Montana. The envelopes bore postmarks from around the country.

Love letters? The man who would become her great-grandfather, courting her future great-grandmother.

She had never seen any of these. The curse of a packrat family. She set the box back in the trunk, careful of a few rolled-up photos, wondering what else it held.

What was that? She lifted out a Whitman's Sampler box and removed the lid. Inside lay letters addressed to Mrs. Cornelius McCaskill. A few envelopes had return addresses in Deer Park—Old Mill Road, the Stage Road, Mrs. B. F. Taunton on Second East. They'd lived on Second East, before they moved to the Victorian, but she didn't remember the house number. The light was too poor to make out the date on the faded postmark.

Beneath the letters was a leather-clad notebook in a lovely golden brown. She set the box and lid aside and stroked the soft, smooth cover.

Caroline Sullivan McCaskill, the signature on the flyleaf read. This had been her great-grandmother's journal. She squinted at the opening entry, wishing for that flashlight.

Sunday, May 21, 1922
Our first morning at Whitetail Lodge. Con has taken Tom and little Harry out for a walk along the lakeshore while I write at the desk in our bedroom, my darling Sarah Beth asleep in the nursery.

Of course. The sewing room had once been a nursery. Connected to the master bedroom by a pocket door, it was perfect for that.

We wake to marvelous views of the lake and mountains through the French doors, and I opened one a few inches, to let in a cool breeze.

She flipped ahead, pausing at an entry from June 1924.

Mrs. O'Dell made the most wonderful sponge for Con's birthday, topped with strawberries—a gift from one of the young Society women. (What fun to put it that way!) I told her it was unnecessary, but she insisted—she grew them herself and they were divine.

Mrs. O'Dell. Holly was named Helen O'Dell McCaskill—Holly was a nickname—after a family friend, but Sarah had never heard anything more about the woman. Who was this mysterious "society woman" who grew the strawberries? And when were strawberries ever unnecessary?

She flipped ahead to the last entry, dated 1926, though several empty pages followed. Why had Caro stopped writing? Were there other journals?

She'd take the journal with her and explore it under better light. She returned the box and tray to the trunk, closed it, and stood.

Heard a sound. Held her breath. Were those footsteps? Heavy footsteps, drawing closer. She stared at the door. Who might be coming up here? Why? There was no escape.

"Who's there?"

No one answered.

Then a shadow filled the doorway. Her heart all but leapt into her throat.

"Sarah?"

"Oh, Connor." She stepped into the light. "You scared me for a moment. You find more damage? I'm not surprised." Her breath was returning to normal, but it hadn't caught up with her voice yet. "I'd like to bring this trunk into the lodge. It's awfully heavy. I don't know how you two managed to haul it up the stairs."

"We didn't," he said, his brow furrowed. "That one was already in here. I didn't open it."

"It's filled with old albums and scrapbooks, keepsakes I think belonged to our great-grandmother. Could you and Matt—uh—uhh." She raised her elbow to her face and sneezed.

"Sure. But—"

"Connor, what is it? What—?" She sneezed again.

A half-smile crept onto his lips. "I'll get Matt."

* * *

In the lodge, Sarah left the journal and pliers on the kitchen counter, then headed for the bathroom to wash off the dust.

A few minutes later, she heard a clatter outside and rushed to open the front door. "Don't worry about your boots," she called. The men lugged the brass and leather trunk through the front hall and set it in Grandpa Tom's office.

"Why don't you start limbing those spruce?" Connor asked Matt. Sarah thanked the young man, then turned to her brother.

"What's up? I can see it on your face."

"I need to explain. About Lucas."

She perched on the corner of their grandfather's desk and crossed her arms. "I just didn't realize he'd done any work for the company. Or that you knew him. But it's a small town. And from what Nic says, when it came to lawyers in Deer Park, you didn't have a lot of choice."

"I know what happened twenty-five years ago, sis," Connor said.

No, you don't. Not all of it. Connor had been a kid then, thrilled to meet an honest-to-goodness, real-life college basketball star. Michael had been kind to the gangly teenager, and Connor had been devastated by his death. As far as he knew, as far as anyone around here knew, the wreck was a terrible accident. And he didn't know what Lucas had done to Janine. His ignorance was her fault; they'd kept their mouths shut.

But now the man was dead. And maybe she'd held her grudge too long.

She raised both hands. "Hey, it's okay. You had every right to hire whoever you thought would do the best job for the company, and I don't get to say boo, because I'm not running the business. Unless you killed him. You didn't kill him, did you?"

"God, no, Sally. How can you say that?"

"Joking. Joking. Seems like most of the people who knew Lucas wanted to kill him, at one time or another."

"He could be a first-class ass," Connor said. "But if Jeremy was willing to let it go, maybe you should, too."

"Jeremy?" She straightened. "What does he have to do with this? And don't you tell me how my husband felt or didn't feel."

"Hey, what's this mysterious trunk?" They heard Holly before they saw her. She stood in the doorway, looking from one sibling to the other. "What? What's up?"

Holly's words echoed Sarah's own demands. They were all on edge right now. Sarah cradled the top of her head. She was sick of secrets. Parts of the story weren't theirs to tell. But if it weighed this heavily, it might be time to lift the burden.

They told him about the letters. About Janine racing up to Deer Park to confront Lucas, only to find him dead on his office floor. About Leo's suspicions and Nic's attempt to piece together the truth, to bolster Janine's defense and identify the real killer.

Through it all, Connor kept a closed face. When Sarah finished, he spoke to Holly. "So that's why you're here. This isn't a girlfriends' week to reconnect and comfort Sarah?"

Holly's silence was his answer.

"How do you know the letters came from Lucas?" he continued.

"We don't. Not for sure. But the four of us and Lucas are the only people"—Sarah stopped, correcting herself—"*were* the only people still living who were here that day. And we have no reason to threaten each other."

"But why would he threaten you? I mean . . ." He ran a hand over his reddish-brown hair, in need of a trim. "Why bring it up now? Why do anything?"

"That's what we don't know," Holly said. "One theory is that Lucas had plans to run for office and wanted to make sure we kept quiet."

"About the assault." Connor's gaze narrowed and he glanced between them. "What else?"

"She ran from him, bruised and bloody, crying." Sarah's throat hurt, the rage unspoken for so long. "We were all there. The guys tried to confront him but he jumped in the car. They tried to stop him but . . ."

"And that's when the accident happened." Connor wiped his forehead with the back of his wrist.

"I—" *Guts, Sarah, guts.* "I have never been sure it was an accident. Yes, the moose came out of the borrow pit. Yes, Lucas was angry and even afraid. But . . ."

"You think—oh, God. You think he crashed that car on purpose," Connor said. "Killing one man and nearly killing another."

"I never knew you thought that," Holly said. "I thought that was just my crazy theory."

"I suspect each of us came to that same conclusion. The girls. Not Jeremy. Never Jeremy."

"Holy crap," Connor said. "I never would have hired Erickson . . ."

"I know," Sarah said. "I know. The story never got out. Janine decided not to press charges, after what happened. We all thought he'd go to prison for the wreck. We never imagined he'd get off scot-free."

Connor's eyes were guarded, and she saw in this giant man the little boy who'd chased after his sisters on the lakefront lawn, who'd stepped into the family business young, working alongside their ailing father for years, keeping it going against all odds. And now, apparently, expanding it.

They heard the front door open. Connor poked his head out, then back in. "It's Leo."

A moment later, the uniformed sheriff joined the siblings in their grandfather's office, forgoing the usual hugs, kisses, and handshakes. This was serious.

"If you're here to see Janine—" Sarah began.

"No. Ms. Lund made crystal-clear that I was not to say anything more than hello to Ms. Chapman outside her presence," Leo said.

"You're treating her as a serious suspect," Connor said.

"Everyone's a serious suspect," Leo replied sharply.

"We've told him everything," Sarah said.

"All right. Good. I'm sending the letter and envelope to the state crime lab," Leo replied, "for fingerprinting and a formal comparison to the others. Though it seems identical. Tell me about it."

"It came to the house. I don't remember seeing it, but either the housekeeper or I must have thought it was another condolence card and tucked it in the bag with the rest."

"Where it stayed until last night," Leo said, and she nodded.

"If Lucas Erickson was the kind of man who would threaten a woman whose husband had just died," Holly said, "then he deserved what he got."

"Probably not the best thing to say in front of the sheriff," Sarah said, "even if he is our cousin. But I appreciate the sentiment."

"Problem is," Leo said, "that kind of logic gives me a long list of suspects."

Was she imagining that his attention settled on her brother a moment too long? Surely Leo didn't suspect his own family. Surely if he did, he'd bring in outside investigators.

"What if," Connor said, "Janine heard about his ambitions—they're hardly a secret—and decided this was the time to stop him? Times have changed."

Easy to say, hard to believe. As the mother of both a young man and a young woman, she hoped sheriffs no longer told young women to get over it, to think about the man's reputation. Leo would never say such a thing. But the rest of his ilk? She wasn't convinced.

And why did Connor sound like he wanted Janine to be guilty?

A thick silence filled the room. In the distance, the chainsaw whirred.

"What if," Holly broke in, "we misunderstood? The letter said 'only you know what to do.' We took that as a warning to keep silent, but what if it's the opposite, telling us to speak out?"

"But who?" Sarah asked. Holly couldn't mean . . . "No. If Janine decided it was finally time to expose him, to derail his ambitions, why not just do it? Besides, he's run for office before and she didn't say a thing."

"That we know of," Leo said.

So they were checking. "Leo, she's not a terrified girl anymore. She's a grown woman. Not that I believe she's guilty for one minute, but if she'd wanted to kill him, why not just kill him? Why go to all this trouble? And why drag the rest of us into it?"

But it made a certain kind of sense. They hadn't been all-for-one, one-for-all for a long time. What if Janine hadn't been sure she could count on their support, not without manipulating them to rally 'round her.

Leo was eyeing her closely, as if he could read her mind. She wouldn't put it past him—he'd known her her whole life.

But he wasn't necessarily on their side. He'd say he wasn't on anyone's side, that his goal was the truth. Justice. She wanted to believe him, believe that he was better than the sheriff who had subtly, but surely, pressured her and Janine to hold their tongues twenty-five years ago.

"Leo," she said. "I know you have to investigate her. You have to investigate everyone who had a beef with Lucas—his ex-wife, his former partner."

"Unhappy clients," Holly said. "Unhappy not-clients."

"Lucas left plenty of both," Leo said.

As she'd heard that first day back, in the Spruce, when Deb the waitress had aired her grievances and the older couple had chimed in with their gossip. And her own brother was a client, though he'd said nothing to suggest he'd been unhappy with Lucas. Neither had Renee Harper.

She stepped between her brother and sister and looped her arms through theirs. "We trust you to do your job."

"Thank you, Sally. Sarah," Leo replied.

"Speaking of jobs." Connor dropped her arm. "Better get back to mine."

The two cousins shook hands. "I see your crews are working up on Lynx Mountain," Leo said.

Sarah frowned. "Do we have land up there? I know it's a checkerboard, but I thought that end of the ridge belonged to George Hoyt."

"He sold," Connor said curtly and turned to leave, gesturing to Leo to go first.

Now what was that about? She stared at the men's muddy footprints and wondered.

20

idn't matter if it rained buckets. If she came back cold and drenched and shivered and got the flu and spent a week in bed. Sarah needed to get out of this house and clear her head.

The woods were quiet. Connor had left, leaving young Matt to limb the downfall and pile up the debris. A full crew would finish the job next week and haul the merchantable timber back to the yard. But the roads on the property were clear and the threats to the buildings removed. The debris, the slash, they'd burn before the summer heat dried out the woods. She'd tended slash piles with her father in the spring and fall, rakes and shovels in hand, the smell of dank, mossy smoke working its way into her hair, her clothes, her nostrils. She should have hated it, but she hadn't. She'd loved the time with him, time in these woods, time tending the family legacy.

Seems the family had another legacy, too. One whose depth she'd never guessed.

Secrets. And silence.

They were talking now. Could they undo the damage the silence had caused?

The rain had subsided, but the air was still heavy, cool in the way that it always was after a rain, and she caught a whiff of wood smoke from somewhere along the shore. A bald eagle perched on a tall snag.

"Take care of the land," her father had liked to say. "We've been good to it, and it's been good to us."

God, she missed him.

Had she passed that legacy of secrets on to her own children? It was true that they hadn't told the kids right away when Jeremy's cancer came back. His first bout, the testicular cancer, had come months after their marriage, not long after he'd recovered from his injuries in the crash. The accident. Whatever it was. If he hadn't been under close watch by so many doctors, they might not have caught it so early—early enough that he'd sailed through treatment and gone on to father two children. And the second time, the kids had been so young— four and six. They hadn't understood enough to be scared. Or so she'd told herself. They'd teased Jeremy about going bald, seeming to forget all about his illness as soon as his hair grew back. As the kids got older, there had never been any reason to talk about it. It had all been in the past.

Last fall, after Jeremy finally admitted the low back pain wasn't getting better and the physical therapist had sent him to his doctor who'd sent him to the oncologist—well, they'd waited to say anything. Why worry the kids? At least until they knew. Until they had their plans in place, with the doctors and lawyers and financial advisors.

Because the third time was not the charm. The cancer had moved quickly, settling deep into his bones. They'd told the kids before he started chemo, and when that first round failed and he'd decided he didn't want to go through another round if the cancer was going to kill him anyway, just as quickly, they'd been upfront about the options and his decision.

She tightened the hood of her jacket and resumed her trek, following the trail uphill, the blood rushing to the skin of her thighs, the tingling sharp, almost painful.

So yes, they'd kept Jeremy's illness a secret, but not long. Only until they knew that the future would be short.

True, they had never told the kids the details of the crash. Why should they? It had happened before they were born, before Sarah and Jeremy had been married.

But she hadn't told him all her theories, all her conflicted imaginings, about that day. Why? Because she'd known—assumed—Jeremy wouldn't share her feeling that they were both to blame, for not stopping Lucas? It wasn't just because they'd been off together, making love in the abandoned homestead cabin. It wasn't just because Lucas had taken Jeremy's car—why had he left the keys in it, anyway? It was all that, and the dream.

Did she really think he'd have dismissed the dream, called her crazy? Yes. Jeremy Carter considered himself a rational, practical man. And she was young and in love, and while she wanted to share everything—*everything*—with him, she had not risked telling him anything that might tarnish his opinion of her.

She reached the top of the hill, the same spot where she'd stopped a day or two before. Found a stick and sat on the bench, scraping the mud off the soles of her feet. Mud, feet, mud, feet, blood, tears, mud, feet.

It wasn't supposed to be this way. None of it. Losing Jeremy meant losing her own future.

She flung the stick away and slid her hands up her sleeves, warming them on her arms.

What had Connor meant when he said Jeremy had let the past go, but she hadn't? How would he know what Jeremy thought about the crash?

And why was Leo targeting Janine? He couldn't seriously think she'd cooked up this whole letter business as an excuse to kill Lucas Erickson and terrify the rest of them.

No. It was because Janine had run. She'd seen the body and she'd fled to the lodge and hidden. What would she have done if Sarah hadn't found her there?

Would she be dead, too?

Sarah closed her eyes, remembering the terror radiating from her old friend.

Janine was convinced that someone had been in the law office with her. Watching her. Someone who'd slipped in after the secretary left, leaving Lucas there alone, and slipped out before she returned. Someone who didn't expect another visitor to come in the front.

A slow heat rose up Sarah's spine. As if she was being watched right now. The heat became a chill and she froze. Felt her breath go shallow, her jaw tighten. Was it better to act casual, turn slowly, try to fool whoever was watching you into thinking you had no idea, or to whip around and catch them in the act? She and Noah had debated that one time, over biscotti and kombucha at the co-op when he'd felt himself being watched. The eyes, his biology teacher had said, sense information beyond the visual. If you can sense when someone is looking at you, Noah had countered, can the person doing the staring sense when you know?

But there was no one there. No one in the woods, not even a sparrow.

This whole stupid thing had turned her into a blubbering idiot, scaring herself for no reason.

This was why she hadn't told Jeremy about the dream. Why she regretted telling Holly, the day of the attack.

The wind was whipping up again. As she headed for the lodge, the question clung to her brain: had whoever saw Janine leaning over Lucas's body known she'd sensed their presence?

And what would they do next?

But short of a hypnotic trance, Sarah didn't have a clue how to help Janine identify who might have seen her. And after this dream nonsense, she wanted nothing more to do with the unseen world. This one was trouble enough.

Outside the mudroom door, she stopped to wipe her feet on the mat. Glanced at the phone box. Remembered the penny in her pocket.

"Okay, okay." She rolled her eyes, tossing the words into the ether. To the ghost of her dead husband, or whoever was listening.

*   *   *

When had she last eaten?

Where were Holly and Janine?

And where had Caro's journal gone?

"I know I left it right here," she said out loud. On the kitchen counter, next to the plate that had held this morning's coffee cake. Too bad Janine couldn't afford to open a café; that coffee cake alone would guarantee success.

Sarah grabbed an apple. In the main room, Holly and Janine sat on the couch, speaking intently, voices low.

They broke off when they saw her, Holly following Sarah's gaze to the journal, which lay on the coffee table next to the box of letters and a stack of albums and scrapbooks.

"Amazing," Janine said, "that your family saved all this stuff. I've never even seen a picture of my grandmother."

"I'd never seen anything in that trunk," Sarah said. "Con and Caro must have brought it with them when they gave the house in town to our grandparents and moved out here."

To the lodge. Everything came back to the lodge.

"And then"—she was guessing now—"it got stashed in the carriage house apartment and forgotten."

"Amazing. Back to work for me," Janine said, pushing herself off the couch. "Earning my keep."

When the door closed behind her, Sarah said the words she'd wanted to say for so long, but hadn't, wanting to hear them first. She didn't have that luxury anymore, if she ever had.

"I'm sorry, Holly. For everything I've done to keep us apart."

Silence. Then, quietly, "Me too."

Sarah sat beside her sister, the couch still warm from Janine. "What are you going to do?"

"Read those letters. Flip through the albums and scrapbooks."

"I meant back home, after this. Why didn't you tell me you lost your job?"

"You had enough on your plate. I'll figure out something. Does Mom seriously want to sell?"

"I don't think she knows what she wants. She practically begged me to come help her with this place, and where is she?"

"Either she's burning to paint—"

"She would not let me in her studio. No way."

"Or she thinks if she leaves us out here by ourselves, we'll work through our differences."

Like she'd done when they were kids. "Hol, do you know—has she said—is she sick?"

"No. Good God, no. What did she say? Why do you think that?"

"She didn't say a thing. It's just—and you may not want to hear this. But what if the girl in the dream, whoever she is . . . She came to me twenty-five years ago, to warn me. What if she's telling me now that someone else is in trouble? At first I thought it was Abby, because of the light hair, but she's fine. I mean . . ."

"Except for the dead dad. Which is horrible. It's hideous. No kid should have to lose a parent at eighteen. But she'll be fine, Sarah. You know she will." Holly's voice shook as she went on. "I'm so sorry for what I said this morning. Forgive me?"

Sarah bit her lower lip and nodded. "Then I thought the woman in the dream might be you. But what if it's Mom?"

21

She'd come to the lodge expecting to be alone, but now that she finally was, Sarah wasn't sure what to think or feel. Nic was still in town, Janine out cleaning cabins. Holly had gone for a run, saying it was time she shook off her self-pity and got moving.

As intrigued as she was by the finds in Caro's trunk, she had work to do. She couldn't inventory dirt. And if her mother did decide to sell, they had to know what work the place needed. She took her notebook and phone to the top of the house. Room by room, she snapped pictures, took measurements, and made notes. In between rooms, she made trips to the cellar to move laundry—sheets, towels, and curtains Janine brought in from the cabins.

She set a basket of towels on a kitchen chair. Mundane tasks like folding laundry could be meditative. Other times, they opened the cracks that let sadness creep in, the spidery, many-fingered tendrils of sorrow in a life. All the things that were supposed to be perfect, but never were.

When had she become such a mope?

She reached for the next towel. It didn't come and she gave it a tug.

"Meeow."

"Oh. Bastet." She scooped up the cat, one claw catching on a thin white dish towel that fluttered up with her. Fluttered like the nightgown on the woman in the dream.

Sarah loosened the cat's claw from the fabric. "Who are you?" she asked. "What do you want from me?"

But she wasn't talking to the cat.

"Sarah?"

"Nic. You're back." Sarah set the cat on the floor and picked up the towel. *Saturday*, the stitching read, beneath the outline of a girl hanging laundry. Apt. She tossed it aside to rewash, then turned on the heat under the teakettle. "Perfect timing. The cat and I were just about to take a break. What did you find out in town?"

"I hardly know where to start. I met Dan Fleming for lunch at the Spruce. Nice guy."

"So why was he in business with Lucas?"

"You cynic, you." Nic cracked a wry smile and sat. "They kept separate clienteles. He had no idea Lucas had done any work for McCaskill Land and Lumber."

Curious. Sarah plunked bags in two heavy white mugs.

"He's been interviewed at length, of course," Nic continued. "He was meeting with clients when Lucas was killed."

"What about Misty?" The kettle whistled. Sarah filled the mugs and set them on the table. She checked her chair for the cat before she sat, but the creature had disappeared. "They live in Whitefish, right?"

"Right. She keeps an office above the shop there, where she was holed up all afternoon. Dan says the sheriff's office confirmed both alibis. Thanks." Nic spooned sugar into her tea.

"He's adamant that there was nothing going on between him and Misty until after she left Lucas, but Lucas didn't believe that."

"Was Lucas serious about a congressional run?"

"Dan doesn't think so. Lucas was really good at shaking hands and making promises, but the job is a lot more work than that."

Sarah frowned, wondering why her brother had done business with the man.

Nic took a quick sip, then set her mug down, holding it with both hands. "I was in the prosecutor's office when she got a call from the state crime lab."

"About the letters? That's the only physical evidence they have now, unless they've found the gun and matched the fingerprints."

"No. No gun yet. And it's harder to get prints from a gun than you think. Plus, it's a common model. How did your cousin put it? 'Guns are like pine cones in Montana. Shake any tree and at least one will fall out.' There's probably a .38 in half the houses in the valley."

Her mother hadn't wanted guns around the kids, so her father kept his deer rifles and the shotgun he used to hunt ducks in a safe in his office. And the handgun he always carried in the woods. You never knew what trouble you'd run into, he'd said. You might hit a deer on the highway and need to put it down. If Connor did the same, he'd left it in his truck when he came inside.

"They can't seriously believe," Sarah said, "that Janine would ever own a gun, let alone use it. Not after what happened with her mother."

"We know that, and I reminded Leo and the prosecutor. But our beliefs don't prove anything."

"And you called me a cynic."

"They have to be skeptical. Because people aren't consistent. Our observations aren't as accurate as we think they are, and they're influenced by what we want to believe," Nic said. "Every single one of us has done something even our closest friends never imagined we would do."

Not a reminder she actually needed.

"Here's where things get ugly. Two things. I probably shouldn't tell you either one."

"Nic. Tell me." Sarah put her palms on the table and leaned forward.

"They got a search warrant for Janine's apartment in Missoula. That's routine. They found a file in her desk drawer. Filled with clippings about Lucas over the years."

Sarah sat back. "What the—"

"Every time his name made the paper—for some lawsuit, when his father died, when he ran for County Attorney—she kept the article. It's a thin file, but . . ."

"But it's a file. Holy cow. What's the second thing?"

"The secretary, what was her name?"

"Renee Harper."

"Right. She told you they'd taken the computers and printers to check for evidence that Lucas wrote the letters to you, Holly, and Janine. They also took a laptop from his house, and according to Dan Fleming, quizzed both him and Misty on whether Lucas had access to any other computers, in their home or offices. This is preliminary"—she held up a hand—"but they don't think Lucas wrote that letter."

"Well, of course they didn't find a copy. He didn't save it. Any idiot would delete it, and Lucas Erickson was not an idiot."

"As I said, this is preliminary—they're still searching hard drives and automatic backups for evidence of the letter itself.

But they can match documents to keyboards and printers. Not like in the typewriter days, but pretty close. And no match."

"What about fingerprints on the paper, or DNA on the envelopes. From licking."

"No such luck. These were gummed. You pull the strip and press to seal. Same with the stamps. But they don't match any envelopes found in Erickson's home or office." Nic scratched her cheek, in front of the ear. "But here's where they got lucky, sort of. They found a partial print on one of the envelopes that matches a print on the stamp from the other envelope. Meaning the same person sent both."

"But it wasn't Lucas . . ."

Nic spread her hands, the gesture and the somber expression in her eyes asking one question.

If Lucas Erickson hadn't sent those letters, then who did?

* * *

From deep in the cellar came the buzz of the dryer. Sarah picked up her basket and fetched the last load of towels. Could Janine really have sent the letters, sending one to herself to send the rest of them down the wrong track?

She'd never imagined her old friend could be so devious.

But then, she'd been wrong about so much lately.

When she reached the kitchen, Nic stood at the window, the two ironstone mugs in hand. Without a word, Nic put them in the sink, wiped her hands, and began folding towels. This wasn't the time to ask about the clippings, and if Nic thought there was a snowball's chance that Janine was behind the letters. Later.

The basket half empty, Sarah glanced up. She had forgotten Nic's habit of biting her lower lip when she was worried. She was practically chewing a hole in herself right now.

"It was kind of shocking-not shocking to hear about what happened at your house," Sarah said. "I guess I don't really know what kind of backlash you get from your work, and just from being who you are. I'd like to hear more, if you want to talk about it sometime." You couldn't be irked at people for not telling you things if you never let them know you were interested.

"Thanks." Nic glanced up, her eyes soft. "That means a lot."

"You get hold of Kim?"

"Yeah." Nic exhaled heavily. "Turns out not to have been the best time to leave town."

Sarah stopped folding. "Not more vandalism?"

"No. There was an—incident at school. It's our fault. My fault." Nic snapped the wrinkles out of a hand towel, but didn't fold it. "I get so fired up. I want gay and lesbian couples to have the same rights to jobs and housing and health care as straight couples. I want queer kids to know they're worthy of love and respect and not be afraid when they walk down the halls at school."

"You sound like you're running for office," Sarah said lightly.

"I've been approached. I said no—I think I can make a bigger difference as a lawyer and an activist. And my wife doesn't want that public a life."

Sarah reached for the towel in Nic's hand, folded it quickly, and added it to the stack. Sat, and so did Nic. "What happened at school?"

"Tempe might not be my apple, but she didn't fall far from the tree." Nic flashed a crooked smile. "She's straight, but there's a trans girl in her class who's been getting grief from other kids and Tempe stood up for her. Someone shoved a note into Tempe's backpack calling her a lesbo loser with lesbo loser friends and parents. It happened Monday afternoon, after I'd left to come up here. She didn't tell either of us, but the school called Kim yesterday."

"Two days later? Why did they wait? Abby and Noah's school had a zero-tolerance policy against bullying, whatever the reason was. Not like when we were kids." When kids like Lucas could torment weaker classmates and get away with it. She'd bet good money.

"Because my kid—and I can't decide whether I'm proud of her or mad at her—didn't report it. Instead, she and her friends took matters into their own hands."

"What? What did they do?"

"They knew who left the note—a boy who makes a habit of going after kids who are different. Kim got the story from the principal but confirmed it with Tempe. One of the girls lured the boy into a corner of the parking lot, where the kids formed a circle and Tempe confronted him." Nic ran a hand through her close-cropped hair. "Same high school I went to. I never would have had the guts. Anyway, she told him he couldn't talk like that. He said he could say whatever he wanted—free speech. She gave him a lecture about every right carrying a responsibility and how he had no right to say mean things."

"Sounds like something Abby would say. How did the school find out? Any chance he's the one who smashed the mailbox?"

"He says no about the mailbox, but Kim did make sure the cops knew. Anyway, big bully peed his pants. A teacher saw him borrowing a friend's running clothes and pried the story out of him."

Sarah covered her mouth with her hands. "I haven't even met your kid, and I love her."

"She is pretty great. And it is pretty funny."

Sarah stopped trying to hold back the laughter, and Nic joined her. A few minutes later, they wiped their eyes, exchanging glances as the giggles subsided.

"Sounds like she handled it perfectly," Sarah said. "You're doing a good job."

"Like you're doing with Abby."

But Abby was eighteen, not fifteen. Flying the coop, leaving the nest. Though to Sarah, she was still that little girl in the blue princess dress. "Text her. Tell her you're proud of her. Tell her she did the right thing."

"The principal wants to talk with all the parents—the boy's, the trans girl's, and us. Tomorrow afternoon. I could make it if I leave tonight, or the crack of dawn. But I don't want to leave Deer Park while Janine is still under suspicion."

"Can you reschedule?"

"Kim's gonna try." Nic leaned forward, almost pleading. Brave, smart, confident Nic. "Just don't tell Janine."

Then another voice interjected. "Don't tell me what?"

22

How had they not heard Janine come in, Holly behind her?

"You have to go," Janine said after Sarah poured fresh tea and Holly set out cookies they didn't touch and Nic repeated the story.

"I do, but not tonight, and not for the reasons you think. Not because supporting my kid is more important than proving your innocence. No." Nic held up her hand. "Don't tell me I have to choose. I don't. The meeting can be rescheduled."

"Your kid needs her mother," Janine said.

"My kid's doing pretty awesome on her own. And Sarah's right. Being a good mother doesn't mean fighting your kid's battles for them, or abandoning other commitments. Tempe needs to see me fighting for what I believe in. For her, yes, when necessary, and for you."

Sarah was almost afraid to breathe, afraid she'd shatter the moment. She snuck a sideways peek at Holly, only to see the same uncertainty on her sister's face.

"Thank you, all of you, for believing me. Believing in me." Janine's gaze stopped at Sarah. "But I need to be alone for a few minutes." She pushed back her chair and headed outside.

What about that file of clippings? "We need to ask her . . ."

"Let me," Nic said. "As a lawyer."

Holly laid Sarah's keys on the table. "I was too out of shape for more than a short run, so I took your car into town."

"Did you see Mom? The studio?"

"Yes, and no. She was taking a break so we took a walk. I asked about her health. She says she's fine."

"I'll let you two talk," Nic said.

"No," Holly replied. "Stay. I believe her. She may look fragile, but she walked my tail off. I also asked if she was planning to sell the lodge."

Was she ready for the answer? "And?"

"Turns out, she's asked a real estate agent to come out tomorrow, tell us what our options are. That's the meeting she was headed to the other day when I showed up unexpectedly."

"It's always good to know your options," Nic said.

"Options," Sarah replied, "mean change. And I've had enough change."

"We walked by the old Lake Hotel where that café wine bar place was," Holly said.

"Why did it close?"

"Mom said the owners got a chance to take over a bigger place somewhere else and left on short notice. The Spruce is fine, but a decent town needs more than one café. It would be perfect for Janine."

"In Deer Park? Are you kidding? Why would she want to come back here?"

"You may be tired of change, but she's ready for one."

"She's actually mentioned it," Nic said. "Her son's fiancée is from this area. They're talking about moving after they get married, and suggested she move up too. She's always wanted to run her own place, but it's daunting."

But if Janine couldn't afford a new phone, she couldn't afford to open a restaurant.

"She would never take money from me." Sarah bit into a molasses cookie, soft and moist, sweet and sparky.

"We can figure out a way," Nic said as Holly said "Think about it."

She grunted. They were teaming up on her, and it might work. But they would have to step carefully. "Dinner time. We can't expect Janine to cook for us every night."

"Why not?" Holly said. "One more thing. Two things. I called the local vet and the animal shelter. No reports of a missing cat who fits Bastet's description."

"Huh. So how did she get here? She's too sweet not to have been someone's pet."

"Dunno. The other thing. On my way back, I saw a car pulling away from the roadside shrine."

"What? Who?"

"Big white SUV. Woman driving, I think. No passengers that I could see."

Like the one she'd seen.

"Did you see where she went?"

"Down the road to the Hoyt place."

The same rig George spotted Sunday evening, or someone else? White SUVs were popular.

"Did you know George sold some of his land, on the east end below Porcupine Ridge?" Sarah asked her sister.

"Not until Connor just mentioned it. Who bought it? And why? You wouldn't want to live up there."

"No idea, though it sounds like the company is logging it."
She frowned. George had not liked her suggestion that he ask
Connor to clean up the storm damage on his home place. Was
there a connection?

*   *   *

They ignored all talk of murder and suspicion over dinner on
the deck. They talked kids, the lodge, the cat, old friends, old
times. The good times—and most of them were good times.

No grief support group, Sarah decided. She didn't need it.
She needed this—spinach salad, perfectly done pork chops,
grilled peaches glazed with thick, sweet-tart balsamic vinegar.
She needed friends talking about their lives, working things
out together. She had friends back home, good friends. But old
friends were the best friends.

After the dishes were washed, the air had picked up a chill
and they settled inside to watch night descend on the lake
through the big windows. So peaceful. For a moment, Sarah
almost forgot that they were only here because of tragedy.

"So tell us about this mysterious trunk," Nic said. "It
belonged to your great-grandmother?"

"Yeah. They met in Butte. Caro's father was a bigwig in one of
the copper mining companies, where Con worked. He wanted to
build a business of his own and started buying land with his sav-
ings. The story is that when they got married, her father staked Con
so he could grow the lumber company. That's why they moved up
here in 1916, the year my grandfather was born. Then the war came
and that boosted production, which really took off afterwards."

"In the Roaring '20s," Holly said.

"When did they buy the lodge?"

"1922, I think. A railroad exec built it as a summer home
and fishing camp, a couple of years earlier," Sarah said. "Why

he sold, I don't know, but I always heard Caro fell in love with the place, so they bought it. Good business move—they entertained a lot of clients who came out on the train. They even had their own bus to pick people up. They kept horses and boats, and threw lavish parties.

"Every community had a few mills," she continued, "but McCaskill had the resources to expand and buy out competitors, even during the Depression. The Hoyts ran a smaller mill until sometime in the '80s, when construction tanked and our family bought them out. The conglomerates dominate the market now—Weyerhaeuser, Georgia-Pacific—but Connor's managed to keep things going."

Janine was flipping through an album. "Caro was quite elegant. I always wonder how couples like that handled money. Of course, it's easier when there's plenty of it."

"She had money of her own, though what she used it for, I don't know. Supposedly her mother believed every woman should have a private fund that her husband couldn't control."

Sarah picked up the journal and returned to the rocker. Life was simpler back then, right? The ink had faded from black to purple in places, and the formal script wasn't easy to decipher. She leaned closer to the circle of light cast by the old bronze floor lamp with its parchment shade.

She picked up where she'd left off this morning, with Caro's description of the family's first morning at Whitetail Lodge in 1922.

We are so fortunate to have been able to buy this place, though I grieve deeply for Ellen Lacey, the girl, and their losses. The lake. I cannot fathom her desperation. Why powerful men feel they can do such wretched things, I cannot imagine. Thank goodness Frank L did not put up with it and sent H packing. Con has said H will never darken our doors. It is beastly unfair that we women must be so constantly vigilant.

That was intriguing. She turned the page.

But I do not want to write of these things or even to think of them, on such a glorious morning in such a beautiful place. The children and I will move out here for the summer as soon as Tom's school year ends. He is getting to be such a big boy, tall and graceful like his father. I'll have my hands full keeping an eye on those boys during the week, while Con stays in town to manage the mill. Fanny will be with me, of course, to help mind the children, and Mrs. O'Dell to run the household.

Ahhh. The mystery of Mrs. O'Dell, solved. She opened her mouth to tell Holly, but her sister had vanished.

She kindly recommended her friend, Mrs. Burke, to deliver hot meals for Con at the house in town, as I know he will tire quickly of eating at the hotel, and to clean once or twice a week. Thank goodness my husband is a tolerant man who does not mind making his own coffee or insist that I iron his shirts and collars. Heaven knows, I botched the job more than I succeeded, and it's been such a relief to have Mrs. O'D take over. Once we're truly settled, we'll start entertaining. The lodge is too small for three children and guests—at least, my children! Con's been setting aside timber from the road construction to build guest cabins, though we might not get them built for a year or more. We will have to invite only guests who are likely to be charmed and let those who insist on crea-ture comforts cluck their tongues at our primitive ways—

The entry ended abruptly, as if Caro had heard a cry from the nursery or Mrs. O'Dell had interrupted her musings.

"Fanny the Nanny"—she remembered Grandpa Tom telling stories about her. Stories that had made her want a nanny, though her mother had howled when she'd asked for one.

Frank and Ellen Lacey. If they were the people who built the lodge, had they—Ellen, most likely—put together the construction scrapbook? She set the journal on the side table and dashed up to the sewing room. Found the scrapbook and opened it. Inside the flyleaf was the name Ellen Granger Lacey. She carried the scrapbook downstairs, along with the stack of framed photos, and set them on the coffee table.

Who were H and the girl, and what were the losses Caro mentioned? Connected to the war? The 1918 flu epidemic? But both were long over by the date of the first journal entry, and Sarah got the sense from her great-grandmother's words that the Laceys' losses were too recent and terrifying to linger on. A miscarriage or the death of a young child, perhaps in the lake? Life a hundred years ago had been full of dangers.

Still was. Just different dangers.

She returned to the journal. She was about to ask Nic for her reading glasses, but they were firmly on the other woman's face, a thin sheet of paper in her hand, the Sampler box of letters open in front of her.

Readers. Another sign of change. Another thing to add to the shopping list.

Holly came out of the kitchen with a glass of wine and sat in the peeled log chair, gazing out at the lake.

Caro's words became easier to decipher as the loops and links of her handwriting grew more familiar. The next entry was nearly two weeks later. *We are HERE! All of us, together at Whitetail Lodge!* she'd written with a flourish.

"Oh, my gosh," Nic said, a letter in hand. "Listen to this."
They all turned to her.

Dear Mrs. McCaskill:

*Enclosed herewith please find twelve dollars and fifty
cents. Thanks to your kindness and—*

"Generosity, spelled g-i-n-e-r-o-c-i-t-y."

*Thanks to your kindness and generosity, I was able to
pay a man to help me rebuild my homestead cabin and
replace necessary items destroyed in the fire. I will get the
rest of the money to you next month, after my hens begin
to lay.*

*You will never know how much I appreciate your will-
ingness to help someone such as me. My—*

"Sincere, spelled with two s's."
My sincere regards to the ladies of the society.

"Signed, Hulda Amundsen."
"It's a thank you note," Holly said. "No big deal."
"Listen to this one," Nic replied. She laid Hulda's letter on
the table and picked up another envelope. Slid out a piece of
heavy linen stationery.

Dear Mrs. McCaskill,

*My husband and I extend to you our deepest gratitude
for your kind assistance in aiding our beloved daughter, Elizabeth, in leaving her unfortunate marriage and returning to*

us. While she is, naturally, mortified by the situation in which you and your friends found her, she is grateful to once again be among those who cherish her.

Enclosed is a draft, payable on our account at the First National Bank of Cincinnati, for the amount of your generous advance along with an additional sum which we wish to contribute to your endeavors.

"Signed, Mrs. Charles Pennington." Nic rested the letter in her lap.

"They were repaying loans," Janine said. "One to rebuild after a fire, the other to go home to her grateful parents."

"Hulda's letter mentions 'the ladies of the society.'" Nic said. "Who, or what, was the society?"

"Wait, wait. I saw another reference." Sarah flipped through the journal to one of the entries she'd skimmed in the carriage house. "Here it is. That same summer. Caro writes that Mrs. O'Dell—she was the housekeeper—made Con a birthday cake and decorated it with strawberries. 'A gift from one of the young Society women,'" she read. "Then, in parentheses, like she was laughing, 'What fun to put it that way!'"

"Mrs. O'Dell was the housekeeper?" Holly asked. "I was named for the housekeeper?"

"Obviously well-loved," Sarah said. "I don't know this society they're referring to, but it sounds like our great-grandmother was lending money, at no interest, to women in trouble."

As if drawn by a magnet, the four friends stared at the photograph of Caro in her silk dress. Kind eyes, yes, but oh, the firm set of that jaw.

23

ost of the letters were postmarked Deer Park or White-fish, although a handful, like the note from Elizabeth Pennington's parents, had been sent from other parts of the country.

"Two cents." Janine held up a thin envelope. "It cost two cents to mail a letter in 1924. What is it now? Forever stamps don't have an amount on them, so you forget how much you're paying."

"With inflation, it might not be much higher," Nic said. "We've got about three dozen notes, dated from 1924 to—let's see." She flipped through the envelopes, a mix of small squares, large squares, and rectangles, white, gray, and ivory, thin paper and heavy linen stock. The handwriting varied, too, from ornate script to a round hand to simple printing. "Looks like the last letter came in 1938. Right about the time the worst of the Depression was over."

"Some loans may have been repaid in person, without a note," Sarah said.

"And the recipients might not all have been literate," Janine added.

"This woman certainly was," Nic said. "Her penmanship is exquisite." She read out loud.

Dear Mrs. McCaskill,

Oh, how I wish you could have seen my children's faces when they saw the feast delivered to us on Christmas Day. A roast goose and plum pudding! Had it not been for your generosity, our table would have been nearly bare, with not much more than our daily fare of eggs, if the hens are in the mood, rye bread, and boiled potatoes with cabbage. Your Mrs. O'Dell is quite the treasure—

"See, Holly," Sarah teased. "She was a treasure."

Not only is her cooking superb, she showed me a few tricks to make good use of the extra provisions. My son played with his new spinning top until late in the evening, and my precious little girl fell asleep with her arms around her new doll.

The men at the mill and their wives have been good to us, knowing as they do the hardships of such work, but there is only so much they can spare, their own paychecks often being stretched to the limit. Your thoughtfulness in including toys for the children and the bottle of rose water is particularly touching, and shows what a truly good and gracious soul you are.

Nic paused and lifted her head, glasses low on her nose. "I'm guessing her husband was a mill worker killed on the job. Little known fact: Montana had one of the first workers' comp laws in the country, but it was voluntary and the employers all fought it. It was years before the constitutionality of work comp was upheld and employers were required to participate. But I can easily imagine that in 1927, the benefits for a widow with two children would have been pretty minimal."

She read on.

I have decided that we should return to my late husband's mother's home in Denver. Although our relationship has not always been a smooth one, she is very fond of the children, and I will be able to find suitable employment. I hope you will allow the children and me to visit you before our departure.

Yours with a deeply grateful heart,

Mrs. Olaf (Olga) Johannsen

"Olaf and Olga," Holly said. "I wonder whatever happened to her."

"Here's your answer." Janine held up a card showing a young girl, in coat and hat, carrying a brightly wrapped package up a snowy hill to a cottage, beneath a full moon and a starry sky. "Postmarked December 10, 1928. It's a Christmas card."

Dear Mrs. McCaskill,

I think of you often and with gratitude . . .

She skimmed ahead.

You will be pleased to hear that both children are thriving. My mother-in-law has moved to her daughter's home a few blocks away, leaving the children and me in the house in which their father was raised. Thank goodness the school district permits widows to teach. Although my salary is sufficient, it does not extend to luxuries, but thanks to your gift, there will be joy around our hearth on Christmas morning.

"First we've heard of gifts, not loans, right?"

"For women with children? Or particularly touching stories."

"Or particularly gracious thank you notes."

Other letters detailed similar tragedies. Several loans allowed women to leave abusive or alcoholic husbands, as they presumed had been the case with Elizabeth Pennington. Others told stories of depression and isolation, of husbands and suicide. One 1932 letter thanked Caro for sending "young Tom" to replenish the wood pile.

"You said your grandfather was born in 1916?" Nic asked. "That makes him sixteen. Almost a man back then."

"If she was sending Mrs. O'Dell and Grandpa Tom on her errands," Holly mused, "then Con must have known. Besides that one contribution, was she using her own money, do you think?"

But that, they couldn't answer.

The most heartbreaking note came from a woman who thanked them for helping her take care of her husband after he was kicked in the head by a horse, then finally died.

"It's a microcosm of the problems women faced back then. Before Social Security and welfare and other programs from the New Deal took hold," Nic said.

"Same kind of problems women face today," Holly said. "Except for being kicked in the head by a horse."

Sarah stepped out on the deck, away from the lights of the lodge. Full dark now, though a smattering of stars blinked into view as her eyes adjusted. She'd been the kid who loved hearing the family stories, who'd sat at the big dining table in the lodge long after her sister and brother and cousins had asked to be excused and some of the adults had begun to drift in and out, who'd sat listening to their grandparents tell tales, some tall, some true. Reminiscing about the colorful characters who'd visited the lodge over the years. Which lumber company client shot that one-eyed bull elk who winked down at them from above the fireplace. Which of Grandpa Tom's war buddies sent the oversized Navaho rug that still lay on the living room floor, a thank-you for a long-overdue vacation with his wife. Which cousin commandeered the baseball autographed by Joe DiMaggio for a pickup game and sent it through the kitchen window. Where was that baseball, anyway? She hadn't seen it in Grandpa Tom's office.

The McCaskill kids had been taught to be proud of their family legacy, how they'd taken care of the woods and provided jobs through the Depression and always supported progress in the tiny town of Deer Park.

But she had never heard these stories.

Was it the late night, the wine, or being together with her old gang after the stresses and sorrows of the last few months? Or the romance of a historic lakefront lodge and the discovery of secret letters, that had her thinking the house was talking to her? The house, and Caro.

And the woman in the dream.

But what were they saying? What were they telling her to do?

Back inside, the other three huddled together on the couch, poring over Ellen Lacey's scrapbook. Sarah perched on the back of the couch and leaned in. As in Caro's album, the photos and clippings, brittle with age, were mounted on black paper and captioned in white ink. In roughly chronologic order, they started with a shot of the shoreline taken from Bitterroot Lake, aboard the steamer *U. S. Grant*.

"There's the point." Holly dragged her finger across the photo to the outcropping just east of their property line. "And here's where they built the lodge. The trees came nearly down to the lake."

In the next photo, stumps and piles of logs, some as much as five feet across, dotted the slope above the shore. Every log and post and stick in the place had been cut right here and milled with a portable head rig.

Another series of photos and a clipping from the *Deer Park Dispatch* showed blasting and rock removal, by horse-drawn wagons using a series of ropes and pulleys and winches, to create a narrow road.

"The beginnings of the North Shore Road," Nic said. "Not that it's much of a road now, but construction must have been a bear."

"It didn't go all the way around the lake until the late '30s," Sarah said. "The WPA finished it. You wanted to get west of here, you had to take the steamer. In Caro's journal, she says Con spent the week in town during the summer, while the family stayed at the lodge. Town's minutes away now, but back then, getting there took hours."

Ellen Lacey had listed men who'd worked on the project and their wages. She'd pasted in receipts, the paper yellowed. Sarah almost whistled at the cost of the staircase. And seriously? Was the lamp over the game table in the corner, the one some tall McCaskill lad or his friends were always bumping with his head when penny ante poker got antic, a genuine Tiffany?

Someone—Ellen, she presumed—had added sketches of a bird's nest found near a felled tree. On other pages, she'd drawn spring grasses and wildflowers—yellow glacier lilies, red paintbrush, bluebells. And a bitterroot, the state flower, for which the lake had been named. Page by page, they watched the lodge take shape—the ridgepole, walls, and windows, until finally, what they saw in the scrapbook matched what they saw around them, give or take a hundred years.

"The Laceys," she said at the photo of the couple standing on the front steps with their children, the boy beaming at the photographer while pointing a stick at the date 1920 carved in the stone foundation. It was still there.

What joy for Ellen to see her vision come to life, this stunning retreat on the edge of the lake. To descend the grand staircase, preside over picnics and parties, smile as her children tumbled down the lawn.

"I wonder what ever happened to them." Several rolls of heavy paper lay on the table next to the journals and albums. "Are those the pictures from the trunk?"

Holly set her glass on the end table. "You know, sis, we're sitting on a mother lode of historical info. The county museum would kill for this stuff."

But it was their family history. Another decision to make.

Holly unrolled the first picture and they all took a look. A black-and-white panoramic view of the lodge, taken from the dock. No cabins yet. A name in white on the lower right indicated the work of a professional photographer, a name familiar from early family portraits. Holly let the picture curl gently back on itself and picked up the next photo. This one had been taken indoors.

"Oh, wow. It's like Downton Abbey, in a log house."

Sarah recognized the Laceys at the foot of the steps, a boy about six and a girl a year or two older standing in front of their parents. Con and Caro stood on the step behind them.

"I'd kill for that beaded dress," Holly said, pointing at Caro.

"You find it in one of those trunks in the carriage house," Sarah said, "and it's yours."

213

Other guests gathered around their hosts or stood on the staircase, the pine garland wrapped around the banister a clue that this had been a holiday gathering. To the left stood the household staff. A housekeeper wearing a formidable expression and a stiff black dress, an older man in a butler's tuxedo, a younger man, and two young women.

The back of her neck prickled. *That face . . .*

* * *

In her yoga pants and sweatshirt, feet bare and a book in hand, Sarah came down the staircase slowly. Riser by riser, tread by tread, craftsmen of a century ago had built it with pride, under Ellen Lacey's watchful eye.

The scrapbook lay on the coffee table where they'd left it. If they sold, what would they do with it, and the guest books and other photos and furnishings? The museum was one option, as Holly had said, but they belonged to the place as much as to the family. Would a future buyer appreciate them? Where was the line between responsibility and burden?

And why was she so drawn to that photo of the holiday party?

In the kitchen, she found a clean wine glass and a bottle they hadn't finished. They were going through the wine almost as fast as Bastet was going through her Ocean Whitefish Paté.

"At that rate, you're not going to be little for long," she told the cat, then returned to the main room, giving the lamp another glance. A genuine Tiffany, in the wilds of Montana? She'd give it a closer look in the morning, maybe send a few photos to an antique dealer friend.

What other treasures had she overlooked through familiarity? That parchment shade on the brass reading lamp? Hand-painted with ferns and pink flowers, while the one in her grandfather's office was more typically Western, the edges whipstitched with brown leather cord. And what about the chair? She'd always assumed it was a Stickley knockoff, but now she wondered if it wasn't the real thing. Tomorrow, she'd flip it over and search for identifying marks. Another reason to get reliable Wi-Fi, so she could consult a few websites.

Everything in the lodge looked different now. History—one more thing to note in her inventory.

Sarah sipped her wine, the cat in her lap, stroking the soft fur. The jumble of noises in her head began to quiet. It had been hours since she'd reached for her useless phone, irritated over not being able to call or text the kids. But this couldn't go on. If the phone company didn't send someone out in the morning, she'd go into town and see if she could find an electrician to fix it. Or wire for splicing. Not that she knew how, but at least she had the pliers.

She shifted and the cat's claws dug into her thighs. "Hey, let go." The chair wasn't uncomfortable, but her mid-back had been bothering her ever since Jeremy's death. Nothing a massage or a visit to the chiropractor could fix. It was just a hollow feeling, the place where her sense of loss had decided to settle.

She picked up her book and switched the lamp up a notch. The bulb sizzled and sparked and went out. She swore softly and set the cat on the floor. In the kitchen, she rummaged in the bulb stash to find the right size. The door swung open, revealing Holly in her long sleep shirt, legs bare, hair mussed.

Sarah held up the bulb.

"Figures," Holly said. "Like every time you move into a new place, or come back from vacation, a light bulb goes out. Usually in the middle of the night, like when you've taken a late flight and stumbled home and all you want to do is take off your makeup and crawl into bed, and poof!"

"One more strike against makeup."

"It's like the house is protesting," Holly said, padding after her. "I came down to see—well, after last night, I thought you might—I don't know."

Sarah knew. Her sister thought she might be afraid to sleep, afraid of another nightmare. She fumbled in the dark, screwing in the bulb, flinching involuntarily as the light came back on.

"I'm happy to sleep on the couch again," Holly added.

"No, you go up. You need your beauty sleep."

Holly stuck out her tongue and headed for the stairs.

"Hol," Sarah called. "Thanks."

Without turning, Holly raised a hand in acknowledgment.

Sarah picked up the cat and sat. Instead of the novel she hadn't been able to get into, she opened Caro's journal.

June 17, 1922

Con has taken the steamer back to town, leaving me alone with the children, and dear Fanny and Mrs. O'D. I know he is worried about us out here on our own—three women and three small children. But it was ever thus, was it not? Women have been left home while the men have gone off to work and war since time began. Why else was Eve sitting alone under the apple tree, if not because Adam was out hunting for the wooly mammoth or some other of God's wild creatures? I do not fear temptations of the sort she faced, although I well know that loneliness can lead a woman—or a man—into foolish choices. I shall not be lonely, even without the bustle of Deer Park or my women's club.

I do have the Model T safely stored in the carriage house, if necessary, and I am an excellent driver—Con brags about me to his friends, who doubt their wives could manage—but the road is challenging at best, and treacherous more often than not. There is talk about the lumber company deeding the land to the state for an official highway, as the blasting and grading needed to extend it in a fashion suitable for automobiles would be terribly expensive. Many in Deer Park advocate for this, but Con urges caution—we must be prepared for the changes a year-round road would bring.

Sarah's eyes sped over the rest of the entry, as Caro described the family's plans for the summer, including the high-walled tents Con had found for the guests they hoped would join them for two weeks in July, although naturally her sister and her family would stay in the lodge.

But what caught her eye was the reference to her women's club. The society?

She took another sip of wine—Holly had made some good finds in Deer Park's state liquor store. One more benefit of the changes in town. That reminded her of Holly's idea that Janine reopen the vacant restaurant space. Though the building hadn't been a hotel for decades, the location was ideal for tourist traffic, by car, foot, or boat.

Then, in midsummer 1922, this.

Over sherry after dinner, we spoke of H. He's laid out his demands to complete the deal. Con is reluctant; he is convinced that long-term success depends on holding the land and managing the timber. But it has taken this long to force the man to relinquish his interest, and if this is what it takes . . .

The H of the early entry, whose "beastly" behavior had triggered the Laceys' departure? And what deal was Caro referring to?

Mysterious, but delicious, to eavesdrop on her great-grand-mother's most personal thoughts.

"Oh," she said out loud. "What if she wrote about . . ." She flipped forward, turning pages until she found the date she was searching for, two weeks before the earliest thank-you note, in February 1924.

Well, we have done it. We have made our first loan, to the Norwegian woman whose home and most of her belongings were destroyed by fire. I know there are some in town who say she deserved her fate, being willing to live with a man to whom she was not married. That is for God to judge, not us. I only wish the sheriff had been willing to arrest the man, but he said it is not arson to destroy one's own property, even if it is also the home of another, and that the woman had no legal right to the structure, in truth little more than a shack. Who owns the property now that that wicked man has left town, I cannot say, but we could not let the woman starve or go without a roof over her head.

I do not know whether we will be repaid. The possibility does not worry me—the amount was small. My biggest concern is that word spread only to those in genuine need, women of good character but unfortunate circumstances, and not become general knowledge. There will be men who oppose us, who criticize us for being too modern, and I fear such talk would keep women from seeking our help. That's why it's so important that Fanny, Mrs. O'D, and Mrs. Burke are part of our efforts; too many women in need would never dare speak to someone they view as above them, but would speak freely to a housekeeper or another woman who works to support herself.

Holly had wondered how much Con knew about the loans. "What do you think?" Sarah asked Bastet. "Even if she used her own money, they seem to have been quite close." And from her comments in that first journal entry about his refusal to tolerate "beastly" behavior by another man to a young servant, and that he trusted his wife with the Model T, it seemed clear that Cornelius McCaskill had shared his wife's "modern" views.

"We" could refer to the household staff. But a society implied more than that, didn't it?

She flipped forward, scanning for other mention of the loans. Here it was, a simple note, two weeks later.

Our faith and our money have been repaid. What a relief.

The next few entries focused on the children, then the subject returned to the loans.

Mrs. Smalley thinks our club should join the state federation, but the rest of us have voted her down. It does us no good to be so public with our mission. I am happy to keep the Lakeside Ladies' Aid Society—

The society. And Mrs. Smalley—Becca's great-grandmother?

—a private endeavor. Heaven knows Deer Park has plenty of other clubs for other purposes. The Medical Auxiliary has been spreading word of new treatments and fund-raising for a local hospital, and the Ladies' Literary Society is soliciting funds for a library. I am on both committees. There is even a mah–jongg club. Con thinks I should cut back on my outside commitments and let others raise their hands and voices, and perhaps he is right. But wealth carries responsibilities.

Some things never change, Sarah thought, recalling similar conversations with Jeremy.

The clock struck midnight. She closed her eyes and rolled her shoulders back, careful not to rouse Bastet, queen of the sharp claws. God, she was tired. But Holly had guessed right. She didn't want to risk another nightmare. She blinked, clearing her eyes, and focused her attention on the pages, skimming accounts of house parties, the children, of Fanny the Nanny becoming engaged to a lumber company accountant. "Beware!" Caro joked. "That's what I did and look what happened!"

Then she reached the end of the journal, two entries made in February 1926.

The first expressed concern about Sarah Beth, who had a fever and swollen throat.

I know my daughter is not well when she loses interest in her precious dollhouse, the gift Con arranged for the shop foreman to build for her sixth birthday. Con tells me she will be better in the morning, that I am over-anxious because of the blizzard, with its high winds and driving snow. Besides, the telephone lines are down and it would be difficult to summon the doctor.

The dollhouse, tucked away in the carriage house.
And the last, lengthy entry, made the next day.

I saw the girl again in my dreams last night. I'm sure it's the Swedish housemaid, the girl who died so tragically. Anja, she was called. There is no reason to tell anyone, and certainly no reason to leave the lodge. It has drawn us here, and it means too much to the children. It should stay in the family.

Anja, with a j. But Swedish, so Anya, said with a y?
Then Ellen Lacey returned to Caro's thoughts.

Ellen blamed herself for not listening to the dream, for not realizing the girl was so deeply troubled. I am not inclined to believe in premonitions, and certainly not to be haunted by them. There is a simple explanation, I am sure.

So Caro and Ellen had had disturbing dreams too.

Con ran into H today at the hotel. Apparently he plans to build on his land, clearing it this next summer. Distressing news, though not entirely unexpected. I am sure the conversation triggered my dream, though perhaps the sherry after a rich dinner contributed. And of course, my worry over dear, sweet Sarah Beth . . .

Sarah scrambled for the rolled-up photos. Grabbed the shoreline shot, then traded it for the photo of the house party. Laid it out as carefully as she could. Despite the new bulb, she couldn't see the faces in detail.

In the bright light of the kitchen where Caro and the estimable Mrs. O'Dell had once presided, Sarah got a good look at the face of the young woman—a girl, not much older than Abby—in the black dress and frilled white apron standing a few feet apart from the rest of the household staff. *Anja.* Ellen Lacey's handwriting on the back of the photo was in pencil, faded and smudged, but Sarah managed to make it out. Besides, she didn't need the name to recognize the face. She'd seen it twice—last night, and twenty-five years ago.

FRIDAY

Twenty-One Days

24

"And you didn't think you should tell me?" Janine's tone was low and controlled, but her eyes were wild.

"I thought it was just a dream," Sarah said. "It wasn't until—until after the attack that I realized it might have been a warning. And now . . ."

"No," Holly said. "If we're coming clean, we're coming clean." She turned from her sister to Janine, parked in front of the kitchen sink. It was morning, all of them up early. "Sarah told me about the dream. She was convinced it was telling her someone was in danger. I'm the one who dismissed it. Who went all Miss No BS and said dreams were, I don't know, misfirings in the brain while we sleep, or the result of too much wine. Then afterwards . . ."

"Afterwards," Janine said. "Afterwards, you disappeared. Acted like nothing had happened, like I wasn't even here." She glared at Holly, then directed her anger at Sarah. "And you talked me out of filing an official report. You and that sheriff. You were more concerned about what would happen to Lucas and his reputation. No one gave a damn about me."

"Janine, that's not true," Sarah said. "I knew how fragile you were—"

"Fragile? You're calling me fragile?" Janine was ablaze. "I'm the girl who practically raised herself because her father left her mother without a backward glance and her mother was too busy screwing any man who would buy her a drink to stay home. I learned to cook so I could eat. And no one"—she jabbed at the space between them—"no man has ever taken care of me. No tech genius who made millions while I stayed home having babies and playing with houses. When my mother was in and out of rehab, or in and out of jail, I took care of myself. When my husband left me with nothing but a toddler, I worked my tail off to raise my son on my own. I am not fragile."

Her words hung in the air like smoke after the fireworks on the Fourth of July, thick, their sharpness piercing the nostrils and watering the eyes.

"I'm sorry, Janine," Sarah said. "I have always regretted what I did, especially since finding you here. All I can say is that I honestly, truly believed letting it drop was the best thing at the time. I never imagined Lucas would skate on the crash— I was absolutely positive he'd be charged and convicted and do time. And I never imagined we would let it tear our friendship apart."

Or bring us back together, but for how long?

"We were all upset," Nic said in her rational lawyer tone. "Over Michael's death and Jeremy's injuries. We didn't know whether he would live or die. We were young and upset and we didn't know what to do."

Janine dug her fingers into the flesh above her elbows. Her lips tightened and she turned her head away. After a long moment, she faced her friends.

"I appreciate the confessions. But what about now? What are the dreams saying now?"

"Right." Nic pulled a notepad out of her tote bag. "Let's go over what we know."

"If you're making notes," Holly said, "I need coffee."

Minutes later, over coffee and scones at the kitchen table, Sarah described the nightmare of two nights ago in detail, the young woman in the white nightgown fleeing down the staircase.

"Who was she?" Nic asked. "Where was she going?"

"Toward the doors to the deck. I don't *know* that she was going to the lake. But I knew. You know?"

"That's dreams for you," Janine said. "They totally make sense, until you wake up."

"My first thought," Sarah said, "was that it was Abby. That she was in danger. But she's fine. Well, fine-not fine. She's an eighteen-year-old grieving her father. Then—then I thought maybe it was my mother, but that didn't make sense, either."

"So who?" Holly said. "I mean, you said the face resembles Anja, but if you're right and the tragedy Caro was referring to was Anja's death, that was a hundred years ago. Why is she coming back now?"

Nic wrote the number one and circled it. "The first dream, that we know of, was Ellen Lacey's, shortly before Anja's death. Exactly what she dreamed or when, we don't know. Tell us again what Caro said."

Sarah read the journal entry out loud.

"Sounds like H," Holly said, "whoever he was, attacked Anja. Caro called him 'a powerful man.' Whether he was local or a guest, we don't know. Clearly, the Laceys believed the girl's account of whatever happened, but that wasn't enough to save her."

"Caro and Con wanted nothing to do with him, either," Sarah said. "I'm assuming that's the same H she mentions later, when they were discussing how to complete the deal. Though what deal, we don't know."

"We can assume that the incident involving Anja occurred sometime between December 1921, the date on that photograph"—Nic pointed her pen at the house party photo—"and May of 1922, when your great-grandparents bought the lodge. Right? Ellen's dream occurred before the incident with H. Caro's dream came four years later. The journal's short on details, but we know she believed the woman in her dream was Anja. And that her dream was the same as Ellen's."

"Oh, God," Sarah said, bolting upright. "That was the last entry in the journal. She mentioned the dream, and that she was worried about her daughter. Do you remember when Sarah Beth died? Or of what?" she asked Holly. To the others, she explained. "Our grandfather's little sister. I'm named for her. She was only six when she died, so 1926 is about right. But of what?"

"I remember seeing her gravestone in the family plot," Holly said. "but what happened, I don't know. The dollhouse was built for her."

Sarah opened the journal and read the symptoms.

"That could be anything," Nic said as Holly picked up her phone and started punching buttons.

"Which would make it worse," Sarah said. "You know how, with kids, you can't always tell if the symptoms are serious or no big deal."

Holly set her phone back on the table. "I thought I could look up those symptoms, but my friend Google is playing dead."

"Then there was the third dream," Nic said, bringing them back to the topic at hand with a glance at Sarah. "Yours, twenty-five years ago."

"Right. There was a woman screaming, then running. Through the trees, across the lawn. But I knew the dream was referring to you." She laid her hand over Janine's. After a long moment, when the air in the room did not move, Janine turned her hand over, her palm touching Sarah's, and gave a gentle squeeze.

"There's a partial pattern." Nic tapped her notes. "If we assume that Ellen Lacey's dream foretold the attack on the housemaid, and maybe her death, and that Sarah's first dream foretold the attack on Janine. But how does Caro's dream fit, even if it was foretelling her daughter's death? Unless there was some attack we don't know about—that's when she stopped writing in the journal."

"Powerful men," Holly said, "taking what they want. Although Lucas wasn't powerful then."

"Powerful enough," Sarah said. "But Nic's right. Ellen's dream meshes with my first one. If Caro's dream was a warning, too, then of what? And what about my dream Wednesday night?"

Her coffee had cooled and when she took a sip, it had that bitter edge that puckers the mouth.

"This may sound crazy," she continued. "Though lately, my life's kinda redefined crazy. Is the girl, Anja, warning us? Or is it the lodge?" They'd gone beyond pennies from her dead husband, sweet reminders of the past, and electronics that didn't work to cut wires and photographs stashed in locked trunks that echoed dreams that made no sense. Dreams that foretold danger. Dreams meant to spur the dreamer into action.

She stared into her cold coffee, hoping for a sign. But all she could see in its darkness were her own terrified eyes.

* * *

227

Sarah stood on the deck overlooking the lake and arched her back. Closed her eyes, worked the knot in her spine. There must be a yoga studio in town. Though a friend had dragged her to a class last week, her muscles contradicted the memory, telling her it had been years since she'd unrolled a mat.

Twenty-one days since Jeremy died. When would she stop counting?

Truth was, she feared that day. Counting kept her connected to him and to who she used to be. As long as it hurt, she was alive.

She exhaled and swept her arms overhead to salute the sun, opening her eyes as her hands met. Then hands down. She had to bend her knees to touch the deck, carefully extending one leg behind her, then the other. She managed two rounds before sinking to a seated position, the muscles in her legs pulling and twitching, even the soles of her feet sore.

Her mother had urged her to come home and rest. The woman could not have known the visit would be anything but restful. Where was she, anyway?

This afternoon. When Peggy came out this afternoon with the real estate agent, she'd ask her mother. Ask what was so freaking important in town, in her studio, that she'd all but abandoned Sarah to the place.

Even stranger, now that Holly was here.

Christ. Humans. What could you do? Those had better be Peggy's best paintings ever.

Sarah snared one tennis shoe, then the other. Slipped a foot in and tightened the laces. Did anything feel so good as the morning sun on the skin? She tied the other shoe and wrapped her arms around her knees.

If you took a picture, compared one calendar photo to another, then the north shore of Bitterroot Lake might barely be a blip on the register of beautiful places. But Caro was right when she said a place drew you to it and wanted you to make it home. Holly and Nic had gone into Deer Park on a fact-finding mission, hoping to learn more about both Sarah Beth's and Anja's deaths. Tragedy had sent Ellen Lacey running, but Caro, of the bigger heart, had not been daunted by Anja's story, whatever it was, or by her dreams.

Caro had understood that tragedy didn't scar a house, but shaped it. Made it yours.

Maybe it was time she understood that too.

25

nside, she scooped up clean rags and grabbed a pair of buckets. Said a quick prayer to the household gods as she walked
out the mudroom door that this was the day the phone company techs deigned them worthy of service.

Why were the carriage doors open? Had Janine gone for a
drive? Nic and Holly had taken Nic's car. She set the buckets on
the gravel path and walked into the carriage house. Janine's
white van stood next to her SUV, cool as the proverbial
cucumber.

From deep inside the building, she heard scraping sounds,
the clink of metal on metal.

"Janine?"

"Over here," came the reply and Sarah peered through the
semidarkness. Picked her way to the workbench near the stairs,
where Janine stood, hands on her hips. She'd pulled her long
curls back in a bright red scrunchie.

"You said this was the most likely place for phone wire, so I
figured I'd rummage around. No luck."

"Half dark, all this dust, who knows what's out here."

"I was actually hoping to find a ladder, so we can reach the second-story windows."

"Outside. At least, that's where they've always been." Sarah led the way. Wood and metal ladders of different lengths hung along the exterior wall. A squirrel had left a stash of pine cone bits and pieces in the rail of a paint-spattered aluminum extension ladder, and after they lifted it off its wooden prongs, they flipped it over to dump the debris. Carried it back to the lodge and hoisted it upright.

"You should have told me," Janine said, as they stared at the dull, dry logs and the mud-spattered windows, the sills caked with dirt and moss. "About the dream."

"I know. I'm sorry."

Janine did not reply. After a long moment, she stuffed a couple of rags in her pocket and picked up a bucket. Tested the bottom rung and climbed up.

In truth, Sarah was surprised Janine had stayed. But despite everything, despite the distance they'd let grow between them, when Janine was in trouble, she'd sought refuge *here*.

Sarah picked up the other bucket and started on the kitchen windows, careful of the peonies and spirea. Her grandmother had sworn that the best way to clean a window was with damp newspaper, but every time Sarah tried that, she'd ended up with a lump of wet mush, stained hands, and ink on the window sills. Happily, she'd found a wicker hamper in the laundry room full of rags. Had no one in the family had ever thrown away an old towel, T-shirt, or diaper?

No. No one in this family had ever thrown away anything.

That brought her back to the letters and Caro's journal. What had prompted Caro and her friends to start the Ladies'

Aid Society loans? Caro had wanted word to spread to women in need, while avoiding talk that might stymie their efforts. She poked her thumbnail at a glob of sap glued to the glass.

Had there been no group of church women willing to offer food, shelter, and a little cash? No one could be judgy-ier than a group of women, even good church women. Had the Society stepped in where the usual folks feared to tread? Not every letter writer fell outside societal norms, but widowhood was one thing, living in sin another. A larch cone, about the size of a strawberry, hit her on the arm.

"Sorry," Janine called. The ladder creaked as she descended. She dumped the dark, flat water from her bucket into a juniper. Sarah dumped hers, too, then rinsed both buckets from the spigot on the side of the house.

It was a long moment, the woods around them oddly quiet, before Janine spoke.

"The first time I came out here with you, it was almost Christmas and the snow was falling." Janine gave the lodge a long, sweeping gaze. "I thought this place was magical."

Just listen. You owe her that.

"When Roger left me," she continued, "we'd been living in New Mexico where he had a job on a ranch. It came with a house, he said, but it turned out to be an ancient metal trailer that rattled like a snake when the wind blew. Drove me half crazy. Sixteen miles out of town, not a tree in sight. Zak turned two there." Janine wrapped her arms around herself and shuddered. "When Roger took off, with the truck and the last of our cash, the ranch manager's wife took pity on me. She knew I'd worked in restaurants and got me a job in town at the café. It was a jelly doughnut-drip coffee kind of place, but I knew I had to make do until I had the money to leave."

She sat on a big boulder. Untied her hair and bent over, shaking her head, then straightened and slipped the scrunchie onto her wrist. Sarah sat on the ground a few feet away.

"The problem," Janine continued, "was where to live. There was nothing I could afford except a cabin by the creek on the edge of town. Practically a twin to the cabins here." Her face softened.

Sarah waited.

"I stayed in that town way too long because of that cabin. The most comforting place I have ever lived. Or that I've ever been, except for here, at Whitetail."

Janine leaned forward, hands clasped between her knees. "They made that job for me. They didn't need me. They didn't know me, they had no reason to trust me or help me, but they did. Customers brought in stuff for Zak—books, toys, clothing their kids had outgrown. The crankiest old lady gave me the most beautiful handwoven blanket—I've kept it all these years. No questions. No judgments. Just . . ." Her voice trailed off.

"They helped me heal. And up on that ladder, looking in at the bunk room where you and Holly and I used to sleep, I realized it was like you and your family. Like coming to the lodge."

"But—this is where—"

Janine held up a hand and Sarah stopped. "This is where the healing started. Where I started to feel I was worth something. Lucas tried to take that away from me. For a long time, I thought you had, too, by denying my voice. But washing the layers of grime off the old glass, I saw that my shame had built up in layers, too. From my childhood, the attack, Roger's abuse. I married a man who abandoned me and our son, just like my mother had done. The lodge helped me heal from my childhood, the same way that little nowhere town helped me recover from my broken marriage."

Sarah began to catch a glimmer of where Janine was going. "So when we found the journal and the letters, and uncovered what Caro and the Ladies' Aid Society did . . ."

"Exactly," Janine said. "I don't know how or why, since you didn't know about Caro's society. But helping women in need is as much a part of the history of this lodge as the steamboat dock or the thirty-six place settings of railroad china."

"But I stopped you from filing a report against Lucas."

"And you weren't wrong. I was thinking, while I was up on the ladder." She wiped her mouth with the back of her hand. "What you said about me being fragile. You were right. I was like glass. Hard on the surface, but if I'd been forced to face Lucas Erickson in court, with him sneering at me and denying everything, I would have shattered into a million pieces."

In and out. Sarah repeated the exercise until she could speak again.

"Are you seriously thinking of moving back up here? I thought you hated Deer Park."

"I thought so too. Turns out, I hated some of the things that happened to me here, but none of that matters anymore. I've got my own experience of Deer Park, and the lodge is a huge part of it." Janine paused. "Nic said she told you about the clippings. I know they look bad. I was just keeping track of him. I kept a file on the case against my mother too. They were part of my story. But I'm ready to let it all go. Live my own story, not theirs."

"Oh my gosh. That's what the dreams are about, aren't they?" Sarah asked. "We're supposed to help each other. Help women in danger. Tell the stories that matter and let go of the ones that don't." She let out a cackle. "In the business, architects and designers like to say a house talks to them. But I don't think they mean it quite so literally."

Then she turned serious. "Ellen Lacey built this house. The first dream came to her."

"She didn't listen," Janine said. "That's what killed Anja. And it broke Ellen."

The question hung in the air, unspoken.

What danger was stalking them now?

*   *   *

The rest of the morning, they washed windows and gathered debris. It amazed Sarah to see Janine work so hard to clean a place that wasn't hers. To restore the magic.

And to keep from obsessing about Lucas Erickson, shot to death on the floor of his own office?

How was that working, she wondered. Because it wasn't working for her. No love lost and all that, but still. The man was dead. People had loved him. His mother and sister. His children. People had depended on him, their lives and businesses entwined with his. Renee Harper and his clients. Which included McCaskill Lumber.

Obviously, someone had hated him. Harper had portrayed him as the classic difficult man—demanding, unyielding— though Sarah had detected a subtler, more complicated side to her feelings. Men like that were often quite charming, and financially successful, which only encouraged their bad behavior.

Entitled, to use the modern phrase.

But clearly not a modern phenomenon. H, in Caro's account of the incident involving the Swedish housemaid, seemed to fit the bill. Who had he been? What had happened to him?

Some got their comeuppance. Others didn't, at least not publicly. She'd worked her way around the side of the lodge and took a step back, scanning for streaks on the office windows. Justice was like physics. For every action, there was an equal and opposite reaction. Even if you didn't get to see it.

But a murder? It had a ripple effect beyond the victim. It affected the entire community.

"Oh," she said out loud. Was that what led to the formation of the Lakeside Ladies' Aid Society? Had they kept it secret not just to avoid talk that might prevent women from asking for help, but also to avoid scrutiny? If a woman who'd been seduced by a married man sought support from a church society, word would spread like wildfire, but a group acting in secret could protect both the woman and the wife, and the child, if there was one, from rumor and scandal.

She picked up her bucket and moved to the next window, careful not to crush the shrubbery. They'd seen no indication that the Ladies' Aid Society had done anything to exact revenge on misbehaving men, but she wouldn't put it past them. Funny that they'd never heard of it until now. Had her father known? She'd have to quiz her mother.

At that very moment, the sound of an engine coming down the lane broke into her thoughts.

"She's here," Sarah told the squirrel who'd been keeping an eye on her. The vehicle passed in and out of view. Not her mother's red sedan but a larger, white rig. "Oh, the phone company. Cross your paws, Mr. Squirrel."

But it wasn't the phone company service truck after all. It was a white SUV, fresh from the car wash.

The one they'd seen near the roadside memorial? Or the one George Hoyt had seen on the lane Sunday afternoon?

Then the SUV made the final turn and she saw two women in the front seat. Her mother, the passenger. And the real estate agent.

Oh, God. Of all the people, of all the agents in Deer Park—and unlike lawyers, you had your pick—why had her mother chosen Becca Smalley?

"Sarah!" Becca said moments later as she crossed the gravel drive, hand extended. Sarah ran her hand up and down her pants leg and held it out apologetically. To her surprise, Becca took it with both hers, warm, soft, and dry.

"I owe you an apology," Becca said. "The other day, in the Spruce, I was so startled to see you. Sitting there, looking—well, confident and serene, as always. My mother told me about your husband's death—she heard about it from yours. But I didn't know you were in town and I didn't know what to say, so stupidly, I said nothing."

Serene? That had been the last thing Sarah had felt. And confident? Ha.

"You weren't the only one who didn't know I was in town," she replied. "I was so worried about how it would feel to be back that I didn't even tell my mother I was coming."

"Oh, Sarah." Becca tightened her grip and for half a second, Sarah feared the woman would hug her.

She freed her hand and gestured toward Janine, standing next to Peggy. "You remember Janine Chapman. Janine Nielsen."

Becca's mouth fell open and Sarah could almost see her mind running through everything she knew, or thought she knew, about Janine, before her lips closed and curved upward. "Yes, of course, Janine. Good to see you. You two were always such good friends."

So that's how it's going to be. Did Becca not remember how hateful she'd been to Janine, and by extension to Sarah and

Holly, not just in the seventh grade but for years? Had she genuinely become this warmhearted woman? Or had she decided the prospect of a sizable commission was worthy of her very best behavior? Wait and see.

Wait and see.

26

"As I see it," Becca said after a tour of the main lodge and a quick survey of the grounds, "you have several options. Whitetail Lodge is stunning—you know that. It could easily qualify for the National Register of Historic Places. But . . ."

They were seated at the dining room table. Janine had made herself scarce.

"But it needs a lot of work," Sarah finished. "Single-pane windows that leak heat in winter and cool air in summer. Logs that need to be cleaned and oiled and rechinked. The soffits, the moss, the roof. Not to mention the damage to the balcony and the gable on the carriage house. Any prospective buyer will see dollar signs before they cross the threshold."

"You sound like you've been making a list," Becca said.

Sarah touched the notebook in front of her. "And you sound like you're going to add to it."

"Well, yes." The real estate agent started ticking off items. It took both hands. "And that's just what you would need to do before listing, if you want to get anything close to its true value.

I always caution homeowners to be careful with improvements if they're planning to sell anytime soon. Most cost more than they add to the value of the house. But others are worth making even if they don't raise the sales price, because they shorten the time on the market."

"How do you know which are which?" Peggy asked. "And doesn't historic listing limit what you can do?"

"Experience. And yes, historic listing imposes some limitations, but it also gives you potential access to funding and tax credits for restoration," Becca replied. "Now, the real challenge is identifying comps. There's nothing like it on Bitterroot Lake. We'll have to consider properties throughout the region—even down on Flathead Lake and in the Swan Valley. Adjust for the size and age of the house, the outbuildings, the acreage."

Sarah was only half listening as Becca outlined the process of setting a list price and devising a marketing plan. She was thinking about decades of McCaskills racing down the steps, running out the doors, and tumbling down the lawn. Jumping in the cold water and screaming in delight. Sailing, canoeing, riding horses. Sledding. Hiking up the narrow trails and gazing out at the lake and the mountains, ridge after ridge and range after range, stretching farther than the eye could see. She was thinking of all the people with more money than sense, who turned classic buildings into nightmares, and those whose eyes were bigger than their budgets, who left the job half done. She was thinking about Ellen Lacey and Caro and Mary Mac. About the Ladies' Aid Society and her own friends. Her daughter, her sister, her niece.

"It's a fabulous place," Becca said, "but realistically, a tough sell. It's going to take a buyer with vision, time, and passion, not to mention the money."

Peggy sighed. "We have some serious thinking to do."

"Take all the time you need." Becca glanced at her watch. "I've got to get going. I should stop to check on the rental next door, but—"

"Next door?" Sarah interrupted her. "George's place?"

"He moved into his mother's house a while back. The little one up near the highway. He put the lakefront house in our rental pool. A woman from San Diego has it for a couple of weeks—she's very nice. I haven't had time to hire someone to help manage the rentals, let alone the second homes. I'm meeting Misty and Dan at the law office. She's ready to sell but I think they're better off waiting."

"Who would want it?" Peggy asked. "After what happened."

"And to think I ran into his secretary right when it was happening," Becca continued. "At the post office. She was in a gabby mood. Hard to get away, but I didn't have time to talk."

Since when did Becca let that stop her? Though Sarah was beginning to find her chattiness endearing. Still, it was hard to imagine Renee Harper going gabby, and her description of the encounter was just the opposite of Becca's.

"I'll leave you with our brochure and a sample listing agreement." Becca slid a folder toward Peggy, who slid it over to Sarah, and they all stood. "By the way, I hear you met my son."

Sarah tilted her head, puzzled.

"Matt," Becca said with a smile. "Looks just like his father, doesn't he?"

Sarah's gaze flicked to Becca's left hand. Sure enough, a slim gold wedding band. Not that she knew who every high school classmate had married—the reunions had never come at a good time, and she only kept up with a few girlfriends—but Becca and Matt, one of the nicest men she'd ever met? Or had she just never noticed Becca's good side?

"Good job, Becca," she replied. "Good job."

"What do you think?" Peggy asked as Becca drove away.

"I think we have a lot to think about." She held the front door for her mother. Inside, Peggy ducked into the powder room.

Everything Becca had said—and she could hardly believe this, but it was true—made perfect sense. The lodge needed serious help. Serious capital. Serious commitment.

It was crazy. Nuts. What would Jeremy think?

She glanced at the coffee table where the scrapbook and albums lay next to the box of letters. When she remembered Caro's words, she knew Whitetail Lodge belonged in the hands of a woman. Her hands. Though the lodge had come to her mother through JP, it had been Ellen Lacey's vision and Caro's passion. Mary Mac's domain. She, Sarah McCaskill Carter, could not be the one who let it go. How she was going to manage, how convince her mother, and her brother and sister, she had no idea.

She didn't care. It was what Caro would have wanted. It was what *she* wanted.

An empty wine glass sat on the side table, left over from last night. She picked it up and caught a glimpse of something shiny. Caught her breath as she stared, open-mouthed, at the penny that lay on the Navaho rug.

And knew in a flash what Jeremy thought.

* * *

"Mom," Sarah said as she, Peggy, and Janine admired the windows Janine had shined to a sparkle. "What do you know about our great-grandmother, Caroline? Caro?"

Peggy's brows arched well above her zebra-striped glasses frames. Specks of green paint dotted the gray-blond hair at her temple. She ran a hand through her hair, remnants of more green paint in her cuticles and under her nails. Funny that she hadn't minded Becca seeing the paint. More likely, she hadn't noticed. She'd ridden out with the real estate agent, planning to take Sarah up on yesterday's invitation to stay for dinner and get a ride back into town.

"Caro is the reason I married your father," Peggy said. "I was crazy in love with him, of course. But when I met her, I knew I wanted to be part of this family. Years later, Mary Mac told me she'd had a similar feeling when she married Tom. Her mother died when she was seven and her father didn't have a clue how to raise a girl. She always said Caro taught her what it meant to be a woman, and to tend to a family. When we told Caro your name, she cried. She died a month later."

"I'm so sorry I never knew her."

"Now you'll dismiss this as woo-woo," Peggy said. "You kids all like to be practical. But I think that once she met you, she was ready to go."

"Mom. You can't mean that."

"Peggy, seriously?" Janine said. "Like Sarah was her daughter come back to life?"

"Well, I wouldn't go that far. More like she knew that with a great-grandson, Leo, and now a great-granddaughter, Sarah, the family legacy was in good hands."

From the kitchen, they heard the oven beep, and Janine excused herself.

"Does the name Lakeside Ladies' Aid Society mean anything to you?"

"Sarah, what is this? Where are all these questions coming from?"

She showed her mother the box of letters.

Peggy took the top envelope from the stack and read the address. "'Mrs. Cornelius McCaskill, Whitetail Lodge, Deer

Park, Montana.' Back when that was enough to get your mail to you. They still name houses in England."

Sarah flashed on the letters sent by owl to Mr. H. Potter, the Cupboard Under the Stairs, 4 Privet Drive, informing him of his acceptance to Hogwarts. Letter after letter, owl after owl, until Uncle Vernon screwed the mail slot shut, and the owls began shooting letters down the chimney. Her eyes darted involuntarily to the stone chimney, thirty feet high.

And she sometimes thought her mother was a bubble off plumb.

H. Caro's journal mentioned H, but there was little chance they'd ever know who H had been.

"We named Connor for him, you know," Peggy was saying. "For Con. The McCaskills love naming themselves after themselves, but I could not call my child Cornelius."

Sarah smiled, then told her mother about the trunk. About Caro's journal and how they'd pieced it all together. "The letters in the Whitman's Sampler box are mostly thank-you notes for loans the Society made to women in need. Women who'd been abandoned, or who wanted to leave an abusive marriage. Small loans, from what we can tell, repaid promptly. No interest, so it was clearly a benevolent undertaking."

Peggy stared at her, the envelope from Mrs. Pennington of Cincinnati now forgotten in her lap. "And who—who was this girl? You said her name."

"Anja. It's spelled A-n-j-a, but Caro described her as the Laceys' Swedish housemaid, so we're saying the j as a y."

"Anja," Peggy repeated. "And she died tragically?"

"We think so, but we're speculating, based on Caro's comments. Nic's in town, asking questions about the murder. Holly went along to see what she could dig up in the old records that might help us identify Anja and what happened to her."

"I thought all those files were online these days."

Sarah held out her hands. "No phone, no internet."

"Oh, for Pete's sake. Those nincompoops haven't come out to fix the line yet? Well, come in and use my Wi-Fi if you need to."

As long as she didn't set foot in the studio.

"And how are the loans related to this Anja's death?" Peggy asked.

"Not sure they are, except that Caro was involved in both. They might have pooled their money to send the girl's body to her family and that got them started. We don't know."

"Her body."

"If we've put it together right, she drowned in the lake." Sarah took the rolled-up photo from the coffee table. "We found this photo of a house party the Laceys threw during the Christmas season of 1921. Some of the names are written on the back—by Mrs. Lacey, we presume—though they're pretty faint. Con and Caro were at the party, but it isn't Caro's hand-writing. This is Anja." She pointed at the ghostly blonde in the somber uniform, with the wild eyes and the coronet of braids, then glanced at her mother.

Who had gone as pale as the ivory linen envelope in her hand.

*   *   *

"You knew her," Sarah said a few minutes later, trying not to hover as Peggy settled into a chair outside on the deck. "You recognized her."

Peggy spoke with her eyes closed, her face lifted to the sun. "After your father died, three years ago, I came out here for a few days' respite. In all the years I've been a McCaskill, I don't think I'd ever spent a night alone in the lodge until then." She opened her eyes and accepted the frosty glass of hibiscus iced tea Janine handed her. Janine took the chair next to Sarah's.

"That's when I saw her," Peggy continued. "Anja, though I didn't know her name until today. But it was her face. And those blond braids—so distinctive." She paused for a sip. "The first night, I got a vague sense of someone. It didn't mean anything. The second night, it was more unsettling, but still unclear. I didn't get the real sense that she was coming to me for a reason until the third night."

"Three nights?" Sarah's voice cracked. Her mother had just described the same sequence she'd experienced earlier this week, from a vague image to a tug to a compulsion. From an unsettled sensation to a full-blown nightmare. Way back when, she'd only seen Anja once. Had she been too oblivious? Was the danger closer now? Why was Anja, if it was her, getting more insistent?

"What aren't you telling me, Sarah?"

She told her mother about her own dreams. "At the time, twenty-five years ago, I was certain the girl in the nightmare was Janine, because Lucas had been pestering her all weekend, and he was clearly bent on trouble. Now I'm convinced that the girl I saw then is the same girl I saw this week. And the same girl you saw."

Peggy reached for her hand, fingers cool from the iced tea. "When I went back to town, the dreams stopped. The only person I told was Pam Holtz. She's so sensible. She assured me I was just overwrought, worn out by those last few weeks with your father."

What Sarah had thought, too, at first. But it was more than that. Both the nightmare this week and the nightmare twenty-five years ago were demanding something. She'd ignored the message back then. She couldn't ignore it now. But first, she had to figure out what she was being asked to do.

"Makes sense," Janine said from the chair next to Sarah's. "Anja worked for the Laceys, and we think this is where she died. She had no connection to the house in town."

"When I got back from Seattle," Peggy said, "after Jeremy's funeral, I came out for a couple of days, intending to start cleaning so we could use the lodge this summer. You and the kids."

Peggy's eyes drifted shut and Sarah had almost decided she'd fallen asleep when she opened them.

"She came to me again." Peggy's voice was soft and distant. "Different this time. Not the nightmare you had, though I knew it was the same girl I saw after your father died. This time, she let me see her face. She wanted me to see her face." She tightened her grip on Sarah's fingers. "I never imagined she would terrify you like that. If I'd had any idea, darling, I never would have suggested you come to the lodge."

"You couldn't have known. You knew about the attack, but not the dream. You had no reason to think she—Anja—had appeared to anyone besides you."

"All this is why I haven't let you girls into my studio. I've been trying to paint what I saw. That's why I went back to town after only one night, so I could paint her. Why I've spent every minute I can working. These pieces"—Peggy hesitated—"aren't like anything else I've done. You'll think I'm nuts. Or nuttier than ever."

"Mom, you know I think your work is terrific." Over the years, she'd booked several shows for her mother in an upscale gallery on Seattle's Eastside and sold pieces to friends.

"Your show in Missoula practically sold out opening night," Janine said.

"The point of a landscape, for me, is to capture the light and movement in a way that gives people an emotional connection to the place. Similarly, in portraiture, I want the viewer to see something essential about the subject and connect to it emotionally. But these paintings . . ." Peggy paused. "They go a step beyond. It's not me providing emotional content for the viewer. It's my emotional connection to what no one else can see. Does that make any sense?"

"Yes," Janine said.

Not one bit, Sarah thought. Not one bit.

But then, neither had anything else in the last twenty-one days.

27

"So, we were right," Holly said. "Not that we can prove it."

The four friends and Peggy gathered in the kitchen after Holly and Nic returned from town, so Janine could hear what they had to say while she cooked. Once again, she'd refused help. Easier, Sarah suspected, to do it all herself than direct the rest of them, especially in an outdated space nothing like the commercial kitchens she was used to.

"Turns out records clerks love a good mystery," Holly continued. "And the county was small enough back then to make searching a breeze." She laid a photocopy of a State of Montana Standard Certificate of Death on the table.

Sarah summarized what the form called the "personal and statistical particulars." "Anja Sundstrom, age twenty-one, born in Sweden, drowned in Bitterroot Lake on Sunday, January 1, 1922. Single, a resident of Whitetail Lodge, Deer Park. Informant, Frank Lacey, Whitetail Lodge. It asks for parents' names and birthplaces. Mother is blank. Father, Carl Sundstrom."

"I always forget," Nic said. "This lake doesn't freeze over, does it?"

Sarah shook her head. "Some of the shallow bays freeze, but not up here. Too deep."

"Does it say what happened to the body?" Janine asked.

"Buried in Valley View Cemetery, Deer Park," Holly replied. "We interpreted Caro's journal entry to mean that she threw herself in the lake because of whatever happened at the house party. But in this column"—she ran her finger down the right side of the form, filled out with a finer-nibbed pen, in a compact backhand—"the medical doctor says cause of death was drowning, and where it asks 'accident, suicide, or homicide?' he wrote 'accident.'"

Sarah frowned. "You saying he didn't want to call it suicide? Why—stigma?"

"Maybe. Look at the time of death. One thirty AM. Or maybe it was an accident," Holly speculated. "She was just running. Trying to get away, not noticing where she went."

Or not caring.

Sarah sat back, stunned. She'd been right about her dream—her nightmare. No one went swimming in a mountain lake at one thirty in the morning on the first day of the year. Not even a hardy Swede. Especially not a servant, expected to work late and early when guests meant extra household duties. Anja had come back to lead her to the truth.

"There was an investigation," Nic said. "If you can call it that." She laid a single photocopied sheet on the table, another printed form completed by hand. "Not easy to decipher, but the upshot is the sheriff was called to Whitetail Lodge in the early hours on New Year's Day after the body of a lodge employee was found in the lake. Frank Lacey was interviewed, and the body delivered to Massey and Sons, Undertakers. End of story."

"What was she wearing?" Sarah asked, sure she already knew. "Who saw her last? What was her mood? Had she been upset about something? Was anyone else present when she went into the water?"

Nic glowered. "Methinks the good sheriff left a few things out. Whether he was lazy or protecting someone, I have no idea. If he made any notes, they're long gone."

"Would the undertaker have records?" Janine asked.

"The Masseys sold to the Newmans ages ago," Peggy said. "Their building was destroyed in a gas explosion when you girls were babies. Flattened the whole block."

"We may never know what happened to Anja," Nic said. "But at least we know her last name and date of birth."

"Oh, we know," Sarah said. "We may not know the details or who drove her to her death, but we know."

One dream, one tragedy, she could dismiss. But not all this.

"What did you learn about Sarah Beth?" She poured herself a glass of iced tea and took a long swallow, the cold constricting her throat with a pang.

"Diphtheria," Holly said. "Ten days after Caro's dream."

It was as if the house itself, every log and timber, every window and shingle, even the deck where they sat, gave a collective shudder.

"But not here, in the lodge," Sarah said, perching on the edge of her chair. "Even Caro couldn't have hung onto the lodge, much as she loved it, if her little girl died here." She pictured the baby book, so lovingly tended. The dress. The funeral roses.

"No," Holly said. "In the hospital, in Whitefish. Different county, but the clerk found her death certificate for us and printed off a copy. That was before the hospital in Deer Park was built—remember Caro's comments in her journal about fund-raising?"

"You kids were born in the McCaskill wing," Peggy said. "It was torn down when they built the new hospital. Mary Mac was so angry she refused to give them any more money. You know how she was."

"Fierce," Sarah said. "Despite her sweet look. Grandpa used to say her needlework was an excuse to stab things without getting sent to jail."

"She scared me half to death," Peggy confided. "Unlike Caro. But she was generous, too, and once she saw that I made John Patrick happy, she completely accepted me."

Like Jeremy's parents when they first met Sarah.

Two dreams accounted for. Three, including her first dream, the day before Lucas—

"Oh my gosh, I forgot to ask." She threw an apologetic look toward Janine, then turned to Nic. "Did you get an answer from the prosecutor? They aren't going to file charges, are they? And did you reach your daughter?"

"Yes. We hope not. Yes." Nic ticked off fingers in the air. "Bottom line, the meeting with the principal is moved to next week. Tempe insists she's got everything under control."

"And the kid?"

"Keeping his distance. Now that the principal and his parents are involved, I think he'll back off. Too chicken for revenge. Or maybe she's right and the other kids think he's a dipstick who deserves a dose of his own medicine."

"You should be there," Janine said. "You don't need to stay here and babysit me. This crew can do that."

"Nothing's going to happen at school before next week," Nic replied. "As for charges, like I told Janine earlier, the prosecutor acknowledges that they don't have any direct evidence to incriminate her—just her admission that she was there and that she fled the scene. Bottom line is, we've agreed that Janine can go home, but she'll keep me posted on her whereabouts and make herself available for additional questioning any time she's asked."

"So she's not in the clear," Peggy said.

"It's as good as we can hope for, until they have evidence incriminating someone else. They confirmed that they have other targets, but we can only guess who. Lucas Erickson was not a popular man."

"Didn't stop Connor from doing business with him," Sarah said.

"You know about that?" Peggy said.

"Not the specifics, no. Routine stuff, I guess." But her mind wasn't on lumber. It was on the lodge, and murder.

* * *

"I've asked too much of you," Peggy said as Sarah pointed the car up McCaskill Lane late that afternoon. "The lodge is too much."

Yesterday, she would have agreed. Today, though, a sense of mission had come over her. It wasn't just that the house was asking her to protect someone.

The thought struck her with the force of certainty, despite its oddity. The house itself, Whitetail Lodge, wanted her protection.

Breathe. Breathe. She slipped a hand off the wheel and squeezed her mother's.

"Both hands, Sarah," her mother said, but not before squeezing back.

She drove slowly, avoiding the ruts. What would regrading the road cost?

She grunted, remembering that the phone company service tech still had not shown up.

If Peggy was nutty, painting her dreams, was she nutty, too, thinking the house was asking her to save it? Blame the shock and grief. Her therapist would respond with soothing comments, suggesting that labels weren't helpful and that perhaps the dreams were messages from her subconscious, pointing her in a healing direction.

Oh, God. She was nuts, putting words in the mouth of a woman who wasn't even here.

Though if she were, that's what she would say.

She might also say that Sarah herself needed Whitetail Lodge. The way Caro had needed it, after the deaths of the Swedish housemaid and her own young daughter.

Sarah had let her ties to the lodge fray. The source of so much childhood happiness, the place where she and Jeremy had fallen in love. The place where she and her friends had broken their promises to each other.

Could she mend all that?

"No idea yet who's decorating the cross?" Peggy asked as Sarah drove past the roadside memorial. Sarah recapped their theories, but her mother had no good explanation.

On Lake Street, she passed the brick hotel, the FOR RENT sign in the first floor window. "Oh, darn it. I meant to ask Becca about that space."

"You thinking of opening a restaurant?"

"Not me. Janine." At the lift of her mother's brows, she explained. "She's making noises about moving back here. Holly thinks I could help, but she won't take money from me."

"Proud," Peggy said. "Like her mother. I wish I'd been a better friend to Sue. You can find a way."

Now there was a challenge if she'd ever heard one.

* * *

Sarah parked in front of the Victorian, wondering how to ask her mother to show her what she was working on.

"I suppose you want to see the paintings," Peggy said.

"If you'll let me."

"Why not? Since the dreams are coming to you, too. Maybe you can tell me what they mean."

Sarah followed her mother through the house. Peggy's style had evolved over the years, always relying on a strong sense of line and movement. Her ten thousand hours painting water had paid off, and when galleries hung work showing reflections, whether of mountains, grasses, or trees, they sold quickly.

What to expect now, though? The refrain of the day: *no idea.*

In the upstairs hallway, her mother opened the studio door and stood aside. Three feet into her old bedroom, Sarah stopped abruptly. This painting was unlike anything she'd ever seen.

Big, eighteen or twenty by forty, resting on the sturdy wooden easel. Rich, dark colors—reds, blues, and greens— receded into the background, paler splashes at three corners creating the impression of shadow and pulling the viewer in. Off-center, as if on the edge between the deep woods and the deeper lake, stood a pale figure in white, the soft fabric of her nightdress billowing around her legs. Shadow draped the woman's face as she looked over her shoulder, at something or someone behind the viewer. Her light hair flowed loosely down her back and her arms and hands seemed ready to push against a danger she knew would overwhelm her.

"That's her," Sarah whispered.

"I know." Peggy slid an arm around her waist and Sarah leaned into her mother's embrace.

A few minutes later, they sat outside, on the wide front steps that faced the lake. Peggy had shown her several sketches working out the composition and two smaller finished canvases portraying similar scenes, but with the female figure glazed over, almost hidden, in layers of green and midnight blue.

"The effect I was after was like when Monet changed the composition of *Woman in a Garden* and painted over two of the original figures. You can still see them ever so faintly." Peggy pressed her hands against the invisible air, miming the disappearing figures. "In the first two pieces, I'd made her too distant. I knew it. I knew I had to keep painting, as if she was pushing me, until I truly saw her. Thanks to the photograph you and your sister found, I know I have."

"What does she want? What is she telling us?"

"I think she simply wanted me to know her story. Because we own the lodge."

"Do you know if anyone else ever saw her? Grandma? Any of the men in the family?"

"Mary Mac never mentioned it," Peggy said. "Men—well, not if you girls are right and she was hounded to death by a man visiting the Laceys for their New Year's Eve bash."

H, whoever he had been.

Sarah blew out a breath. "So now that we know her story, now that you've put it on canvas, she'll be satisfied? Because I'm done with the nightmares."

"I think so. I hope so. This has all been quite the revelation."

"Mom, why didn't you tell me Holly lost her job?"

"She asked me not to. Said you had enough on your mind," Peggy replied. "I think she was embarrassed. Afraid you might think she's a flake who can't hold a job."

"I would never think that," Sarah protested. "Museum work is cutthroat. You'd think the art world would be genteel, but I've been on boards. I've watched her over the years. I know better."

"She worries about what you'll think of her. Whether she'll meet your standards."

Ouch.

"So, what will you do with the paintings?" Sarah asked. "Will you show them? Our theories about Anja's death aside, they are really striking."

"I haven't decided. I'm hoping Anja will tell me."

Sarah stood to leave. Peggy gripped her shoulders tightly, then kissed her cheek. "It's good to have you girls home. And with Connor feeling less pressure, now that he's bought the land below Porcupine Ridge, I hope the three of you can spend some time together."

"He bought the land? I thought—" She tried to remember the conversation between Connor and Leo, in the office. Connor had said George had sold the land on Lynx Mountain, below the ridge. To whom, he hadn't said, though he had rushed out with Leo, as if avoiding the subject. As if he wasn't sure she would trust his judgment. "Is that what's behind this expansion of the company? Got to be a lot of board feet up there. Anyway, doesn't matter. See you tomorrow."

In the car, she sat, hands on the wheel. The news of the land purchase was curious, but her mind was still on the mystery of the Swedish housemaid. Peggy had said—how had she put it?

That Anja wanted Peggy to see her. Now that she'd been seen and heard, Peggy thought, the girl could rest in peace.

The rest of them—Sarah, most of all—had interpreted the nightmares as a sign of physical danger, as when Anja appeared to Ellen Lacey before her death, and when she came to warn Caro that Sarah Beth was sicker than they thought.

And when, twenty-five years ago, she'd wanted Sarah to protect Janine from a man with trouble on his mind.

If Anja had been satisfied with being painted, why come to Sarah now? Why had the latest nightmare been so vivid, so demanding?

What were they missing?

Sarah turned the key in the ignition. The only way to find out what Anja wanted was to ask her.

* * *

The wind had picked up by the time Sarah reached Valley View Cemetery on the southeast edge of Deer Park. She didn't remember when she'd last been here.

Her phone buzzed with a text from Abby. *The Paper Place offered me my old job for the summer!!!!!!!*

That's great, honey, she texted back. *Just saw your grand-mother's new paintings—stunning!*

Cool! Love you, Mom!

The screen went dark. She stared out the window at the branches shivering in the cold wind. The sky had turned a hard gray. It wasn't going to snow, was it?

The place was deserted. She zipped up her jacket, cinched the belt, and stepped out, bracing herself against the hard wind. The cemetery dated back to homestead and railroad days. In the older section, granite crosses and statuary were common, gradually giving way to a mix of styles and materials—granite, marble, bronze, every grave a story.

She found the McCaskill plot easily, the small stone markers for Tom and Mary Mac, the gray-and-white marble monument for Con and Caro, the stone lamb for Sarah Beth. She crouched, fingertips grazing the smooth white marble. What had it been like, losing the much-loved little girl? Caro had responded by making the lodge and her family her refuge.

"Is that what all this is about, Caro?" she said. "The dreams, the discovery of the old trunk. Are you telling me, as your daughter's namesake, that I'm the one to continue the legacy of Whitetail Lodge?"

But the stones kept their tongues.

She stood, aware that she wasn't quite as steady as she ought to be. *Breathe in, breathe out.* Where to begin? Swedish housemaids got no grand markers, no stone angels. She wandered past familiar names—Holtz, Hoyt, Smalley.

Holtz. Hoyt. H.

Then, as if a hand beckoned, she wound her way toward a section where simple graves marked by small flat stones lay beneath the outstretched arms of a weeping birch.

There it was. *Anja Sundstrom, 1900–1922. God has called His Angel home.*

The tears surprised her, and she blinked them back. "What happened, Anja? What happened to you? And what do you need from me?" She brushed away a few of last year's dried birch leaves. "If you want us to tell your story, we can do that."

She could persuade her mother to display the paintings at a local gallery. At the wine bar, or whatever shape the restaurant took, if she and Holly convinced Janine to let them help her pursue her dream. As investors, or advisors. Who knew what else they'd find in the old trunks? Holly could track down the Lacey family and see what details the descendants could provide. They could tell the story of the girl with the crown of yellow braids, and of the Lakeside Ladies' Aid Society, dedicated to making a woman's lot a little less rough, a little less lonely.

Was that it? Was that all Anja wanted?

Sarah wasn't sure. She had more questions to ask, questions that might make the story a little more complicated.

A lot more complicated.

She bowed her head and made a promise to the girl, the young woman, in the simple grave.

28

"He's on the phone, Mrs. Carter," Steph, the lumber company desk clerk, told Sarah, and she could see her brother through the window between the front desk and the office. Connor held up two fingers, an inch apart, signaling that he'd just be a minute.

Not telling her the daily details of the business she understood, but they'd been talking about expansion and land and George Hoyt and he hadn't said a thing.

The front end of McCaskill Land and Lumber was as far from the hip showrooms of designer Seattle as you could get. Scuffed linoleum floor. A patchwork wall, lengths of rough-cut lumber tacked up next to samples in various finishes, and another displaying varieties of molding. A Mr. Coffee as old as the one at the lodge perched on a 1950s step table in the corner. The acrid odor of sawdust drifting in from the shop floor, accompanied by the whine and whirr of saws and sanders and planers.

Refreshing, to know your stuff was so good that you didn't need to prove how cool you were.

Connor was standing now, his broad back to her. That minute was stretching itself out.

The final waiting room wall was hung with photos that had been there for decades. Her great-grandfather Con, looking the part of the prosperous early twentieth-century businessman in his dark suit and starched collar. Two lumberjacks wielding a crosscut saw standing next to the largest old-growth Ponderosa she'd ever seen. And in a thin black frame, a yellowed newspaper article with a photo she'd never paid attention to, three men posing before a giant machine, men in work shirts in a half circle behind them.

She leaned in to read the caption. "Deer Park Lumber Company founder Cornelius McCaskill, Frank Lacey, and G. T. Hoyt show off the new electric circular sawmill installed recently at their Deer Park lumberyard, the largest of its kind in the Inland Northwest."

Their dark business suits were quite different from the tuxes they'd worn in the photo of the Laceys' New Year's Eve party, but she recognized them in an instant. Con, Frank, and the man who'd stood on the steps looking down at the young housemaid, the man whose name on the back of the photo had been smudged into obscurity.

A date had been handwritten on the side of the clipping and she tilted her head to read it. June 21, 1921. Six months before Anja's death.

"We gave that old sawmill to the historical society ages ago," Connor said, coming up behind her. "Getting it there was a bugger."

"G. T. Hoyt," she said, turning to him. "George's grandfather?"

He reddened and held out his hands. "Mom told you. I know, I should have sat you down, explained, but you've had so much on your mind, and we needed that land to continue expanding our production—"

"Connor, stop. I don't care that you bought land from George Hoyt and didn't tell me. Well, I do care." But that could wait. She needed to know who G.T. Hoyt was, his role in the company a century ago, and whether he was H.

Get a grip. He's not gonna know all that.

"Come into my office," Connor said, away from Steph's curiosity. He closed the door and gestured to an oak chair, his own chair new and sturdy, the only modern touch in the room other than his phone and computer. A wall-mounted shelf held books and memorabilia, and the autographed baseball on its heavy metal stand. So that's where it had gone. Good.

Where should she start?

"Sit. You're making me nervous."

She was too nervous to sit. She kept her words slow and deliberate as she tried to separate the lines of connection swimming before her eyes. "The photograph in the showroom. The caption says the men with our great-grandfather were Frank Lacey and G.T. Hoyt, and refers to 'their lumberyard.' Were they business partners? What do you know about that?"

"Not much. Lacey managed the sawmill the Great Northern built to supply ties to the railroad. You know, the one downriver that became the Superfund site. They bought timber from McCaskill, and I think Lacey invested in the company for a while."

"What about Hoyt?" she asked. "What did he have to do with McCaskill Land and Lumber?"

"Not sure I ever knew." He opened a desk drawer. "A volunteer with the historical society put together a history of the company when we donated the old mill and other equipment, and a bunch of photographs and papers. I've got it here somewhere."

As he flipped through the hanging files, a metallic glint in the bottom of the drawer caught her eye. A revolver. Their dad's old .38? Connor slammed the drawer shut. Crossed the room to a green three-drawer metal cabinet. Opened and closed the first two drawers, then crouched to flip through the lower drawer.

"Con bought Lacey out at some point," he said. "Obviously. And if Hoyt was an investor, that was short-lived, too. Why does it matter now?"

"It matters," she said. "When matters." She alternately clenched her fists and flexed her fingers. Finally, Connor plucked out a file. Sarah stood next to him as he laid the file on his desk and opened it to the typed summary of the company's history. So much she didn't know.

She needed to know.

She also needed reading glasses. The print was too old, too indistinct, the onion skin paper brittle.

Connor dragged a finger down the page. "Here. 'In the 1920s, Cornelius McCaskill consolidated his ownership, renaming the company McCaskill Land and Lumber.' That's all it says. Nothing about Hoyt or Lacey."

"Do you have the sale documents? I need to know when he bought them out." She already knew, from Caro's journal, that Lacey cashed out and the family left the area because of Ellen's distress over Anja's death. If Hoyt sold his interest to Con near the time Caro wrote about their debate over how to deal with H, then she could safely conclude that H stood for G.T. Hoyt.

Then what? Would that knowledge alone satisfy the ghost of Anja Sundstrom? What good would come of telling George that his ancestor had been a predator who drove a young immigrant girl to her death a century ago?

She'd figure out what to do about that later. She'd lay it out for the family and they'd decide together. No more secrets.

"Yes. They're all here." Connor closed the file and laid his big hand on the cover. "Sarah, I am so sorry. It was the only way to save the company. If we didn't get that land, we wouldn't be able to compete. We'd be forced to sell out to one of the international conglomerates and let control of the company leave not just the family but the valley. I know, the way Deer Park's grown, not everyone thinks the lumber company matters anymore. But I do. Tourism is great, and I love a good microbrew as much as the next guy, but jobs making burgers and beer will never pay what working in the woods or the mill does. We want this valley to keep growing, we need this company to keep growing so families can afford to stay here. It's my responsibility. Jeremy understood that. I don't know why you think the date we gave the Hoyts Porcupine Ridge has any relevance to buying it back, but—"

"What are you talking about? What does Jeremy have to do with any of this?"

"I had to do it." Connor swiveled his chair toward her and leaned forward, elbows on his thighs, pleading with his hands. "I hated the subterfuge, but Hoyt wouldn't do business with us directly, and we needed that land. If Lucas hadn't set things up the way he did—"

"Lucas?"

"Oh, God." Connor raised his hands. "I told him he should tell you, but he said you'd never agree."

Somehow, Sarah got to the old oak chair. Somehow, she managed to listen without screaming as her brother told her what he and her husband—her dead, sainted husband—had done. How George Hoyt had asked Lucas to find him a buyer for Porcupine Ridge. How Lucas suggested that the obvious buyer was McCaskill, but Hoyt said no; the McCaskill family cheated his a hundred years ago, leaving them land-rich and cash-poor and refusing to buy Hoyt timber, then forced them out of the business altogether a few decades back, and he'd be damned before he did business with the McCaskills.

"That is prime timber land," she interjected. "Yes, it's in poor shape, but that's on George. He could never be bothered to manage the timber. He let blowdown rot. When fire blackened Lynx Mountain, he could have harvested, then restored the land and planted seedlings, but he did nothing. Dad and Grandpa bought that mill to save George, not to punish him."

"I know." Connor stood. "I know. Lucas came to me and said Hoyt wanted to sell, but not to me. I was terrified that one of the internationals would snap it up. Not only would we lose out on the land, we'd be giving a major competitor a foothold in our back yard. Literally, right next to the family's main holdings."

"Connor, no. You didn't put the lodge up as collateral on a loan to buy the Hoyt land." One of the questions she had come here to ask.

"No, I—"

"And what about Jeremy?"

They stopped, interrupted by a knock on the door. Connor gestured and young Matt Kolsrud, in Carhartts and heavy work boots, opened it, glancing at Sarah before speaking. "Boss, I need to talk to you about that extra time off. You said we'd work it out this afternoon."

"Right, right. Tell Steph what you need"—he gestured toward the woman watching them from the other side of the window—"and that I said it's okay."

"Um, sure. Great. Thanks." Matt backed out and shut the door.

Connor sank heavily into his chair and it squeaked in protest.

"Lucas knew how badly I wanted that land." he said. "And that George Hoyt would sell it to the girl making ice cream cones at the Dairy Queen before he'd sell it to me. So, being Lucas, he figured a way around that."

What would her brother say next? She wanted him to hurry up and explain, explain what Lucas had to do with George Hoyt and Porcupine Ridge and the H of their great-grandmother's journal. And Jeremy.

And Jeremy.

But at the same time, she wanted him to shut up. To not say another word. To pretend her husband had not kept something so big, so terrible, from her.

"I meant to tell you all this yesterday, when we were in Grandpa's office at the lodge, but then Holly came in, and I wanted you to know first." Connor rested his forearms on the desk, on top of the file that documented the company history. "Lucas proposed setting up a shell company to buy the land. Every acre, from the ridge down to the lake, including the Hoyt home place. It was a solid plan. The buyer would have no visible ties to McCaskill Land and Lumber, and George would never know we were behind it."

"Until you started working on the property."

"The deal would be long closed by then, and our involvement could be easily explained. The mysterious out-of-state buyer would contract with us to clean up the property, blah blah blah. Happens all the time. Usually it's eighty acres or a couple hundred, not several thousand, but—same difference. But for a purchase that size, we needed financing."

A sour heat began to grow in her stomach.

"You borrow money all the time. Businesses finance growth every day."

He eyed her seriously. "We needed a lot of money. And I was afraid that if we requested a loan that size anywhere in the area, word would get out and one of the big boys would swoop in. So we went to Jeremy."

"My husband loaned you—this shell company—the money to buy Porcupine Ridge?"

"And funds to upgrade the mill. He understood what we needed to do and why. Gave us good terms, a competitive rate. The land itself was the collateral. If we defaulted, he would take title. And he was my brother-in-law. He wasn't going to screw me and unload it in a fire sale to Georgia-Pacific."

"When was this?"

"Last summer. Before he got sick."

When she couldn't pretend he was under the influence of stress, or chemo. And not telling her after the deal was done, leaving that gnarly task to her brother? She couldn't decide if that was kind or cruel. One more win for cancer.

"Did he tell you why he didn't want me to know? Did he tell you what Lucas did?"

Connor made a noise meaning yes. Not everything she and Holly had told him yesterday about the assault had been a surprise.

"George Hoyt. All these years," she said. "I never suspected he hated us. The other morning, after the storm, he drove down to check on the place and he couldn't have been nicer. When we were kids, he let us ride all over the ridge. Anywhere we wanted."

And the first time she'd slept with Jeremy had been in the Hoyts' homestead cabin, on the land he'd helped her brother buy. Jeremy, who always swore he wasn't sentimental.

"We gave him a life estate on the property between the highway and the lake," Connor said. "He was just about broke. He'd already moved into the smaller house up by the highway and started renting out the lake house. Now that he's getting a hefty monthly payment from us, he could move back down. It's not fancy, but nice enough, and it's on the water."

"What was in this deal for Lucas? Let me guess. He wanted help funding his campaign."

"Initially, yes, but Jeremy talked him out of running. How, I don't know—I wasn't part of that conversation."

"Oh. Ohhh." She raised a finger to her mouth, her eyes filling. "Jeremy knew that if Lucas stepped into the public eye, we would all have to make a decision. About what to say . . ."

"About the crash, and the assault," Connor filled in, understanding now. "Makes sense. So Lucas contented himself with legal fees for the corporate work, which added up. Plus the commission—less than a real estate broker would have asked, but substantial, and a monthly service fee for transferring funds."

"And this fictitious company he created?"

"Oh, it's not fiction, big sister. It's real." A smile tugged at one corner of his mouth. "And you own it."

29

Turned out Jeremy had been savvy as well as secretive. He'd set up a company called KB Properties, named for *Knuffle Bunny*, a book Abby had adored and the name she'd given her favorite stuffed animal until she discovered princesses and cast all other toys aside. KB then lent Deer Park Lumber—Connor had resurrected their great-grandfather's original business name—the money to buy Porcupine Ridge, including Lynx Mountain. And Sarah owned KB, in trust for Abby and Noah. She would retain sole control of the company and its only asset—the loan to Deer Park Lumber, in reality McCaskill Land and Lumber—until Abby, the younger of the two kids, turned thirty or Sarah died, whichever happened first.

Lucas had been clever and capable, if a bit conniving.

The low rumble of heavy equipment that had been droning in the background since she arrived faded away. Employees waved through the window as they paraded by. Steph at the front desk turned out the lights and left. Sarah and Connor sat in the office, alone with the ghosts of the past.

Connor laid out his plans for the expansion, investing in new equipment and processes for using small-diameter trees and developing new markets. "We're expanding and diversifying. Focusing on sustainability will keep us competitive. And, I hope, profitable."

"You convinced Jeremy," Sarah said, "and you've convinced me." Then she finished telling him what they'd found in Caro's trunk, who she now believed H to have been, and what she suspected of his role in Anja's death.

Connor opened the manila folder and slid out a receipt for a single burial plot, dated January 4, 1922. "I always meant to track down who this plot was for, but never got around to it."

"Apparently log walls are more than good insulation. They're good at keeping secrets, too."

"Now I understand why George didn't want to sell us that land," Connor said, rolling his chair back and resting his big feet on the corner of the desk. "If you can understand holding a grudge for three generations and a hundred years. George resented Dad and Grandpa Tom for succeeding when business got tough forty years ago. But well before that, G.T., which I assume also stood for George, resented Con for forcing him out of the company in 1922."

"Give Con and Frank Lacey credit for listening to their wives," Sarah said, then switched gears. "How much of this does Mom know? I mean, about the loan and you buying the Hoyt land."

"She knows I bought the land, but I didn't tell her where I got the money. She never would have agreed to keep that from you."

"She's better at keeping her mouth closed than you think. Not one peep about the dreams, until today. Or the paintings—have you seen her new work?" Sarah described them to her astonished brother.

"If it were just Mom," Connor said, "and you know I love her, I could call those dreams woo-woo and wave it off. But not you. And not twice." He glanced at the brass clock on his desk, a gift to their grandfather from some association or another. "I gotta go. Almost dinner time, and I promised Aidan I'd watch the NBA playoff game on TV with him later. You're coming to their soccer games tomorrow, right?"

"You bet. We'll bring Mom." Sarah started to rise, then stopped. "Basketball. Do you have any idea who's been tending the roadside memorial for Michael Brown? It's all done up in Griz colors, UM keychains, his picture."

"Wow. No. No idea."

"One more thing. You told Leo all this, right?" Sarah asked. Her brother's face went blank. "You know, our cousin the sheriff. Investigating your lawyer's murder. You did tell him, didn't you?"

But she knew the answer before she asked the question. Leo wouldn't have kept the secret, either. He'd have quizzed her, hunting for any facts, no matter how trivial, that might point to a suspect.

"There was no reason to tell him, Sarah. George doesn't know about the ruse or the loan. Even if he did, he wouldn't have gone after Lucas, who made plenty of enemies on his own. George would be coming after me, screaming bloody murder and yelling about fraud."

"Why? He got his money. He got his grandfather's revenge."

That should have been enough. Unless there were ghosts haunting him, too.

*　*　*

Twilight in the mountains was a magical time of day, and it came on quickly. Sarah stayed on alert for whitetail and other wildlife as she drove down Mill Road. You never knew what might jump out at you in these woods.

Or anywhere else.

"Oh, Jeremy," she said out loud. He'd been protecting her and her family, making a business deal she would have refused because of an old resentment. A valid one—Lucas had caused deep pain and had not been punished for it. And some of that was Sarah's fault.

Grateful as she was for Jeremy's willingness to help Connor save the business, she was furious over the deceit.

Whoa, girl. He hadn't actually lied. He just hadn't told her what he'd done. It wasn't the same thing.

The irony was that she and George Hoyt were caught in similar binds, not wanting to do business with someone they resented, though any sensible person would have jumped at the opportunity.

She liked to think she was a sensible person. But here she was, holding the past in a death grip. And believing in ghosts.

At the edge of town, she made a left. If she was going to keep digging for secrets in her family's archive, she needed reading glasses.

Did it make a difference that her grudge was grounded in more recent, personal offenses, not ancient history like George's? Not really. If she were honest, she had to admit she was driven as much by her own guilt as by a compulsion to protect Janine.

In the shopping center lot, she parked between two white SUVs. Jeremy had been willing to navigate waters he knew she would have resisted wading into—and had done so brilliantly. Like he'd done almost everything.

Damn the man for making her miss him so much.

Inside the pharmacy, an instrumental remake of Bob Dylan's "Knockin' on Heaven's Door" played, just loud enough to be noticeable and annoying. She paused to scan the bulletin board for "lost cat" notices. Nothing. The reading glasses were on the far wall near the nail polish. Vanity clustered with vanity? She pried a pair of tortoiseshell frames off the rack. Maybe someday she'd be one of those women who, like her mother, wore zebra stripes or red frames with blue and yellow dots, but not yet.

You'd think there would be reading material next to the display of reading glasses, but no. She scanned the nearby shelves for a box or jar with print in different sizes. Picked up a bottle of nail polish remover, then did a double take. At the end of the aisle stood the Black woman she'd seen at the Blue Spruce earlier in the week. The woman she'd seen at the wheel of the white SUV pulling away from the roadside memorial.

Now the woman was standing in Deer Park Drug, holding a helium balloon on a silver cord. A maroon and silver balloon in the shape of a football, UM emblazoned on both sides. Perfectly reasonable. And perfectly telling.

While Sarah debated how to march up and introduce herself, the woman stared straight at her. The football balloon bobbed and wove above her head.

Sarah shoved the bottle back onto the shelf and whipped off the glasses. Strode down the aisle and held out her hand.

"I don't think we've met yet," she said. "Sarah Carter. Sarah McCaskill Carter."

"I know who you are," the woman replied. She did not take Sarah's hand. "Vonda Garrett."

"Vonda Brown Garrett?" It had been twenty-five years since she'd heard Michael Brown talk about his big sister. His "little-big sister," he'd called her, two years older but small like their mother. His height had come from their father.

A few minutes later, Sarah waited on the sidewalk while Vonda tucked the balloon in her car, also a rental, twin to Sarah's except for the color. They walked silently to the grocery store coffee bar. Despite the tempting smells of coffee, Sarah bought two Pellegrinos and drank half of hers before Vonda had the cap twisted off her own bottle.

Now what? She set her bottle on the table and flicked a cookie crumb off the surface.

"Michael was a lovely young man," she finally said. "Jeremy and I talked about him often, wondering what he would have become. What kind of life he would have had."

Vonda said nothing, her deep brown eyes glistening.

"My sister and I have been wondering," she went on, "who's been decorating the cross. We thought it had to be someone local—a basketball fan who knew about the anniversary. But it was you, the woman from San Diego renting the place next to the lodge."

"Yes. I got here Sunday. Misread the directions and drove down your road first. The lodge is every bit as impressive as my brother said."

The vehicle George had seen? The lights, the presence she'd sensed watching her?

"I heard about your husband's death," Vonda continued. She took a drink and swallowed quickly. "My condolences. My parents never forgot the flowers your family sent to Michael's funeral. I hope you and Jeremy understood when they asked him to stop sending Christmas cards. It was too painful."

Because, to return to the Harry Potter metaphor that had bounced into her brain earlier, Jeremy was The Boy Who Lived, and Michael the one who died.

"I'm sorry for your loss," Vonda finished, and pressed her lips together.

Sarah reached out and covered the other woman's hand with hers. "And I for yours." She could feel Vonda's fingers twitch, as if she wanted to pull her hand away. Sometimes, she'd learned over the last twenty-one days, a comforting gesture made the ache throb more. She took her hand back and picked up her mineral water.

"My parents are getting on," Vonda said, tucking her hands in her lap. "It was only the two of us, and now that they're in their eighties, I think they're feeling the loss more acutely than ever. Their only son, part of their legacy. Though they adore my boys."

"How old?" Children. Common ground.

"Twenty-five next month. Twins. My mother believes she and my father will be reunited with Michael in the afterlife, but he's not so sure. They want to know the truth before they die."

The buzz around them hushed, the cash registers and squeaky cart wheels and the swoosh of the electric door all gone silent. The smells of coffee and apples and a hint of floor cleaner drifted away and the bright lights and low hum of commerce dimmed. It was as though a key slid into a lock and opened a door and beyond the door lay a world that looked nothing like the one where she'd been standing.

"You sent the letters. Why? What do you want from us?"

"Nothing. What do you mean?" Her hands flew to her mouth. "No. Ohmygod, I didn't mean—"

"What did you mean?" Sarah leaned forward, her confusion turning to anger.

"I wanted"—Vonda's voice became a thread to the past. "I miss him so much. All the things he never got to do because of Lucas Erickson."

Sarah's senses snapped back to life. "Stay right there," she said, and marched to the counter where she ordered two double-shot lattes. Pulled her phone out of her pocket and texted Leo. *I'm in the grocery store having coffee with the killer.* Studied her screen as the espresso machine buzzed, watching Vonda Brown Garrett out of the corner of her eye.

On my way, he replied. *Stay safe and keep him talking.*

So Leo didn't know, either. Who did he think the killer was?

After minutes that seemed like hours and years, the lattes were ready and she carried them to the table, hoping, praying that her fear didn't show.

How could this petite, grieving woman be a killer?

You never knew. And like they said of the Old West, a gun was a great equalizer.

"Tell me everything," she said. To her astonishment, Vonda drew the hot coffee toward her, gripping it like the proverbial lifeline, and began speaking.

She'd been pregnant at the time, not due for weeks but having trouble. Afraid that the shock of Michael's death would trigger premature labor, the elder Browns had opted to stay in San Diego with their daughter rather than travel to Montana. What could they do anyway? They'd visited a few times to see their son play, had just been here for his college graduation, but had never wanted to come back and see where he'd died. To make the pilgrimage, as she called it.

"They wanted to remember him alive," Sarah said.

But Vonda's own desire finally compelled her to act. She'd flown into Missoula last week, walked the campus, found his face in the team photos lining the halls of Dahlberg Arena. "I asked around, talked to people who knew him. That's when I heard that Jeremy had died, and I realized if I was ever going to find out the truth, it had to be now."

That's why the letter had been addressed to her, not to them both.

"I didn't know I was going to come up to Deer Park yet," Vonda continued. "I went to the library and wrote you and your sister. And Lucas."

"And Janine."

"Later, after I found out her married name." Vonda sipped her coffee, her plum lipstick leaving traces of color on the paper cup.

That answered Nic's question about how the letter to Sarah had arrived before she left Seattle on Sunday, when Janine didn't get hers until Monday.

"Why leave Nic out? I'm sure you didn't mean to hurt us, but what did you think would happen? What did you think we'd do?"

"I hoped . . ." She lifted her gaze to Sarah. "The whole thing never sounded right. We had the highway patrol report—that's where we got your sister's name and Janine's. Of course, we knew yours and Jeremy's. Michael had told Mom and Dad that he was going up to the lake with Lucas and another guy, to see some girls. What was your other question? Nick? I don't know who he is."

Sarah had never seen the crash report. In her mind, they'd all been there together, the four girls, but that wasn't true, was it? She and Jeremy had been out riding. Holly had been sunbathing, and Michael and Nic had just come in from canoeing on the lake when Janine managed her escape. When they heard the crash, Nic had stayed at the lodge, near the phone. Her name wasn't in the report, even though she'd made the call, because she hadn't seen anything, hadn't been up on the highway with the rest of them.

"What happened? Why did the three boys race away in the sports car? Michael's things were still in the cabin. The sheriff packed them up and sent them to my parents. What didn't they tell us?"

Vonda didn't know. How could she? They'd kept quiet about the attack, about Michael and Jeremy trying to stop Lucas from leaving, afraid that he'd hurt himself or someone else. But she wanted to hear what Vonda had to say before getting tangled up in all that.

"Why did you come up here, to Deer Park?"

"To confront him. Lucas." Vonda's hands tightened around the cup. "I needed to know the truth. Why my baby brother died. He owed me that."

Out of the corner of her eye, Sarah saw Leo walk in. Though his manner was as casual as his jeans and fleece pullover, he quickly scanned the area, sizing up the situation. He was alone, but she was sure backup waited outside. She couldn't see his gun, but he always carried one. He pulled a chair from the table next to theirs and sat.

"What did Lucas say to you?" Sarah asked the woman across from her.

The hurt on Vonda Garrett's face deepened. "He sneered. He had no intention of telling me a thing."

"And you shot him?"

"Oh, God, no. No." Vonda's eyes darted from Sarah to Leo, as if just noticing him and his interest. "No. I would never . . ." Her mouth formed the perfect O of a choir singer.

And though two minutes ago, she'd been convinced the woman was guilty, Sarah believed her.

"Then what happened?" Leo asked quietly.

"I told him my parents deserved to know the truth before they died. And he said . . ." She paused, as if not wanting to repeat Lucas Erickson's words. "He said I shouldn't be asking him. I should be asking the moose why it rammed into the car. I should be asking Janine Nielsen why she was such a prick-tease. He laughed, a mean, nasty laugh. And then I left. I ran out."

"Was anyone else in the office? Did you see or hear any-one?" Leo asked.

"No. My phone rang, just as I got in the car. It was my mother and I always take her calls. With elderly parents . . ." She didn't finish the sentence.

"What time?"

She dug in her black croc bag for her phone and started scrolling. Found what she was looking for and held the phone out to Leo.

"I wish you had come to me with this the moment you heard that Lucas Erickson was dead," he said.

"Vonda Brown Garrett, may I introduce my cousin, Sheriff Leo McCaskill." To him, Sarah said, "If you put that together with the time Janine arrived . . ."

"Narrows the time of death. You're sure you didn't see any-one?" Leo asked Vonda, who shook her head. "Anyone see you?"

"That I couldn't say," Vonda replied. "I was too shocked. If that's how he treated people . . ." She let the words trail off, but Sarah knew what she was thinking. She felt the same way.

If that's how Lucas Erickson treated people, then she wasn't surprised that he was dead.

And she wasn't sorry.

30

This time, the lights in her rearview mirror were a good sign.

But if Vonda Brown—Vonda Garrett—hadn't killed Lucas, then who had? Had the killer seen her? Was she in danger too? As Janine might be.

Sarah parked in the turnout, leaving room for Vonda's car. The two women picked their way down the narrow shoulder, the balloon sailing above them. Together, they unwound the ratty, wind-torn ribbons and tied the balloon to the post, below the cross. Vonda leaned in and kissed Michael's picture.

"Rest easy, baby brother," she said.

Minutes later, on the steps of the lodge, Vonda hesitated. "I'm not sure I should be here. I've caused you all great pain, and it's not my intention to blame anyone."

"We owe you the truth. It won't change the past, but you deserve to know."

"Hey, sis, I think we found the link," Holly called as the two women walked in. She was sitting at the game table, a notebook and the Sampler box in front of her.

Nic and Janine entered from the kitchen, the doors thwunking behind them.

"And I've solved another mystery," Sarah said, and introduced Vonda.

"It's you who's been decorating the cross," Holly said.

"Michael deserves to be remembered. He died during a difficult time for my family, and I never wanted to come up here until now," Vonda said. "As time went on, I wanted to put the pain of losing him in the past. My boys were born prematurely a few weeks after his funeral, and my energy was focused on getting them healthy. They're fine," she said, smiling. "Almost as tall as Michael was. And older than he ever got to be."

"How much does she know?" Janine demanded. "What did you tell her?"

"That's why she's here," Sarah said. But when they were seated on the old leather couches and chairs, Vonda held up a hand.

"My turn first. I sent the letters to the three of you, and to Lucas. I never meant to frighten you, and I am so sorry. I—I wasn't thinking straight."

"That partial fingerprint on the envelope will probably turn out to be hers," Sarah said.

"What did you mean?" Nic asked gently. "What did you want?"

"I hoped one of you would reach out and fill in the blanks. Lucas had been his friend, his roommate, and I wanted him to take responsibility."

"Why not sign the letters?" Nic continued. "Give them a chance to respond?"

Vonda's expression was mortified. "All I can say is, being in Missoula, where Michael went to school, where he played ball, where he lived for four years, it made me a little crazy. I wasn't thinking straight."

Sarah could understand that. Grief made you do the inexplicable, sometimes.

"The letters had nothing to do with my mother," Janine said. "Thank God."

"My parents never believed they'd been given the whole story," Vonda said. "The coach and some of Michael's teammates came to San Diego for the funeral, and you all sent cards and flowers, but we always thought we were missing pieces of the puzzle."

Piece by piece, they filled in the picture for her. How Lucas had baited Janine and finally attacked her in one of the cabins. How she'd run from him, how Michael had tried to help her and stop Lucas. How Lucas swore he wasn't going to go to prison for a slut—Sarah couldn't bring herself to repeat what he'd really said—from the wrong side of the tracks and jumped in Jeremy's car just as Sarah and Jeremy returned from their ride. How the two boys raced after Lucas, trying to keep him from what seemed like suicide, only to become the victims themselves.

Vonda covered her mouth with her hand. "The sheriff didn't tell us any of that. Was he charged with what he did to you?"

"No," Janine said. "He'd already been accepted to law school and the sheriff implied that I'd be ruining his future. That it would be he-said, she-said and did I want to put myself through that? I decided no, I didn't. Sarah will tell you that's her fault, that she discouraged me from pursuing it, and I used to think that. But the truth is, I made the decision. She acted out of love. I acted out of fear."

"When the crash was ruled an accident and no charges were filed, my parents were devastated. I remember Dad saying 'It's 1996 and there's no justice for a young Black man in a white state.'"

"I can't say that race wasn't a factor," Nic said, "but Michael was a star. People all around the state loved him. I'd like to think the highway patrol investigators honestly did see it as a tragic accident. They didn't know about the assault, either."

"And the assault?" Vonda asked. "'Boys will be boys'? I'm the mother of two sons. Boys don't attack girls."

Janine kissed the top of her head. "This girl's got dinner almost ready. You're staying."

Being tired of secrets, Sarah told herself, didn't mean she had to blurt out everything all at once. There was no need to tell Vonda about her nightmares. And she wasn't ready to tell her sister and her friends, old and new, about the deal Connor, Jeremy, and Lucas had worked out. Later, after she'd worked out what it all meant for her.

* * *

"So here's what we found," Holly said, leading Sarah to the table where she'd been sorting the letters. "It's the link between Anja and the Ladies' Aid Society."

"Darn it, I never did get reading glasses," Sarah said.

Vonda dug a pair out of her handbag and held them out. Leopard print. Figured.

"*December 1, 1923*," Sarah read.

My dear Caroline,

Forgive me the long delay in thanking you for your kindness during those dark, difficult times last year. You could not have been a better friend to me and my family. I trust Con received Frank's check for our dear Anja's burial plot and gravestone.

"So the Laceys paid for it," she said, glancing up.

You are the perfect custodian of my beloved Whitetail Lodge. I know that you will love it as much as I did, and make it the best home in the world for your family.

We are finally settled here in St. Paul, in a large home on Summit Avenue near my brother. The children love to regale their friends and cousins with tales of life in the wilderness. I am sure their parents think we lived among the savages.

Sarah made a face, then continued.

I have one more great favor to ask. Had I paid more atten-tion to the well-being of our household staff and not dis-missed my premonitions, Anja would still be with us. Her final days would not have been plagued by unwanted atten-tions, and worse. I know there are many women in difficult situations who cannot afford to leave them, even to save their lives. I am enclosing a check for one hundred dollars and ask that you use the funds at your discretion to benefit those in need. Women who are unable to seek help or whom others are unwilling to help.

"Oh my God. This makes so much sense. When was the first loan made? Caro mentioned it in her journal."

"The loan to Hulda Amundsen," Holly said. "In February 1924. I think that hundred would be around a thousand today."

"Guilt money," Janine said.

"Maybe at first," Sarah said, "but it's obvious they loaned out far more than Ellen sent. And they did it for years."

They were solving all the mysteries. Except the one that had brought them all together.

Who killed Lucas Erickson?

And was it one of us?

SATURDAY

Twenty-Two Days

31

"Still no luck." Sarah dropped the rusty needle-nose pliers on the kitchen counter, along with the coil of old phone wire she'd snared from the mill's tool room on her way out Friday afternoon. "I guess I do need glasses."

"And no chance the tech guys make house calls on Saturday," Holly said. She was dressed casually, in leggings and an oversized T-shirt, and purple running shoes with no socks. "You ready to go?"

"Five minutes," Sarah said, and raced upstairs to change. She'd meant to scrub her once-white shoes before the games, but there wasn't time. Despite her fears that they'd roused the ghosts of the lodge, she'd slept soundly and woke to clear blue skies and a calm lake. She'd taken her coffee down to the shore, away from the others, to have a little talk with Jeremy—or rather, the part of him that lived in her mind. Then she'd tried unsuccessfully to splice the wires in the phone box.

"You sleeping on the job?" she asked her dead husband. "I could use some help here."

No reply. Which was probably a good sign, all things considered.

Now they drove toward town, Holly at the wheel so Sarah could text the kids. The balloon she and Vonda had tied to Michael Brown's cross bobbed lightly above the wild grasses.

They passed power company crews working on downed lines and road department crews slinging branches into a giant chipper.

"It could be years before all this storm damage is cleaned up," Holly said, pointing at a fallen spruce, its root ball the size of a Volkswagen bug. "So many owners don't live here. Not that they don't care, but they're not eyes-on. And it's hard to make all the arrangements long-distance."

"Becca's real estate agency does property management too. They have more work than they can handle."

For all that she hated the finagling, Connor, Lucas, and Jeremy had saved Porcupine Ridge, but there were still a few other large holdings in the area. What would happen to them in the long run? And then there were the residential properties. The Hoyt place, with its lake house, two smaller houses, and out-buildings, would be safe in her family's hands. As Becca had said yesterday, some of these old homesteads would be cherished for what they were, but others were ripe for trophy homes and overdevelopment.

Everyone here is excited to see you! Sarah texted her daughter. *We need to make plans!* The plan had been that the kids would come here with her to sprinkle some of Jeremy's ashes on Bitterroot Lake. Now she understood, more than ever, why he'd been so insistent that she bring a bit of him back to Montana.

Dot, dot, dot, her far-off daughter replying.

What? No! I promised I'd start my summer job the week after finals!!!

She pushed CALL. Abby picked up on the first ring. "Hi, honey. We're heading into town to watch your cousins' soccer games. What are you up to?"

"Trying to finish my paper for psych. Tonight's the Meryton ball."

"Oh, I'd forgotten. Sounds like fun. And your dress is perfect." Abby had sent her photos from the visit to the costume shop with her roommates, English majors who'd talked her into attending the Jane Austen Club's annual dance party. Easy to do, with Abby's love of pretty dresses.

Two weeks until Abby finished her first year of college. So much happening so fast, and no way to slow it down.

"I miss Dad, Mom."

Twenty-two days. When was it supposed to get easier?

"I know, honey. I do too." They'd turned off the highway toward Deer Park and the south end of the lake came into view. "I know you're excited about the job and about getting back to Seattle, but I'm only asking you to come here for a few days. Spend some time with your grandmother and your cousins. We've been sorting out the family stuff. Aunt Holly found some great dresses in an old trunk, though you might have to fight her for them."

"Mom, you're not staying there, are you?"

Was she?

"A little longer, anyway. When you and your brother get here . . ."

"Oh, good luck with that. Mom, you have to come home. You can't stay in that dusty old place. What would I—how would I—" She broke off, and Sarah heard girl chatter in the background. "I have to go. But Mom, you have to come home. You have to."

The line went dead.

"That went well," Sarah said after a long silence.

"Look at it from her point of view. Going back to Seattle means life going on as normal. But only if you're there."

"Life is not normal." Sarah heard the brittleness in her voice. "It is not going to be normal for a long time. She has to understand that."

"Yes, but you're not at that point yet. Not anywhere close. Don't expect her to beat you to it." Holly parked in front of their childhood home and shut off the engine. "You coming in?"

"No. I want to sit for a moment. Maybe call Noah." What had Abby meant, wishing her good luck getting Noah to Montana for a few days? What did she know that Sarah didn't?

Was she losing her kids, too?

No, she told herself. Don't be dramatic. Holly was right. Abby was afraid of losing *her*, and that meant being where she was supposed to be, doing what she was supposed to be doing.

There was no playbook for any of this.

Noah didn't answer, no surprise, so she left him a voice mail, putting on a chipper tone, about how beautiful Montana was this time of year and remember, they'd talked about the kids coming here for a week or two after school got out, blah blah blah.

What was taking her mother and sister so long? She was halfway out of the SUV to go check when the front door of the blue Victorian opened and her mother emerged, Holly behind her. She waited while Peggy got situated in the front seat, then opened the back door. Holly stopped her before she climbed in.

"She showed me," Holly whispered. "The paintings. Is that what it looked like?"

Sarah nodded.

"I don't know whether to be jealous that the dreams didn't come to me," Holly said. "Or grateful."

* * *

The soccer fields sat between the grade school and the junior high, two blocks east of the courthouse and across the street from the law office. Children, adults, and dogs swarmed the place, while kids in brightly colored uniforms and knee-high socks clustered on the field. Sarah exchanged greetings with a couple of old friends, accepting condolences and making promises to get together.

"Nice to have a brother who stands out in a crowd," Holly said of Connor, head bent, listening to his wife, one big hand resting on her back.

"Sarah!" Brooke rushed forward and enfolded her in a warm embrace as Holly and Peggy greeted Connor. "My big goof husband told me he finally 'fessed up to you. I won't ask how you're taking the news. I can imagine the answer and I don't want to make you swear in front of your mother."

"Not that she hasn't heard all the words," Sarah replied. "But thanks. I owe your parents a thank-you note for the flowers and the hospice contribution."

"No worries," Brooke said. The kids, nine and eleven, rushed up and Sarah found herself wishing her kids were that age again, not caught up in the zig-zag whiplash of launching their own adult lives while reaching with a back foot for the security of the one they'd left.

The one that no longer existed.

Aidan and Olivia ran back to their teams and the adults drifted toward the bleachers, Sarah lagging behind with Brooke.

"Oh, there's Misty Erickson and her mother-in-law," Brooke said at the sight of a trim blonde in her mid-forties, a broad-brimmed straw hat shielding her face, a gray-haired woman beside her. "I barely know her, but I should say something." They watched as an older couple greeted the Ericksons, he enveloping Lucas's mother in a hug, she embracing Misty, and the opportunity was gone. Sarah could feel Brooke's relief.

"Hard to know what to say, isn't it?" she said, and her sister-in-law flashed her a grateful look. It wasn't just this moment, or Misty's loss, that they were acknowledging.

"Now that he's told you about his deal with Jeremy," Brooke said, "I'm hoping Connor will feel less stressed. It's a big job, trying to keep the company relevant, as he likes to say."

"Work and family are a tough balance sometimes," Sarah replied. "But it's good to have a husband who believes in what he does."

Her husband had put his trust, and a big chunk of cash, into her family's business. On the field, Aidan and Olivia and their teammates were going through warmup exercises led by one of their coaches, a thirtyish woman with a ponytail and killer quads.

Jeremy had invested in their future as well as hers and that of Abby and Noah.

She changed the subject. "Hey, I can't believe all the packing you two did in the lodge."

"We didn't get very far. But wow, some great old stuff."

"One thing I haven't found yet is my grandmother's china and stemware. White porcelain dishes rimmed in gold and dark red crystal—it's called ruby glass."

"Oh, yes! Olivia was helping us one day and when she saw those glasses, she was smitten. You know," Brooke said, as if confiding a secret, "she's not a girly-girl. Which is fine."

"Abby would have run track in a frilly dress and a tiara if she could have gotten away with it." It was fun to share a moment with Brooke over their unconventional daughters.

"That fabulous dollhouse that's a replica of your mother's house? I loved it. She couldn't care less. So when she fell for the dishes and glasses, we took them. She eats her cereal out of one of the porcelain bowls and drinks her juice from one of the red-and-gold tumblers every morning. I'm sorry—I should have told you."

"No, no reason for that," Sarah said. "But she and I need to have a good long chat about Grandma Mary Mac, so she knows the history."

Brooke's face lit up. "That would be wonderful. Let's grab our seats."

A prickling sensation kept Sarah from moving. But when she turned to see who was watching her, she saw no one. *Strange . . .*

"Sarah?" Brooke's words pierced her fog. "You look like you've seen a ghost."

Or a ghost saw me. "Sorry. I'm fine." She took her sister-in-law's arm. "Let's go root for your kids."

Aidan's team played first, losing to the visitors from White-fish three to one. In the second game, Olivia shone, running up and down the field with ease, defending, scoring, cheering on her teammates. She had her father's height and that same easy stride as Abby. Kids at play, on a bright spring day. Life went on, and life was good. As the game wound down, the home team well in command, she glanced at her beaming brother. She clapped her hands and turned back to the field, her irritation with her husband and her brother over their secret business deal a thing of the past.

Minutes later, the game was over, the Deer Park kids jumping up and down in victory. Olivia had scored the winning goal and had the ball in her arms when a boy from the other team ran up and tried to jerk it loose. She tightened her grip and pulled the ball closer. The boy kicked her in the shin. She yelped and dropped one hand to her leg, while he grabbed the ball and dashed away. Connor sprinted onto the field, along with one of the coaches, while other kids and adults corralled the offender.

Brooke clapped one hand over her mouth and Sarah slipped an arm around her.

"She'll be fine," she said. "They're taking care of her. She's a brave girl."

Olivia refused to sit or to lean on an adult, putting her hands on her hips and shaking her leg to ease the pain. A minute later, she took to the sidelines, clearly trying not to limp. Then the kids dispersed and the next pair of teams, the oldest kids, took the field.

"What was that all about?" Sarah asked Brooke.

"Luke Erickson," Brooke said. "I'd like to say he's behaving badly because he's upset about his father's murder. But he was in Olivia's class until Misty moved the kids to Whitefish last year, and he's always been a bully. Can't stand a girl being better than him."

Just like his father. She started to chide herself, then stopped. You weren't supposed to speak ill of the dead. But there was no reason you couldn't think it.

32

"Someone better give that boy a good talking to," Peggy said as they left the playfields. Olivia claimed her leg didn't hurt, though she would have a nasty bruise, even with the ice pack a coach had given her. She'd wanted to stay and cheer for the last game of the day, and her parents agreed. They'd join the rest of the family later at the Spruce.

"Not sure it would do any good," Holly replied. "Bullying is in his genes."

They crossed the street in front of the law office and Sarah saw a light on. "You two go ahead. I'll meet you there."

To her surprise, the door was unlocked.

"Hello? Renee?"

No answer. She stepped inside, careful to avoid the spot where Lucas had died. The smell had dissipated, but the place still held a mood. If she owned this building, she'd probably be eager to unload it, too. Years ago, in their first house in Seattle, there had been a murder-suicide in the next block, and the house had been torn down, the lot sitting empty for a few years before a duplex went in.

"Renee? Are you here?" she called again, and again got no reply.

She peered into the conference room. Empty. Across the hall stood Lucas's office, looking no different than earlier in the week. Her eyes locked on the black-framed photo on the credenza, and she picked it up. Were there clues to Lucas's state of mind in the way the three young men stood beside Jeremy's red car? She didn't know if she wanted this picture, or if Vonda Brown Garrett might want to see it. Maybe she should burn it, put the past firmly in the past.

Ha. Like a McCaskill would do such a thing.

"What are you doing in here?" Renee Harper's voice broke into her melancholy.

"Sorry. I called your name and didn't hear you, so . . ." Sarah held up the photograph. "Mind if I take this? Lucas with my husband and a friend. Though I suppose I ought to be asking Leo. Sheriff McCaskill."

"Your cousin."

"My cousin," Sarah agreed, and glanced around the office. "It's a nice space. Close to the courthouse. I imagine another lawyer would be happy to snap it up. Especially if it came with an experienced legal secretary."

The other woman looked surprised, then appeared to realize Sarah meant her. "Not sure I can wait that long. Better talk to your cousin if you want those client files."

"No. No." Sarah held up the framed photo. "This is all I wanted." A minute later, standing outside the front door, she paused to slip the photo into her bag, and heard the dead bolt snick shut behind her.

*　　*　　*

Sarah slid into the booth at the Blue Spruce, the same booth where she and Janine had sat that first day back in town.

Monday. That had been Monday. Today was Saturday. Life had seemed so out of order since Jeremy's death, but the days of the week had a comforting rhythm. If you could remember them.

Holly and Peggy were deep in conversation about Becca's suggestions for staging the lodge, if they decided to sell, for updating if they didn't, and the pros and cons of the historic listing. Deb set coffee and a slice of pie in front of her. She smiled at the waitress. Huckleberry-peach. Thank God for pie and bossy women who knew what you needed even when you didn't.

Sarah took a sip. Not bad, but Holly was right. The Spruce wasn't everyone's cuppa. Could they convince Janine to let them help her open her own place in town? A worry for another day. She picked up her fork.

Two bites in, she set it down. "Mom, what do you know about Renee Harper?" And why the woman eyed her with such distrust. Though it wasn't good to read too much into a short encounter.

"Oh, right—she was Lucas Erickson's secretary. Is that who you stopped to see?" Peggy reached for her coffee. "Renee Taunton. She was a few years ahead of you. One of those kids with all kinds of potential but without much chance of fulfilling it."

"I saw her in the grocery store when I ran into Pam Holtz, and Pam mentioned a problem over a scholarship?"

"I remember. She got a perfect score in math on the college entrance exam and was offered a full scholarship to the University. Judith, her mother, wouldn't let her take it. Thought she should be practical and become a secretary. Your cousin Leo got it instead."

"That's horrible," Holly said. "Not that a good secretary isn't worth her weight in peach pie."

"You remember Judith Taunton, Sarah—she worked at Deer Park Floral for ages. You used to love going in there with me or your grandmother."

Sarah did remember. Her love of the shop and the flowers had been strong enough to overcome her fear of the sour-faced woman who sold them.

"They live in that little gray cottage on Second East, across from where we lived when you kids were born," Peggy continued. "They've had that house forever. Beautiful flower beds in the backyard. You have to drive down the alley to see them."

The image of an envelope flashed into mind, bearing the name *Mrs. B.F. Taunton*. And the image of Renee up by the horse barn earlier in the week, claiming to be looking for wild-flowers for her mother, on a dusty, dry trail, her hands empty, her shoes clean. As if the flowers were an excuse. Why had she really been there?

"Renee couldn't wait to get away," Peggy was saying. "Then her mother's dementia got worse and she came home to take care of her. After the last incident—"

The door opened and Peggy broke off at the sight of the two older women who entered. After the ritual "Where do you want to sit?" negotiation, they set their bags on chairs at a nearby table before coming over to greet the McCaskills.

"Girls, you remember Grace Smalley and Cheryl Kolsrud." Peggy touched Holly's arm, then nodded across the table. "Holly, and Sarah."

Matt and Becca's mothers, out for pie and coffee. Did this sort of thing happen in Seattle, where everyone was too busy for their own good? Or had that just been her?

"So sorry to hear about your husband," Grace Smalley said. "Too young. Such a shame."

"Good for you, though, getting out and about," Cheryl said. "When I lost my husband two years ago, the last thing I wanted was to leave the house. Your mother insisted, and I've never forgotten that."

"Step aside, ladies," Deb called, a heavy tray balanced on one hand as she shook out a folding rack with the other. Burgers and fries for the family crammed in the next booth, the kids in their soccer uniforms. Grace and Cheryl waved and retreated to their own table.

"I hate that phrase," Peggy said, dropping her voice. "'Lost my husband.' It always reminds me of when we were in that shopping center in downtown Spokane—you remember the place."

"River Park Square," Holly said.

"That's it. I came out of Nordstrom's and your father wasn't where we were supposed to meet. I waited, and searched, called his cell. No answer. Finally went to the help desk and had them put out a page. And there he was, sitting not ten feet away. I didn't know whether to kiss him or kill him."

It was a funny story, even if they had heard it before. JP had fallen asleep in a high-backed chair and in her panic, Peggy hadn't seen him. Though he was already ill, they'd decided to make the once-a-year Christmas shopping trip anyway. A month later, he was gone.

Gone. Another phrase not to like.

But what struck her was that these older women—the other two had to be past eighty, nearly a decade older than Peggy—were not afraid to acknowledge that Sarah's husband had died. Unlike the women her own age, all perfectly polite, but on edge. Afraid of the future she represented.

The door burst open and her niece and nephew rushed in, their parents behind them. The women slid over to make room, while Connor grabbed a chair from the nearest table. Olivia appeared no worse for the encounter with the Erickson boy, but Sarah wondered what Connor would have to say about it.

Deb delivered more coffee and postgame ice cream floats, and Sarah felt herself surrounded by a bubble of life going on, happy to drift to the edge and watch. Connor did look more relaxed. Because of the deal Lucas had worked out, using Jeremy's money, or because he'd told her? How would it change her relationship to McCaskill Land and Lumber, now that she was both family and the largest creditor? She'd happily ignored the business for years. No longer.

When the pie plates and ice cream glasses were empty and the young bottoms were growing restless, they headed for the door, Sarah and Connor at the rear of the clan. She heard her brother swear under his breath and looked up to see a girl and an old man. George Hoyt and his great-granddaughter, in her team uniform.

It's only George, she told herself. The neighbor she'd known all her life. Who just this week had stopped by to check on the lodge after the storm.

The man staring into her brother's face with a look that sent a shiver down her spine.

* * *

In the upstairs studio, the McCaskill women stared at the paintings. Since Sarah had first seen them, Peggy had set all three on easels, and laid her sketches and studies out on the work table.

"When this is over," Holly said, "you have to show them and tell the story."

"Isn't it over?" Peggy said. "You two found the notebook and letters and the link to the past. But if I show these pieces, everyone in town will think I'm nuts."

"I think," Sarah said slowly, "that the dreams asked each of us to do something only we could do. For Ellen and for me, twenty-five years ago, they were warnings that women, not much more than girls, were in danger. I'm not sure whether Caro's dream was telling her that Sarah Beth was really sick, or whether it was a call to take action to protect women in trouble in the community. Or both. For you," she said to her mother, "they were a request. Anja wanted you to tell her story, in the way only you could."

And what about now? Anja had come back after they'd found the papers in the trunk, but before they'd put the story together. Why frighten her? Was danger still lurking? Where and from whom? To whom? She suppressed a shudder.

"So the paintings are kinda weird," Holly was saying. "So some people will think you're nuts. Screw 'em."

Sarah left the room, phone in hand, to try Abby again. Their spat had rattled her, and the specter of more danger looming terrified her.

Turned out her sweet princess of a daughter had beat her to it, texting an apology. *I miss him. I miss you. I'm so sad*, her note ended.

Abby picked up on the first ring. "I just want everything to be the way it was, but it's not, is it?"

"No, honey. It's not. We have to make a new normal and stick together. It's what your dad wanted."

A long silence. "Mom, you're not going to stay there, are you? You are coming back to Seattle, right? To our house?"

"Yes, of course. I just don't know when," Sarah replied. "Right now, I need to be here. And I want the two of you to come help me scatter Dad's ashes on the lake." And listen to the family stories, so they'd be safe for another generation.

Oh, God. Would she be putting her daughter in danger by bringing her here?

Or was the danger Anja was warning her about to her daughter's heart, and to her own?

"I'm listening, Anja," she told the long-dead Swedish house-maid after the call ended. "I'm not sure I understand, but I'm listening."

33

"You wanta drive?" Holly held up the keys. "It *is* your car."

"What? No," Sarah said. Wherever her mind was at the moment, it would not be on the road.

They drove through town in silence. As they crossed the old steel bridge, Sarah reflexively glanced downriver to the mill that had dominated both town and her family for so long. High above the river's edge, in a tall cottonwood, a bald eagle surveyed his kingdom.

Good day for fishing, she silently told the bird. He turned his big white head and she swore he was looking right at them. At her.

Her mother wasn't the only wacky McCaskill.

At the roadside memorial, Holly pulled over. "You know, I don't think I ever stopped at one of these in my whole life, and this week, I've lost count."

A few minutes later, Sarah suggested they detour down to the old homestead and ice house. It was time to tell Holly one more thing, one last reason she'd felt guilty all these years over what Lucas had done to Janine. Back then, hearing that she and Jeremy had been hooking up in the rickety shack instead of keeping an eye on Lucas would have devastated Janine, and she still wasn't sure how to tell her. But she was tired of keeping secrets from her sister.

In the last few days, the birch and maple had gotten leafier, the tiny green triangles on the snowberry unfolding into actual leaves, the wild roses bursting with promise.

"I hope George doesn't mind us coming down here," she said as they passed the small clapboard house where Mrs. Hoyt had lived when they were kids. The house George lived in now. No sign of his truck. Still in town, no doubt.

"Oh, he won't mind. He likes us," Holly replied.

That was then, this is now. They owned his property, and he didn't know. Though it was clear from the look on his face in the Spruce that he had suspicions.

As she climbed out of the SUV, Sarah spotted a stone chimney, the top visible through the gaps in the woods created by the blowdown. "Look. You can almost see the lodge from here."

They were standing between the ice house and the pond, the homestead shack a few hundred feet away. "Holly. I need to tell you—" She broke off, listening. George returning? No. His truck had an unmistakable sound. She was hearing nothing more than the noise of traffic filtering down from the North Shore Road.

Holly craned her neck, gazing up at the weathered, two-story building, louvers on the cupola serving as a vent. "This place is fascinating. I've been thinking, Sis." The wooden door creaked as she it pushed open and walked inside, leaving Sarah to follow.

For a long moment, she couldn't see a thing. Light filtered down from the cupola and streamed in through broken boards on the side of the building, where ice had been loaded onto waiting carts through a sliding door. As her eyes adjusted, she could make out metal tools hanging along one wall.

"You said"—Holly's words came from the shadows, and Sarah could just see her, standing in the middle of the main storage room, hands on her hips. "You said Becca needs someone to do property management. To handle rentals and work with the snowbirds. I could do that."

She could. Much of her museum work had been on the operations side. She knew how to maintain and upgrade buildings, many of them historic, and raise the money to keep them running.

"But"—Holly continued—"I'm also loving diving into the history. Not just of our place and family, through the letters and scrapbooks, but the whole valley. The Ladies' Aid Society, the immigrants. Did you know Pam Holtz's grandfather was the last steamboat captain on Bitterroot Lake? Anyway, I could combine the two somehow, helping owners piece together the histories of their homes and land. Not sure how, but I could figure it out."

"That sounds seriously perfect," Sarah replied. A raven flew overhead, letting out a single caw, and left through the opening made by the missing planks. What she needed to tell her sister could wait.

It would have to. Her sister was nowhere in sight.

From the rear, or outside, she heard a loud crack. A floorboard, or a branch? But Holly didn't shout for help, so she turned her attention back to the wall where tools hung on nails pounded into two-by-four crosspieces. She'd seen similar tools in the carriage house. Ice saws, tongs, a pointed bar her dad had called an ice hook. Leather cords and ropes. Splitting bars and forks, long poles with a flat blade or pointed prongs, used to break the slabs of ice apart after they'd been cut. Holly had talked about preserving history. This place was ripe with it.

A shadow flickered across the floor. The movement kicked up dust and she sneezed.

"Oh, there you are," she said when she got her breath back. But the shadow did not belong to her sister. "Renee. What are you doing here?"

"You aren't going to stop, are you? Poking around. You can't help it." Renee Taunton Harper stepped into the dim beam of late afternoon sunlight and Sarah saw the menacing look on the legal secretary's face. "You and your brother, you think the world exists for you. Your whole family."

What was she talking about? And where was Holly?

"You think you deserve every good fortune in the world. You're not as bad as Lucas, but that's not saying much."

"Lucas?" Sarah heard her voice crack. "What does he have to do with anything? Renee, what is this about?" Though she was beginning to suspect she knew.

"This is about"—the woman took a step forward and Sarah steeled herself not to step back. She could not let herself be trapped. Where was Holly? "This is about me getting what I was promised. What I deserve. The entire plan was my idea, you know."

"What plan? Ohhh. The plan for McCaskill Lumber to buy the Hoyt land through an intermediary?"

"Owned and financed by a rich in-law." Renee took another step closer and Sarah's skin prickled. "Now, to be fair, although life never is, your husband didn't make me any promises. Not directly. I doubt he ever knew I existed, let alone that I cooked up the whole thing. Ran the numbers, laid out the steps, showed Lucas how it could work. Not that it would ever have occurred to Lucas to give credit to anyone else, especially not a woman.

If an idea popped into the air near him"—she lifted a hand, fingers curved as if holding a light bulb—"he would snatch it up and call it his." She closed her fingers with a flourish, crushing the imaginary glass.

"There are men like that. Entitled narcissists, psychologists call them." Sarah had seen the term while flipping through Abby's textbook, wondering how the intro to psych class had changed in thirty years. The terms, yes; human experience, not so much. "I'm not surprised. What else did Lucas do to you?"

Keep her talking. That bulge in the woman's jacket pocket, the pocket she kept patting, had to be a gun. A .38, she guessed. The one she'd taken from Lucas's desk before shooting him and leaving the office. A lucky break, running into Becca—anyone who knew the two women would easily believe Renee's lie that she'd been trapped in the P.O. by chatty Becca.

"What he did was break his promise. I"—Renee pointed at her chest—"I was supposed to get half his commission for brokering the deal. And every month, there was a processing fee tacked onto the loan payment. Fifty percent of that was supposed to be mine, though I did all the work. But he wouldn't give me a cent. Not one penny."

"I know you've worked hard for what you have, Renee. Do you know our families go way back, a hundred years or more?" Though the last thing this desperate woman would want to hear was how Caro had loaned money to—who? Renee's grandmother? Great-grandmother?

"Oh, spare me the history lesson. If I'd had half the opportunities you've had, everyone in this town would know who I am like they know you and the rest of your clan."

She heard a scurrying sound somewhere in the distance. Renee heard it too. Too loud for mice. What other wild creatures had taken up residence in the ice house?

"Taking care of your mother must be difficult," she said. "You're a good daughter."

"You don't know if I'm a good daughter or a terrible one. You're just saying what you think I want to hear. That's what people like you do."

"People like me?" Sarah took another step sideways, aware of how far the door was.

"You don't know. You and your millions and your big houses and your perfect life. You pretend to be interested in me. Lucas didn't even bother." She shoved one hand into her pocket.

"I understand why you killed him—"

"Do you? Really?" Renee was moving closer now, into deeper shadow.

Don't lose sight of her.

"A good lawyer—"

"Righhht. You forget, he was a lawyer, too. Not a popular one, but no matter. No one will want to help me. I'll be stuck with the stupidest public defender they can find."

Where was the woman? Sarah was having trouble seeing her, seeing anything, in the fractured light. She had to get out of here. She had to find Holly and get out of here.

"Don't do this, Renee. Your mother needs you."

"My mother doesn't know her ass from a teakettle. She can't even wipe herself anymore. She's run off every home health aide I've hired. I finally talked the memory care facility in Whitefish into taking her, so I could get away from here. Live a little, before I end up like her."

Too late. This was the cost of bitterness. But Sarah was not going to pay the price.

"Then you came back to town," Renee continued. "Lucas said you never would, not for more than a few days. But here you are, making plans. Make Whitetail Lodge great again."

How did she know Sarah's plans? Small towns . . . "Killing me won't help. And you won't get far."

"Maybe not," Renee said, but underneath her cackle, Sarah could hear her feet edging slowly closer. "But won't it feel sweet, taking something from people who have more than they need, who will never even notice. My family's been beholden to yours for a century. What's that old line? Might as well be hanged for a sheep as a lamb? Your sister's around here somewhere."

Did she mean to kill Holly, too? Did her rage and resentment extend to the entire McCaskill clan? And what about Vonda and Janine, who'd been in the law office at exactly the wrong time?

Dust motes danced in the faint beam of light. She'd never make it out alive.

"You've been watching me, haven't you? That's why you were driving down the trail between George's place and ours the other day. Did you tell George about the deal? Did you think that would help you?"

"You can't talk your way out of this, Sarah." Renee raised her arm and pointed the gun, Sarah sensing the movement as much as seeing it.

Could she do it? She'd never been much of an actress, but her life might depend on it.

"Ah-ah-ah-CHOO." The sound gave her cover and she reached behind herself to the wall, fingers scrabbling for something, anything. Touched a metal rod and tightened around it, tugging it free. A nail clattered across the floor and she heard the other woman stop, heard her swear softly.

Outside, an engine? Did Renee hear it, too?

In the shadows, they were quiet as breath. Then came the softest hint of movement and Sarah gripped the tool with both hands, like a baseball bat. *Eyes on the ball.* But she couldn't see it. Could not see the woman.

Another movement and a whoosh of air. She swung hard. Hit the target, heard her cry out. Swung again, aiming the pointed prongs of the splitting fork where the woman's right hand must be. Aiming for the gun, her arm. Anything.

A blast deafened her. She lunged forward, the fork in hand, aiming for the body. And knew with a sickening certainty that she'd found it.

* * *

Where was Holly?

Sarah used the belt from her jacket to tie Renee Harper's hands and dragged her across the room to the sliding doors, where she ran a leather rope she'd grabbed from the tool wall through the handle of a sliding door, then wrapped it around the woman's ankles. Not that she'd be going anywhere, bleeding as she was. And not that Sarah wanted her to die, but she wouldn't mind if Renee lost consciousness and stopped screaming.

Back where they'd scuffled, she'd found the gun and run outside, gun in one hand, splitting fork in the other.

The rented SUV was parked where Holly had left it, listing to one side. The crack she'd heard had been Renee, shooting out a tire.

Another vehicle was approaching, though she couldn't see the road. She ducked behind the SUV, peering through the windows. Out of nowhere came a streak of energy. A black-and-white dog, poking his nose at her. "Shep," she whispered, grateful but confused.

A sheriff's SUV came into view, another behind it, the drivers stopping well back of the ice house, as if according to a plan.

Her cousin slipped out of the lead vehicle, gun in hand, gesturing to his uniformed deputy with the other.

"Leo!" she called, crawling out from behind the SUV. "Leo." Then she ran to him, the dog behind her. Explanations tumbled out of her as she pointed to the ice house door and a whimpering Renee Harper.

"You okay? You're not hurt?" he asked.

"Yes. No. But where's Holly?"

No time for answers, as Leo and the deputy took charge. By the time they had Renee cuffed and were checking out her injuries, George arrived, emerging from the woods to stand next to Sarah. He ran his gnarled fingers over the dog's ears, a shotgun in his other hand. For the first time, she noticed the ancient Chevy truck parked behind the small, square white house.

And then she heard her name and Holly came racing around the end of the pond, past the homestead shack, and into her arms. More deputies arrived, followed by EMTs, and once again, the two sisters watched an ambulance leave the woods and speed down the North Shore Road to town.

"She'll live," Leo said. They'd moved off the lane and into the woods, giving the deputies and medics room to do their jobs. "Whatever you stabbed her with was sharp enough to hurt like hell and make her bleed like crazy, but not enough to do any serious damage."

"Thank God," Sarah said. "I want her to die in prison, and not any time soon. I assume the gun belonged to Lucas. I tucked it on top of the rear tire, in the wheel well. I left the ice splitting fork under the car." She pointed and a deputy trotted over to her vehicle.

Still gripping the heavy black flashlight she'd grabbed in the lodge, Holly explained how she'd gone into the smaller, secondary storage room. When she heard voices, she peeked into the larger room and saw Renee confronting Sarah.

"I didn't know if she had a gun, but I knew she meant trouble. No cell signal, so I sprinted out the back and around to our car, but it had the flat. I checked Renee's car"—she gestured at the blue sedan parked beside the ice house—"but she'd taken her keys. I didn't see George's truck so I ran down to the lodge, intending to grab Nic or Janine's car and drive up to where I could call for help. Didn't know I could still run like that."

"Holly, honey," George said. "I've got a landline. And I never lock my doors. You coulda gone in."

"Now you tell me." Turned out Nic and Janine had managed to splice the landline at the lodge and got it working, so Holly called Leo. Who was already on his way—moments after Holly left, George had arrived home after dropping off his great-granddaughter.

"I saw two vehicles I didn't recognize," he said. "Not that I'm one to worry about trespassers, but I been seeing that blue car prowling around and it felt hinky. I didn't wanta go over there myself, after sitting on those damned aluminum bleachers for hours, but the dog was clueing on danger. So I called you," he said to Leo. "Forgot for a moment you're a McCaskill and I've got my beef with your family."

His old grudge, flared up from news of the recent purchase. How much had Renee told him? "We'll sort that out later, George," Sarah said.

"Then I heard the gunshot, so I grabbed this." George gestured with the shotgun, then continued. "But you three had things in hand, like true McCaskills. You, sir, are a damn fine sheriff," he said to Leo before turning to the sisters. "And you are my neighbors and friends no matter what. No matter what."

"No matter what," Sarah agreed, and glanced down. There, on the duff of the forest floor, amid the pine needles and spruce cones and bits of moss, lay three shiny bright pennies.

EPILOGUE

Two Weeks Later

T hirty-five days. Or was it thirty-six? Was she losing count? Her therapist had said she would, eventually, but what Sarah hadn't anticipated was the mingled sense of peace and sadness that brought.

Jeremy was still dead. But she was alive. She stood on the grass near the water's edge, the sunlight rippling the water as it rocked gently over the colored cobble, and lifted her face to the sun. Raised her hands high above her head, then swept them down and bowed low. Moved through the familiar poses, feeling her muscles stretch.

The world bowed you now and then. Bent you over, brought you to your knees. The pain was like a sharp wind that tossed you from the safe nest you'd labored to build, shattered the glass you'd kept between yourself and the world. If you were lucky, you came through it with your eyes and your heart open. She felt the sun warm her skin. Brighter, warmer, and stronger every day.

Abby had flown in two days ago. Yesterday, they'd hauled the old canoe down to the water and paddled along the shore. They were going riding this afternoon, out to Granite Chapel, and picking Noah up tonight. The day after Renee Harper was charged with the murder of Lucas Erickson and attempted murder for the shot she took at Sarah, the McCaskills finally had their family meeting and opened up the trunks that held their secrets. The three siblings, Brooke, and Peggy had sat around the kitchen table and talked over "the Knuffle Bunny deal" and the future of the lodge. They'd invited Leo, who, bless him, had said thanks but the fate of the family holdings was up to them, and he and his brother would be content with whatever they decided. Connor agreed with Sarah that they would tell George everything about the land purchase and encourage him to stay on the property, living in the house on the lake if he chose, but that they would keep their theories about his grandfather and Anja to themselves.

Peggy confessed her hope that Holly would return to Deer Park. And that Sarah would actively protect Jeremy's investment in McCaskill Land and Lumber by getting more involved in the company, and that she would invest both time and money in Whitetail Lodge. Rebuild herself and her life here on the shores of Bitterroot Lake.

Too soon to say. But the way Abby had immediately been drawn to Janine's cooking and her plans for the space in town, Sarah wouldn't be surprised if she chose to stay in Deer Park for the summer. She'd quickly fallen for Bastet and the adoration was mutual. The cat's owners had not been located, and it seemed clear that wherever she'd come from, however she got here, she too was meant to be at Whitetail Lodge. Sarah was not looking forward to her first wedding anniversary alone, but she vowed that she and her children would celebrate Father's Day together, no matter what or where.

Janine had left her job in Missoula and moved into one of the cabins. Nothing could be done about the attack—too long ago, the assailant now dead. But Leo had given her the department's official apology, and she'd accepted it. Sarah had gone with her to order a stone for her mother's grave, which wasn't far from Anja's, and they'd visited both.

Holly hadn't decided yet whether to accept Becca Smalley Kolsrud's job offer. Right now, she was busy cataloguing the letters, journals, and other ephemera they'd found in the carriage house. Caro's trunk was just the beginning. One day, one project at a time, the sisters were rebuilding their trust in each other.

Nic had gone back to Billings, taking, Sarah was sure, those rusty needle-nose pliers with her. Once school was out, she and Kim would return with Tempe for a week or two.

They were all friends again, forever. And there had been no more nightmares.

Renee Taunton Harper had been right when she predicted that no lawyer in western Montana would want to touch her case. The state public defender's office had ended up assigning one of its brightest stars, a woman with a killer record, who would do everything possible to ensure that she got a fair trial. Good. She deserved that. Everyone did, but being cheated, ignored, and humiliated most of her life was no excuse for murder. It had been Renee whose presence Sarah had sensed in the woods and at the soccer field, Renee who'd cut the landline, and Renee who'd blatantly hinted to George Hoyt that he wasn't being told the truth about the deal for Porcupine Ridge.

Vonda Brown Garrett had returned to San Diego knowing the truth about her brother's death. They'd talked about a visit, with her husband and sons, later in the summer. Sarah, Holly, and Janine were tending Michael's roadside memorial.

And so, in varying ways, justice was being done, with Whitetail Lodge at the heart. The lodge Ellen Lacey had built and Caro McCaskill had made into a home. The lodge now entrusted to her. What the lodge wanted most, it seemed, was justice. And a woman to tend it.

A shadow fluttered near her cheek. A copper butterfly, its iridescent wings shimmering in the sunlight glinting off the lake. She smiled and stepped out of her flip-flops, then crossed the colored cobble into the water.

Readers, it's a thrill to hear from you. Drop me a line at Alicia@AliciaBeckman.com, connect with me on Facebook at LeslieBudewitzAuthor, or join my seasonal mailing list for book news and more. (Sign up on my website, www.Alicia-Beckman.com or www.LeslieBudewitz.com.) Reader reviews and recommendations are a big boost to authors; if you've enjoyed my books, please tell your friends, in person and online. A book is but marks on paper until you read these pages and make the story yours.

Thank you.

ACKNOWLEDGMENTS

W hitetail Lodge, Deer Park, and Bitterroot Lake are all fictional, though I have drawn heavily on the history of northwestern Montana and its logging, its mill towns, and its historic lakeside lodges. The region is home to a small lake called Little Bitterroot and a Deer Park Elementary, but their fictional namesakes live only in my mind, and I hope, yours.

Women's clubs were a critical part of life in the late 19th and early 20th centuries, often providing the only social opportunities some rural women had. While the Lakeside Ladies' Aid Society is fictional, I suspect many organizations did good works that fell far outside their charter.

Book research takes many forms. Thanks to my cousin, Dawn Schwingler McQuillan, for helping me try to solve the mystery of Mrs. O'Dell, known only as a family friend of our great-grandparents, the Beckmans, and a namesake in two generations. We didn't succeed, but it's clear the real woman was as well loved as the Mrs. O'D of my imagination.

ACKNOWLEDGMENTS

Jordonna Dores opened her treasure trove of family albums and scrapbooks, allowing me to connect with and better describe what I had imagined lay inside Caroline McCaskill's trunk. Francesca Droll of Abacus Graphics, LLC created the map of Bitterroot Lake. Our collaboration was a joy, a chance to see how a professional artist and designer can add a critical visual layer to a novel from a rough sketch and a draft manuscript.

My sweet hunny, Don Beans, spent a glorious, clear blue spring afternoon exploring local cemeteries with me and scouting out an old ice house, not far from home but which neither of us knew about before I started researching them for this book. Thank you, love.

What a treat to work again with editor Terri Bischoff, now at Crooked Lane Books, and the rest of the CLB staff. Thanks to Edith Maxwell for reading the proposal, and to the late Ramona DeFelice Long for commenting on a draft. I'm lucky to share a terrific critique partnership with Debbie Burke, who read the proposal and a draft, and brainstormed with me when Terri said "more of this, and less of that" and my brain froze! Mystery writers are the most generous people I know.

My agent, John Talbot, pivoted on the proverbial dime when a series proposal turned into an invitation to write the stand-alone I'd long wanted to write. I deeply appreciate your knowledge of the business and your wise counsel.

Readers, it's all for you. *Thank you.*